"Miss me, F

A hint of a smile curved Raf's lips, then was gone.

He stood, moved toward her so quickly Marina thought for a moment he'd shimmered. Then before she could breathe, before she could sort out what was happening, he pulled her against him.

"No regrets?" he asked, staring down into her eyes. "Not a one?"

Marina shook her head. His fiery scent tickled at her memories, made her want to close her eyes... go back in time.

Her traitorous body swayed toward him. Her knees tried to buckle, but she forced herself to stay upright, fought to ignore the desire pounding through her.

Then Raf's lips covered hers....

Books by Lori Devoti

Silhouette Nocturne

Unbound #18
Guardian's Keep #32
Wild Hunt #41
Holiday with a Vampire II #54
"The Vampire Who Stole Christmas"
Dark Crusade #62
The Hellhound King #82

*Unbound

LORI DEVOTI

grew up in southern Missouri and attended college at the University of Missouri-Columbia, where she earned a bachelor of journalism. However, she made it clear to anyone who asked, she was not a writer; she worked for the dark side—advertising. Now twenty years later, she's proud to declare herself a writer and visits her dark side by writing paranormals for Silhouette Nocturne.

Lori lives in Wisconsin with her husband, daughter, son, an extremely patient shepherd mix and the world's pushiest Siberian husky. To learn more about what Lori is working on now, visit her Web site at www.loridevoti.com.

THE
HELLHOUND
KING

LORI DEVOTI

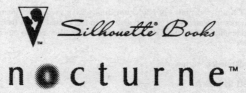

Silhouette Books

nocturne™

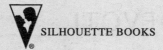

SILHOUETTE BOOKS

ISBN-13: 978-0-373-61829-3

Recycling programs
for this product may
not exist in your area.

THE HELLHOUND KING

www.silhouettenocturne.com

Printed in U.S.A.

Dear Reader,

Thanks for purchasing *The Hellhound King*.

This book takes you into Alfheim, home of the elves. A lot has changed in Alfheim in the past century. The land lost its rulers, and a new body, the elf lords, has moved in. But the residents of Alfheim aren't happy.

In *The Hellhound King*, Marina, whom you may have met in *Dark Crusade*, is brought back to her home against her will. Raf, a hellhound, also first introduced in *Dark Crusade*, follows her—though not with entirely good intentions.

When they get to the land of light, they instead discover a land in chaos. A land neither wants to visit much less embrace. They also discover secrets and a connection to each other and Alfheim no one can deny.

And in Alfheim, the land they think they want to leave behind, dreams they've never dared to dream come true.

I hope you enjoy it.

Lori Devoti

P.S. Stop by my Web site at www.loridevoti.com.

Dedicated to Sherman and Meriwether,
the two best writing companions any author
could ask for. I miss you both.

Acknowledgments

Many thanks to Tara Gavin, Shawna Rice
and everyone else at Harlequin Enterprises
who made this book possible. Thanks also
go to my agent Holly Root.

And huge hugs of gratitude to Jenna Reynolds,
Kathy Steffen and Meagan Hatfield for listening to
my many whines in person and to Ann Christopher,
Sally MacKenzie, Eve Silver, Caroline Linden,
Laura Drewry and Kristi Astor for listening to me
moan virtually. You all make the ride a lot easier!

Prologue

Gunngar

Marina ran her hand over Raf's chest. His heart beat slow and steady under his skin. She pressed her lips to the muscled hardness and breathed in his scent.

Fire and smoke…as if a blaze smoldered deep inside his body.

She'd never met a hellhound before this. She'd been guarded her entire life, told how to live, who to associate with—and hellhounds were most definitely not allowed.

Her uncle, her sister, the elf lords…none of them would appreciate how Raf made her feel…none of them would care.

She took advantage of his sleep to trail her fingers down his chest, to soak in the raw beauty of him.

He stirred and her heart stopped for a second, as if she were at risk of being caught doing something she shouldn't. The sheet draped over him slipped lower, revealing a new wealth of bare masculine skin. Her heart resumed its beating, sped faster.

She pressed her lips to his skin again, let her tongue dart out and taste him…to see if his taste was as tantalizing as his scent.

It was…more so…

She leaned over him, her platinum hair hanging loose, forming a curtain around her face and brushing over his chest.

Enough torture, she would wake him…remind herself he was real and here with her, for her…the only male she'd ever known who loved her, wanted to be with her *because of her* not who she was in Alfheim, or what she could do for him.

A rustle of sound outside the door halted her. She gathered her hair in one hand and twisted it into one long bunch. Just as quickly, she picked up a robe from the floor and slipped it up her arms, tied it at her waist.

Then she went to the door.

The hallway was empty, but sitting on the ground, leaning against the stone door jamb was a tiny plastic box. With a quick look around, she picked it up and hid it in the sleeve of her robe.

Inside the room, Raf was still asleep.

She hesitated, but continued past him, her bare feet making no sound on the cold stone floors. A benefit of being an elf…she could move as silently as a feather drifting on a breeze when needed.

And for some reason, right now she sensed she had that need.

There was a small bathroom attached to her sleeping quarters. She went inside, turned on the water and pushed the button marked Play on the box.

Raf's voice, but not with the playful rough tone she knew and loved, instead with a hard almost cold business edge spoke from the box.

"I've seen no sign she isn't doing as you wish. She's carrying out your orders—hunting the witches."

"Has she caught any?"

At the second voice, Marina stiffened. She knew the accent, if not the male. An elf. Raf was talking to an elf.

A pause, then, "No."

"You will tell us when she does." An order not a request.

"And anything else she does. We missed your report yesterday—we don't want to miss another one, not if you expect your pay."

Marina's skin went cold and her fingers went limp. The recorder tumbled onto the stone floor. Shattered—just like her trust.

The courtyard was quiet, but guards were lurking in the shadows. Marina knew, because she had ordered them to be there.

She licked her lips and glanced around the courtyard.

It wasn't too late. She could still call off the guards, but what would be the point? Raf had lied to her. She could never trust him, and just like her, he was trapped here in Gunngar. They were trapped here together.

The doorway to headquarters opened and Raf stepped out. His dark hair gleamed almost blue in the noonday sun. His shoulders brushed against a doorway built for elves, Svartalfars and dwarves to pass through, not a broad-shouldered hellhound male.

Marina sucked in a breath and forced a smile onto her face. Used it to disguise the tears that formed behind her eyes and the shake of her hands.

She jabbed her fingernails into her palms, concentrated on that pain instead of what she was about to do, had to do.

Stupid lovesick fool that she was, she hated herself, when she should hate him.

Chapter 1

Anger and anticipation warred inside Raf Dolg as his gaze clocked each movement the lithe elfin princess made. Even dressed in dirty dungarees and a stained over-sized shirt advertising some human sports team, Marina Adal was as alluring as ever. He gripped the tree in front of him, his fingers digging into the bark as he spied on her.

Her scent was different than he remembered it, but then her emotions were different, too. The sharp tang of confidence that had emanated from her was gone.

Good. She shouldn't be confident, and she had no reason to be. Marina Adal, elfin princess, had a lesson to learn, and he was here to teach it to her.

She had taken his freedom from him; now he would return the favor.

Marina Adal jerked the heavy bucket up from the sidewalk.

"Why won't you help me?" she murmured to the

witch inside her. "Do you like existing like this? Hiding?"

The witch whose spirit Marina had taken inside her own body refused to speak. Marina would have almost believed the witch, Amma, hadn't really made the transfer, was still locked in that needle back in Gunngar, but every so often, she'd feel her. A tickle. A frown. Always some ugly emotion.

Amma hated Marina. Because of the act she had played in Gunngar, everyone hated Marina now.

Marina had accepted that, made the best of it by striking before being struck. But even that hadn't worked.

Her body was host to one of the most powerful witches in the nine worlds, but she was cleaning toilets at a dive motel in the human world. Stuck here until Amma decided to show herself and release her powers.

Dirty water sloshing out of the bucket onto her leg, she teetered toward a small grassy area next to the office. As she turned the corner of the building, she caught sight of movement behind her. She turned, the knife she kept hidden under her sleeve instantly moving to her hand.

A cat jumped from a tree on the other side of the parking lot. The animal landed with elflike grace on the hood of a car.

Marina bit the inside of her cheek. She was jumpy, had been since she had escaped Gunngar.

Her uncle would surely have heard of her disappearance by now, the elf lords, too. All would be looking for her—and she most definitely didn't want to be found. Not yet. Not weak.

* * *

Raf watched Marina slosh the bucket over onto its side. As dingy water swirled onto the grass, she played with the blade that had appeared almost magically from her sleeve. Perhaps it had. Perhaps the witch Amma was working with her.

His body stilled; his mind whirled.

If Marina had Amma's powers in addition to her own elfin talents, she would be near unstoppable. But if that were true, why would Marina be here, waiting on humans?

Content she couldn't have Amma's powers, he went back to watching her, to enjoying this part of his hunt…anticipating what was to come.

The bucket empty, Marina placed her foot on its bottom edge and flipped it with her toe into an upright position. A lock of her platinum hair slipped from under the scarf she had tied around her head. In that second, Raf saw the elf princess that he'd known in Gunngar—the confident beauty who had treated him as an equal, inspired his trust. A band tightened around his chest. He gripped the bark in his hand and squeezed. Lies.

The bark nothing but dust in his hands, he let the bits fall to the ground and ran his palms over his twill pants. He took a step forward; he'd stayed hidden long enough, used the hellhound talent for blending long enough. Time to face Marina—or more accurately, force her to face him.

As his heel hit the cement sidewalk in front of him, two dark forms dropped from the motel's low roof. Stretched between their hands was a shimmering net.

A snarl lifted Raf's lip.

Someone was trying to steal his prey.

* * *

A whoosh sounded behind Marina. She spun on the ball of her foot, the knife slipping into one hand while the other reached up to ward off any approaching blow.

Two dark-skinned males, svelte by human standards, stocky by elf, stood in front of her. Svartalfars, dark elves, mercenaries. One motioned to the other.

Her heart fluttered. They'd found her.

A sheet of shimmering material…a net…appeared between the two.

Marina took a step back, her knife ready. She recognized the tool, had used it herself. Laced with elfin magic, the net would douse any powers that lay beneath it, render a shape-shifter unable to shimmer, and a witch unable to cast a spell.

It would make her helpless…

She gripped the knife, kept it secure but not tight— ready to throw or slash, whichever would serve her best.

Then she waited, but not for long.

The Svartalfars moved closer, sideways. One reached into his pocket, pulled out a blade of his own. The weapon snapped and popped with electricity.

They meant to stun her, wrap her helpless into the net, then what? Marina blinked away the thoughts, concentrated instead on what she could do to avoid capture.

Her gaze darted behind the pair to the tree the cat had leapt from. It was far, but not too far, not for an elf. She tucked the blade back up her sleeve, bent her legs and forced every bit of energy she had into an upward motion. Her hands held forward, she focused on the lowest branch. As the rough bark bit into her palms, she saw light shimmer below her.

She swung up and onto the tree limb, crouched there, like a bird. From her perch, she twisted and looked down. The Svartalfars had dropped the net. One lay unconscious on the ground. The other still stood, but an arm, solid as the branch she stood on, was pinched around his neck.

Her breath caught. For a second, she could only stare. She knew the male holding her attacker—Raf Dolg, the hellhound who'd wandered into Gunngar. Who she'd let closer than she'd ever let anyone. Who had lied to her and spied on her until she found him out and ordered him locked up.

The hellhound stared at her, too. His dark gaze was hard, unforgiving.

Her hands balled into fists. Unfair, since he'd betrayed her first. But he didn't know she'd discovered his lies. She hadn't explained. Why would she?

As the thoughts spun through her head, Raf twisted the dark elf's neck, let him fall lifeless to the ground. And all the time his gaze held hers, angry and intense, just like the hellhound himself.

When he bent to retrieve the net, she blew a breath out of her mouth and forced her legs to move. Run. She had to run. Her savior, Raf, was far more dangerous than the males he'd just protected her from.

Raf dropped the dark elf to the ground. He'd killed neither of the males…a kindness he was sure they wouldn't repay given a chance. It was the least he could do, though, having stolen their tool from them—and soon their bounty.

He looked up. Marina had already skittered out of view, over the motel's roof, moving with the speed and sure-footedness of one of the multitude of squirrels that seemed to populate the human world.

He took his time rolling the net into a small bundle, so small it tucked neatly into the back pocket of his pants. Elves might not be the friendliest of beings in the nine worlds, but they did make intriguing toys.

And…he glanced up…Marina's scent was even now beginning to wane…equally intriguing females.

Marina's feet made little sound as she raced over the flat roof of the motel. When she hit the drainpipe-lined edge, she spared only a second to glance back over her shoulder. No sign of Raf or the dark elves. If she was lucky the hellhound had somehow became entangled in the net, lost his powers to shimmer at least for a while.

Even as the thought whirled into her brain, she tossed it aside as ludicrous. Not Raf. No, he would be after her, on her and soon.

She squatted and prepared to jump onto the asphalt below. Then she paused. *What would Raf expect of her? To run, of course. Only an idiot wouldn't when pursued by a hellhound.*

She stood, glanced around again. Cars crept down the street beside her. People moved in and out of the café across the road. Everything appeared normal. No one seemed aware of what was happening only a few yards from where they went about their mundane human lives.

Oblivious beings, humans. Easy to catch, she guessed. But she wasn't human. She was an elf. Time to think like one.

She pivoted slowly, quietly, and started creeping back to the area from where she'd come. Raf thought he knew what she would do, but he didn't. Didn't know *her,* not really.

Back atop the office, she gazed down. The dark elves were there, faces flat on the concrete, but Raf and the net were both missing. She leaned forward, checking to make sure the hellhound wasn't hiding under the overhang, then swung herself down to the ground and let out a relieved breath.

She would gather her things and leave. She would find another part of the human world to hide in. Cars came and went along the freeway only a few yards away day and night. It wouldn't be hard to convince a driver to transport her wherever he or she was going.

But first…she took a step toward the downed Svartalfar…she wanted to know who had sent them, who was this close on her trail.

The dark elf wore close-fitting pants, a shirt and a padded vest. All obviously of Svartalfar design. But the net, it had been pure Alfheim.

She ran her fingers over the first mercenary's pockets, pulled two blades and a demi ball free before finding a sealed pouch with papers inside. She slid her thumb under the magnetic clasp, popped it open. Two cards fell out. The first was a digital imager. Six pictures, all of Marina, flashed over it. Four were actual pictures she remembered posing for; the other two were doctored to show how she might look if disguised. She pursed her lips and moved her attention to the second card, an advertisement, the kind usually found posted near portals and nine world bars. Another picture of Marina, but this one with words, too…words that promised a bounty equivalent to three years' earnings for an average mercenary. To earn it, all they had to do was return Marina to Alfheim, to her uncle.

Marina held the last card between two fingers. Her uncle then, that was good. Hopefully, the elf lords knew nothing of what she had done and didn't care about where she had gone.

She was still studying the card when a net dropped onto her head.

From the limb of the tree, Raf smiled down at the now completely encased Marina. She'd come back.

Of course, he'd known she was coming back as soon as her body twisted his direction.

The elf princess had underestimated him.... He dropped onto the ground next to her. Her lips opened to release a curse. He smiled.

"Miss me, Princess?" He reached one finger through the weave of the net, stroked it down the back of her hand. "I'm sorry I had to go away so unexpectedly. Oh, wait." He pulled his finger back, curled both hands into fists. "You sent me to that boxed hell, didn't you?" She hadn't just had him imprisoned, she'd had him locked in a box, hung from the ceiling of a dungeon...for years.

She kicked out with both feet, managed to knock the heel of her boot into his shin. He barely felt the pain. It was nothing but a whisper against the roar of success.

He'd caught her. Now the fun would begin.

Chapter 2

Marina used her heels to inch her body backward, until she could lean against the wall.

Raf had shimmered them both to some dark pit of a room. The walls were bare and water-stained, the floors concrete. He'd told her he meant to take what she valued most—or what he thought she valued most—Amma. Then he'd fallen silent, hadn't said a word for twenty minutes. He just sat in the lone piece of identifiable furniture the room offered, a battered folding chair, and stared at her. He'd glanced occasionally at the only other object in the room, something big and rectangular covered with a tarp, but he'd said nothing about it and said nothing to her.

Her back pressed against the wall, she turned her head to face him. The net pressed down on her, suffocating her even, though the weave was open and the material appeared light. It was the magic in it, pressing against her, sucking up any power she had, making it hard to breathe, and even harder not to scream out in frustration.

But she ignored both sensations, smiled, pretended she didn't feel a thing.

"What now?" she asked.

He folded his arms over his chest.

"What exactly was the purpose of this?" She lifted her hand, tried to motion with it. Her fingers caught in the net. She jerked them free.

A hint of a smile curved Raf's lips, then was gone.

She leaned her head against the wall and stared up at the stained ceiling. She was tired. Tired of pretending all the time, worrying about keeping up whatever facade people expected.

A female voice whispered in her head, a taunt. "Poor elf princess, forced to live a life of privilege. Were you forced to hunt those witches? To kill them?"

It was Amma, stirring in her brain. She'd begged the witch to show herself, and now when Marina was at her lowest, she did. But not in the way Marina needed.

"I have reasons for what I did," she said to Raf, but to Amma, too. "And regrets."

Nothing about Raf changed. His stare stayed steady, his body stiff. Marina couldn't even say if he was breathing. He was like a statue, a cold judging statue.

"My biggest—" she dropped her gaze, stared at her hands—pale and sleek, elf hands, a killer's hands, or so people thought "—is the witch-burning." Her voice shook as she said it.

She'd blocked the memory from her mind, but the smell of the wood came back to her, the terror on the crowd's faces. She had tried to tell herself she'd had no choice, had to carry out the deed as part of her role as Jager leader, the main representative of the elf lords. They'd already sent one spy, Raf; there had to be others. As it was, Marina had taken risks enough. She had put on the performance of her life.

The smoke had billowed when she'd tossed the flame. And everyone had thought the witch was dead, burned to nothing but ash.

Only Marina knew the truth.

Which meant everyone else, Raf, Amma, everyone, thought she was a killer.

"Liar," whispered Amma.

Marina ignored her. She was used to ignoring such things now. If she wanted to survive, stay sane, she had to.

She looked back at Raf. He was beautiful. The word was feminine and he wasn't, not at all, but it fit. Sitting there so still, his beauty was even more obvious. His body was fit, shoulders broad with muscles that couldn't be hidden by the long-sleeved Henley he wore. He was big, big for any male of the nine worlds, except a giant, but compared to the men her uncle would pair her with, elfin royals, he was huge. He made Marina feel safe, or had for that short time in Gunngar when she had let herself forget her role, and hadn't yet learned of his perfidy.

"Anything else?" Raf this time. He'd finally spoken. Marina hid her shock, relief. If he was talking to her…that had to be better than the cold silence. Not that his question was warm, far from it. If anything, he looked more removed.

"You mean like you?" she asked. Her hands trembled.

She hid them under her legs…. "Not a thing. I don't regret a thing about that." Her voice softened at the end, almost too soft for her own ears to hear.

He stood then, moved toward her so quickly she thought for a moment he'd shimmered. Then before she could breathe, before she could sort out what was happening, he jerked off the net and pulled her against him.

"No regrets?" he asked, staring down into her eyes. "Not a one?"

She shook her head. He was pressed against her, warm and hard. His fiery scent tickled at her memories, made her want to close her eyes…go back in time.

She had missed being close to him, touching him. She didn't—couldn't—get herself to regret for even one second the time she'd spent with him in Gunngar. It had been stupid and foolhardy, but for a few brief days, she'd been happy, relaxed. He'd done that for her.

But she also couldn't regret what came after, ordering him locked into that box and put into the farthest reaches of the dungeon. He'd betrayed her. What else could she have done?

"I have regrets, lots of them." His dark blue gaze was intense, snapped with anger. His body seemed to thrum with the emotion, too. He hated her, but he was holding her.

It was all she'd ever wanted, his touch, his arms around her, Raf being with her.

Her traitorous body swayed toward him. Her knees tried to buckle, but she forced herself to stay upright, fought to ignore the desire pounding through her.

Then his lips covered hers and she let reality slip away, let her mind drift back to those few days in

Gunngar, let herself pretend she was as ignorant now as she was then.

His kiss was harsh, not the loving soft movement of his lips she remembered, but the pressure of her lips against his was just as strong and punishing. She was angry, too.

He'd destroyed her trust so thoroughly, destroyed her in a way no one else ever had.

His fingers yanked the scarf from her head. Her hair cascaded down her shoulders, her back. It had grown since she'd left Gunngar. Almost reached the curve of her hips now. It was impractical, flying loose like that. Playing princess, she'd been forced to keep her hair up in elaborate braids; playing Gunngar's leader, she should have had it shorn, but had kept it long. One tiny secret sign of revolt.

Now she reveled in its weight on her shoulders.

Raf grabbed her hair with both hands and cradled the back of her head as he took the kiss deeper. She reached her arms around his waist, up his back. Spread her fingers over the muscles that shifted as he moved against her.

Her breasts flattened against his chest; his heart beat against hers…both beating too fast. She panted for breath, unable to kiss him hard enough, long enough.

She had wanted this for so long, but…one tiny sane part of her brain piped up…*he isn't here to love you, to save you. He's here to hurt you, again.*

Her fingers twitched. She still had her blade. She should threaten him, force him to free her, but she couldn't. She didn't want to. Didn't want to remember that she needed to.

His mouth still close to hers, he took a step back. Then muttered something against her lips—a curse she guessed. She wanted to curse, too, curse him for pulling away, putting even an inch of space between them.

Then he was back. Her breasts smashed against his chest, her groin against his thigh. He smelled good, smoky. She'd forgotten how his scent tantalized her, excited her. How had she forgotten that? Smoky like a wood fire when you were alone in the woods, not the ugly black smoke of that pyre where she'd had the witch tied.

A shudder shot through Marina's body. Even knowing the woman had survived, she couldn't stand the memory, not of the event or the congratulations the elf lords had sent afterward.

As if reading her change of mood, Raf froze. Realizing she'd messed up, was losing the moment, Marina rose on her tiptoes and tried to recapture his lips.

He shoved her aside, and she fell on the net. Physically, she was unharmed, but emotionally she felt his rejection like a dagger slicing her flesh.

She'd lost him again. The few moments forgetting everything that had passed between them were over. She closed her eyes to hold back the regret.

He turned away. His cold dismissal gave her strength, reminded her what reality was, what she had to do—look out for herself, because no one else would.

She reached into her boot and pulled out her blade.

Another bounty hunter, another hellhound, had shimmered into the room. Raf pushed Marina to the floor, instinctively protecting her even, though logic said that was insane, that she was the enemy, not a damsel in distress.

Still, he turned, ready to fight.

The other hellhound hadn't realized he'd been made

yet. He stood in the shadows, thought he was blending into the background. Perhaps he didn't realize Raf was a hellhound, too. Or perhaps he was just arrogant.

Either way, Raf had a surprise for him.

Not even allowing himself a glance down at Marina, he shimmered.

As Raf solidified behind the other male, Raf could smell his surprise. He hadn't expected a forandre, a shape-shifter, the only beings in the nine worlds who could shimmer, to be caught in an embrace with an elf princess.

No one would expect that.

Raf shoved the ugly thought aside, grabbed for the other male's throat instead. The bounty hunter ducked, dropping and spinning as Raf reached for him.

Raf grunted, happy the fight wouldn't be simple. He needed an outlet, needed a way to release the fire that had built inside him as he held Marina. Maybe killing this hunter would kill the insanity, the need he still felt to hold her, protect her.

The other hellhound sprang to his feet, his fist flying toward Raf as he moved. Raf slipped to the side, flung his elbow into the hellhound's head as he did. The rewarding crunch of cartilage breaking put a smile on Raf's lips.

The bounty hunter, shorter than Raf, but stockier, didn't pause, didn't bother to wipe the blood streaming from his nose, just balled his fist and struck again. This time he hit.

Raf's lip split. Adrenaline coursed through him. Blood filled his mouth; he spat. Balled his own fist and swung, connected again. The other hellhound staggered backward. His hand hitting a wall stopped him from falling.

Raf pressed his advantage, grabbed the bounty hunter by the front of his shirt and shoved his fists into his throat to keep him from shimmering. "Find your own princess. This one is mine."

The other male shifted his weight, tried to throw Raf off balance. Raf adjusted, pulled the male forward, then knocked his adversary's head back against the wall.

"Surely, there's an easier bounty to gather. Is this one worth dying for? How much are the elf lords paying you?"

"The elf lords? Is that who you're working for?" With a surly twist of his features, the bounty hunter grinned. "Maybe there are two rewards—a possibility of an auction. What say we work together?"

Raf stared into the male's eyes, let his own go red— let the extent of his anger show. "I work alone, and as I said, this princess is mine."

The bounty hunter's eyes shifted to the side, to the part of the room where Raf had left Marina. "Doesn't look that way to me."

Seeing truth in the bounty hunter's gaze, Raf jerked his head, glanced to where Marina was waiting, *had been waiting,* but wasn't now.

The net still lay where he had left it but the elf/witch was gone. He dropped his hold on the hellhound, stalked to the net and jerked it off the floor. He glared around the room. "How did she...?" The door was locked, the room ten stories above ground.

The bounty hunter he had let loose stood by the now open window. "She's an elf. And soon she'll be mine— at least until the auction." With a grin, he shimmered.

Raf cursed and crossed the room. He stuck his head through the window and inhaled. Marina's scent was everywhere. She'd somehow scaled the side of the deserted brick warehouse with no ledges and no fire escape in sight.

He pulled his head back inside the room and slammed his hand into the wall.

He had completely underestimated her—again.

He returned to the net. As he bent to retrieve it, something small and silver caught his eye.

Cylindrical in shape, it fit easily in his palm, was actually designed for a hand smaller than his—an elf hand. Carefully, he rolled the object over his palm, studying the elfin lettering that was inscribed down its side. He didn't read much elfin, but he didn't need the capability to know what this was; he had one of his own. It was a locator, the kind used by bounty hunters. It was even marked with a service's logo.

Whoever had hired the other hellhound had given him a way to call once Marina was caught. Had he used it?

If so, who might be on their way?

Raf flipped the object into the air and slipped it into his pocket. It didn't matter. Raf was going to catch her first, and Raf was going to turn her over to the elf lords—no matter how strongly his heart and hormones objected.

Marina dropped onto the street. Her bare feet raced over the grit-covered surface as she scurried to where she had dropped her shoes. She'd been forced to take them off. The human footwear she was wearing offered no traction for scaling a wall, not even a brick one with convenient toe holds provided by the mortared spaces.

She was on the opposite side of the building from the

window she'd broken. She'd made her way around, clinging to the brick, knowing if her escape was discovered early, it would be harder for the hellhounds to catch her there. Even their ability to shimmer wouldn't allow them to hang from the brick.

Now she hoped her trip around the building had thrown them off her scent, much like running through water when chased in the woods. If they were unable to follow her path, they would have to travel on the ground around the building searching for her scent to pick back up.

Hopefully, it would buy her time—enough to escape. Her shoes still in her hands, she ran across the street, kept running until she saw two workmen flinging tools and construction debris into the back of a truck. She waited until the men had climbed into the truck's cab and started the engine, then leapt forward and scrambled into the bed. Hunkered down, she took a breath and slipped on her shoes.

The vehicle jerked as it pulled onto the deserted street, sent a paint can careening toward Marina. She stopped it with her foot, but kept her head low.

Four hunters in four hours, if she counted Raf. Which meant her time quietly hiding in the human world was over.

She closed her eyes, tried to fight the panic building in her chest. Hunted, like the witches she'd hunted in Gunngar.

"Like it?" Amma murmured.

Marina gritted her teeth, tried to ignore the witch. But she was right. Marina deserved this, deserved to be hunted like a witch. She was one, after all. A weak one, but still a witch. She had hunted her own kind, more vehemently because they were like her. She'd felt she had to work harder to cover the similarity.

"Elf/witch, like me, but without the power." Amma again, her voice singsong. "Elves aren't supposed to be witches. Bad. Bad. Bad. They'll destroy you when they find out."

Again the damn witch was right, had hit on the fear Marina had always harbored. Elves weren't witches. Other beings were, but not elves. Until Amma had shown up in Alfheim, declared herself half elf and all witch, none had believed it possible. None except Marina, that is. She'd always known, had lived with her secret since childhood.

"Dirty little witch. Not strong enough to hold her own. Not pure enough to be an elf. What will the elves do when they discover your lie?" Amma's voice drifted, as if she was talking to herself, but Marina knew the words were directed at her, that the stronger witch wanted to hurt her.

"What am I to do?" Marina asked herself.

"To do, to do. What is she to do? She spent all that time hiding her talents, thinking the elves would turn on her. And now they've turned on her anyway—because of me."

Marina clapped her hands over her ears, even, though she knew it wouldn't shut Amma up, that nothing could shut her up, not as long as she was inside Marina, babbling in her head. Besides, the witch was wrong. Marina wasn't being hunted because of Amma. She was being hunted because of who she was, because of her uncle's insane plans for her.

Desperate for silence, or at least an inability to hear

the other witch, she started humming…a dead mono-
tone note that made her feel even more alone, desperate.

"You could take me to Alfheim. Reunite me with
my body. Then I'd fight with you, defeat the elves,"
Amma whispered.

Marina dug her palms into her closed eyes. Defeat
the elves. It wasn't what she wanted. She didn't want
Amma's power to gain more power for herself. She had
wanted Amma's power to secure her freedom, to know
she was strong enough to stand up to her uncle and the
elf lords, to fight for her own rights and happiness. To
keep from being a pawn ever again.

But her plan had backfired. Everything had backfired. And now Raf was here, reminding her how good
things had been, could have been, if their time together
hadn't all been a lie.

"Release me," Amma urged.

The truck hit a pothole. Marina's body jerked into the
air. The paint can she'd stopped earlier collided with her
head. And all she could do was lie there, shake with the
disappointment of what her life was, always had been,
always would be.

"Get over it!" Amma's voice broke through her mel-
ancholy. "How do I keep getting stuck in such weak-
lings?" Then there was silence, blessed silence.

Marina waited, sure the witch would be back to taunt
her, but minutes later she hadn't made a peep. Marina
sat up, rubbed dirt from her face and clothes and ran a
hand through her tangled hair.

Amma was right. Marina had to get over it. Running,
hiding wouldn't fix her life. It was no way to lead a life.

Raf had said he was here to take Amma. He must be working for the elf lords. They must know.

If Marina gave the witch up, would the elf lords, at least, leave her alone? Her uncle might still look for her, but Raf would be off her tail. She wouldn't have to struggle with the longing she felt every time she saw him, worry that he might pop up again, and remind her of what she'd thought they had. The idea was solid, practical. She would give Raf what he wanted. In return, why wouldn't he let her go, a head start...something?

Hope flickered inside her. Her resolve began to grow.

And what reason was there to keep Amma? The witch had made it clear she wouldn't help Marina, not unless Marina carried her back to Alfheim herself and released Amma's spirit into her body.

Marina couldn't do that. She would be walking into her uncle's and the elf lords' hands.

So, what good was keeping her?

Marina sat up, peered over the truck's tailgate. They hadn't gone far; she recognized the street.

Not waiting for the truck to slow, she slung her leg over the vehicle's side and leapt to the ground.

She was going back...to Raf.

Chapter 3

Raf paced around the room. He should be chasing down Marina. He was sure the other hellhound was, but Raf had signaled Joarr before Marina escaped. He needed to wait for the dragon to arrive before taking off after her.

Worst case, he'd take her back from the bounty hunter. The other hellhound didn't worry him.

Raf strode back to the window and stared down at the street. Traffic was picking up. A bicycle wove between cars. Two men argued near a mailbox. But no sign of the dragon.

He had almost decided to give up, to leave and find Marina, when the sound of wings beating against the air drew his attention to the horizon. The dragon, cloaked in fog, moved steadily toward him. He landed on a rooftop one building over. His scales shone silver for a second and his silvery blue eyes gleamed, then the fog around him grew thicker, impossible to see through. Raf waited, watching. Slowly, the fog cleared and the ice blue dragon was gone. In its place stood a man, dressed all in white. In one hand he held what appeared to be a lantern. He raised it above his head, gestured at Raf.

The hellhound shimmered, solidified on the roof next to Joarr.

The dragon-shifter frowned. "Where is she?"

"Escaped. There are bounty hunters after her. I let myself get sidetracked."

"Humph." The dragon arched one brow. "By the hunter or the elf?"

Raf crossed his arms over his chest. "I'll get her back. Do you have the needle?"

Joarr reached into his pocket and pulled out a sliver of silver. "The elf lords were quite generous. They insisted I take the needle, the vessel—" he held up the lantern "—and a few niceties for my cavern."

"Did they?" Raf asked. The dragon and the elves had a history, not a friendly one. He knew anything Joarr had gotten from the elf lords had not come freely. "What will you do with her, once you have her?" he asked.

"The lovely Amma?" Joarr ran the heavy chain connected to the lantern through his closed hand. "I may keep her for a while. In lieu of what she cost me—seems a fair exchange."

Raf didn't know what had happened between the witch Amma and Joarr in the past. He had met the dragon when they were both trapped in Gunngar. Joarr, locked in his dragon form, had been positioned by the elves as a watchdog to the chamber where Raf had been imprisoned.

Not a willing watchdog, and not one allowed any freedom.

The elves had put him there, but surprisingly Joarr seemed fixated solely on Amma. Finding her. Toying with her.

Whatever had passed between them, Joarr hadn't forgiven or forgotten.

But Amma wasn't Raf's concern. From all he'd heard she was no more deserving of his pity than Marina.

"I'll contact you when I've found her again. Stay close. I don't want to risk another run-in."

"Afraid of losing her? Not very confident, are you?" The dragon angled his head to the side.

Raf suppressed a growl. "Stay close," he replied, then he shimmered.

One pass around the building told Raf what Marina had done, where she had landed when she climbed down from the room.

The other hellhound had gotten this far, too. Raf could smell him.

Raf's lip curled into a snarl. He wasn't worried about the competition, but that didn't mean he didn't resent it.

Marina trudged through the streets. She'd found a hooded sweatshirt lying on a bus stop bench. She'd pulled it on, jerked the hood up to hide her hair.

The thing smelled of stale cigarettes and wet dog. She ignored the stench, told herself it was added camouflage, hiding her scent from any other bounty hunters.

Three blocks from the building where she'd escaped

Raf her steps began to slow. Something wasn't right. She felt a tickle, an edge of annoyance. She stared at her feet. They refused to move.

Amma.

"You cannot be serious," Marina said. She gritted her teeth. *The witch was impossible.*

"Without me, you will have nothing," the witch said.

"I thought you wanted me to let you go?" Marina argued. She grabbed hold of her pants, tried to tug her leg forward.

"I want you to take me to Alfheim—to my body. Not turn me over to the hellhound."

"I'm not going to Alfheim with you inside me and not helping me. I am not going to Alfheim at all." Marina concentrated, managed to move her foot a few inches. "I'd be walking into a nightmare. The elf lords would have you and I'd be lost somewhere in the middle, stuck between the elf lords and the royals, two dogs who want to own me."

"What's your choice? Staying here in the human world?" Amma scoffed.

"Yes. *Staying here in the human world.* Cleaning toilets and gathering up cigarette butts is a better life than what waits for me in Alfheim—a far better life. Here, I'm free," Marina replied.

The witch seemed to mull this over. Marina took advantage of her silence, and general disappearance, by hurrying toward her goal. She was less than a block from the building when Amma decided to let loose of her magic.

Marina's hands shot overhead; power surged through her body, up her arms and out her palms. She could feel Amma inside her, twisting her, aiming...for what Marina didn't know.

She cursed—Marina and Amma. Marina because she had lost control of her own body. Amma, Marina assumed, because the witch had missed her intended target, whatever it was.

Humans around Marina scattered. Screamed about electrical lines and a woman being struck. It took a few seconds for Marina to realize they meant her, thought she had been hit by a fallen power line. They didn't realize the electricity arching overhead was coming from her body rather than flowing into it.

The street cleared. In the distance there were sirens. Marina lay on the ground, panting, exhausted.

To her right something growled. She rolled onto her stomach, pushed herself onto her hands and knees. A black hellhound, his eyes glowing red, stood staring at her.

Her heart slowed. She pushed herself up, onto the balls of her feet, ready to run. She'd come looking for Raf, but hadn't expected to see him like this. Every hair on her body stood up, every ounce of instinct said flee.

Behind her, she heard another sound, another growl. A second hellhound stood behind her. This one golden. *Which, if either, was Raf? Surely the dark-haired one…but the other hellhound, the bounty hunter, he'd had dark hair, too. Was the golden yet another mercenary? How many could there be?*

Power crackled into her palms. "Kill them," Amma murmured. "I've no desire to be trapped inside a chew toy."

Marina stared at the blue glow of power that colored her flesh. If she killed the hellhounds, it would buy her time. And now Amma was cooperating. She could go back to her original plan, or work out something else with the witch.

Her hands itched; her fingers curled toward her palms, then straightened.

Kill the hellhounds and escape with Amma on her side. It was what she had wanted, except... What if one of the dogs was Raf?

Raf had found the other hellhound. He'd been trailing him more than Marina. Raf had known where she was. He'd sensed her approach and concentrated instead on the bounty hunter who was after her. The other hellhound had shifted. So Raf had, too.

Now the other male had her trapped, or thought he did. He must not have seen the magic streaming from her hands, shooting skyward. Raf had. He knew Joarr had, too. He suspected Joarr, flying hidden by the sudden fog, was the target.

Amma must be working with Marina after all.

The other male leapt, his trajectory clear—Marina. Raf held his breath, waited for the elf/witch to let loose the power he'd just seen shoot from her palms. But she hesitated, glanced over her shoulder at him then back at the hound already too close to touching her.

With a roar, Raf surged forward, knocked Marina to the ground. Then twirled and stood over her as the other hellhound landed and turned, too, his hackles raised, his eyes glowing red.

Raf had stolen his prize and the other male wasn't happy.

Too damn bad.

Raf widened his stance and lowered his head. Let his jaw drop enough his lower teeth would appear. Then he raised his upper lip, letting show his intention to keep the prize as his own.

The other hellhound seemed unintimidated. He paced to the side and back again, his eyes darting from Raf to Marina. He was waiting for her to run, Raf realized, planned on shimmering and grabbing her if she did.

Raf backed up until his hind foot touched her leg. He could have shimmered her then, but that would have left the hunter undefeated, still thinking he could take Raf, and steal Marina. He had to be beaten, taught.

"He wants you to run," he projected the words into the elf princess's head, hoped it was enough to keep her in place.

The bounty hunter lunged, his jaws open, aimed at Raf's throat. Raf bent his front legs, let the other dog land on top of him, then stood, charged forward and flipped the hunter onto his back. As the other male struggled to right himself, Raf moved in, stepped over him and wrapped his jaws around his neck. Squeezed.

"No bounty here," he said telepathically.

The hellhound below him kicked with his hind legs, bucked his weight against the pressure of Raf's jaws. His toenails dug into Raf's stomach; his feet pummeled Raf's gut, making it difficult to breathe. Raf returned the favor, squeezing more tightly around the other male's throat.

"How much are they paying you?" Raf asked. "Is it worth being killed for?" He dug his teeth in deeper, tasted the other male's blood.

The bounty hunter twisted, managed to pull his neck free. He lunged to his feet. Skin tore; a hunk of his fur dangled from Raf's teeth.

Raf spit it out, cursed, then bounded to the side, stopping the hunter from moving closer to Marina. "The hunt is over. You had that—you just didn't get the prey."

"It's not over *until* I get the prey."

"Or I kill you," Raf replied.

The hunter grinned, stalked left, then right. "There is that possibility."

Behind him, Marina shifted, murmured. Power snapped. The surge of magic sent the hair on Raf's hindquarters to a stand. She was at the advantage. His back was to her. She could kill him now, or at least damage him seriously.

The bounty hunter jerked his head to the side. His gaze shot behind Raf…to Marina. "What was that?"

There was another surge, this one bigger than before. Every hair on Raf's body shot upward. His eyes watered. He spun.

Streams of power tore from Marina's palms toward Raf. He dropped to the ground, felt heat sear over his back, past him. The other hound cursed, fell.

Raf sprang to his feet, his gaze locked on the elf princess. Her chest was moving up and down; her eyes were wild. "Tell the elf lords to go to hell," she muttered. Then she turned on the ball of her foot and pointed her palms at Raf.

Marina had lost control of her own body. Amma had convinced her to let the witch take care of the bounty hunter, but Marina hadn't realized that once Amma was given rein, it would be so hard to pull her back.

She struggled against the pull that had made her raise her arms. Her body twitched with the effort. Pain shot through her, brought tears to her eyes, but it didn't matter. She wasn't strong enough. The witch was winning, was going to shoot down Raf just like she'd shot down the bounty hunter. Destroy him.

Magic sizzled down her shoulders, through her arms toward her hands. Raf, in dog form, golden and beautiful—just as beautiful as when he was a man. She'd realized which dog Raf was after he'd spoken in her head, but knowing wasn't enough. Not if she couldn't control Amma.

He stood frozen watching her, not moving. *Why wasn't he moving?*

She wanted to scream at him, but Amma had taken control of her throat, too. Marina was nothing but a puppet, trapped inside her body, forced to watch what the witch was doing, the destruction she was about to unleash.

Marina fought harder, managed to curve her fingers slightly, but she knew it wasn't enough—that the magic arcing through her would blow her hands open, blast out of her into Raf. She squinted, tried to close her eyes to block the sight, but even that didn't work.

As she steeled herself for what was about to come, air hot and humid dropped down around her. The magic building inside her vanished and like a marionette whose strings had been cut she crumpled onto the ground.

Raf reached two fingers through the net and touched Marina's throat. After the dragon had dropped the piece of elf magic on her, she'd collapsed, been unconscious since.

"She's fine," Joarr growled from his position across the room. The dragon, back in his white suit, leaned against the brick wall; the lantern dangled from his hand. "Let's get on with it while she's out. Keep it simple."

Raf let his touch linger, absorbed the steady feel of Marina's pulse beating against his fingers. The even cadence reassured him, as did the up and down movement of her chest. Still, he fought the urge to pick her up and cradle her against his chest.

Joarr pushed himself away from the wall and stalked across the room. "She was going to kill you. You realize that, don't you?"

Did he? Raf pulled his hand away from the elf princess, curled his fingers into his palm, tried to hide the slight shake of them, even from himself. Marina had blasted at the other hellhound without hesitation, could have done the same to him. Like an idiot he'd stood there, given her plenty of time.

But she hadn't.

"Here." Joarr held out his hand. Pinched between his finger and thumb was the needle.

"How do we know it will work?" Raf asked, for some reason reluctant to touch the sliver of metal.

"It worked before," Joarr replied.

"Not really. I was there. She plunged it into her arm over and over, nothing happened." Back in Gunngar, Marina had tried to use the needle to drive Amma into her body, but it hadn't worked. Not until Amma had been forced from her current host's body and been left with no other options had she moved into Marina.

"Not there. In Alfheim. It's how the elf lords pulled Amma's spirit from her own body, before they transferred it to the necklace." Joarr lowered his brows. "Do it, or I will." Then with a huff, he added. "It won't hurt her."

Raf took the needle and kneeled beside Marina. Her breathing was even, but as he reached through the netting, she stirred. The needle brushed her skin. Just that tiny touch left a zigzag of blood behind it. Marina's eyes flew open.

"Yggdrassil's roots!" Joarr leaned forward and grabbed the needle.

Marina's eyes widened and her mouth opened as if to scream, but Joarr ignored her panic and plunged the needle into her flesh. Just as quickly, he jerked it back out.

Marina's hand slapped over her arm where the needle had pierced her; she sucked in a breath. Her eyes rolled upward and Raf thought she was going to faint again. Instead, her spine straightened, hardened as if forged of steel. She sat there, no readable expression on her face.

Raf leaned forward, afraid to touch her. His hands were shaking again; a band had tightened around his heart.

His voice hoarse, he asked, "Did it work?"

The dragon, who had already retreated, was next to the window, holding the needle up to the sunlight.

"Hard to say." The dragon pulled the needle close to his face. "Are you in there darling, Amma? Did you miss me? Maybe I'll use you to stitch up a hole in my sock." With a laugh, he slid open the top of the lantern and dropped the needle inside. It landed on the bottom with a ping. "If she's in there she'll come out eventually. The lantern will give her the ability to see her surroundings. She won't be able to resist that."

Raf growled under his breath. "What about Marina?"

"What about her? Amma's out of her. She should be easy enough to handle now. You shackled her this time, and you have your box." The dragon nodded at the covered glass box Raf had brought with him from Gunngar. It was exactly like the box he had been trapped inside, deep in Gunngar's dungeon—under Marina's orders.

As Raf was staring at the cloth-covered rectangle, the dragon slipped the lantern strap over his head and across his chest. "Time to fly." He strode to the window and threw up the sash. "I have a witch to torment." With no further goodbye, Joarr shot out the window, shifting into a dragon as soon as his human form started to drop.

Raf crossed to the window and slammed it shut. The dragon was a good ally, but an annoying companion.

"Is she gone?"

Raf turned. Marina sat on the floor, flexing and un-flexing her hands. She looked well, fine, beautiful... Angry at his own reaction, he walked over and jerked the net off of her. He didn't need it to control her, not with Amma out of her body.

"She's gone." He paused, waited for Marina's outrage, waited for the sense of joy it would give him. Taking Amma's power from Marina was just the first part of his plan of revenge, but an important part. He waited, but the joy didn't come.

Marina stared around looking lost and unbelieving. "Really?" She smiled.

She smiled. Raf's eyes narrowed. *She shouldn't be smiling. She'd lost what she'd fought so hard to get. What game was she playing now?*

"Raf." Marina struggled to her feet, baby-stepping away from the net. Raf waited, watched, refused to be taken in by her act, refused to feel guilty for the heavy shackles confining her. She would reveal her game soon enough.

She glanced down at her bound ankles. "Is Amma all they wanted? Will you let me go now?"

Her eyes were clear. Green as new grass. Not an ounce of guile in them—innocent as if she expected him to walk over and set her free. And damn everything, he wanted to, but he wouldn't be taken in, not by her.

He raised a brow. "Are you serious?"

She licked her lips and glanced around the room. "You're working for the elf lords, aren't you? The dragon took Amma. That's what they asked you for, right? What they are paying you for?"

"What makes you think I'm working for anyone?" he asked. "You stole years of my life. What makes you think I'm not just here for revenge?" He walked to the box and yanked the cover off of it.

She laughed.

Laughed. He couldn't believe it. He growled.

She shuffled forward again, her body straight and anger snapping from her eyes. "You want revenge on me? I trusted you, and you were working for the elf lords." She glanced at his face and shook her head. "What would you have done? Would *you* have left the spy roaming free? Especially after his lies had been so complete? I trusted. I haven't trusted anyone, not since my parents were killed. But I trusted you. Do you know how much that hurt? Spies get death in Alfheim— did the elf lords warn you of that? My uncle would have had you killed without pause, but weak sap that I am…I just had you locked up. And now you want revenge." She closed her eyes and turned her back on him.

Raf folded his arms over his chest. Didn't let the shock that she'd known about his deal with the elf lords show.

Marina pressed two fingers to her brow. She moved as if to walk then realized her ankles were still chained, stopped and swayed for a second before regaining her balance.

His hand lifted to help her. Remembering himself, he lowered it. He didn't want to understand the reasons behind what she had done to him. He needed her to be the evil female he'd created in his mind; it was the only way he could justify selling her to the elf lords.

And he needed to sell her to the elf lords; he needed the seer stone. He'd tried everything else; the stone was his last hope.

Forcing himself to focus on all the tales he'd heard of her since his release, all the crimes she had committed, he squared his shoulders, kept his gaze cold and distant. "What about the witches? The ones you hunted and burned? Were their deaths justified? Why weren't you generous with them? Why didn't you lock them in a box? Or refuse to hunt them at all?" He put metal into the questions.

She turned back around. Her anger had intensified, morphed, was almost tangible now. "You mean refuse to do what your bosses demanded of me? You work for the elf lords. Doesn't that make you as bad as me?"

He shook his head. "No. It doesn't." He hadn't terrorized an entire land. He hadn't caught and burned a witch for the entire city to see.

Her nostrils flared. "You seem to know everything. Do you really want to hear my side of it? Will it make any difference? Will anything I say make a difference?"

He only blinked. It was the most he could risk without opening himself up to softening, believing her justifications and lies.

"I didn't kill anyone, not anyone who didn't deserve it, didn't threaten me or someone else."

He was sure the witches' families wouldn't agree.

"I am a princess, but you know that. What you don't know is what that meant. I was never a person in my own right. I was always a symbol of something else— something the royals lost and hoped to get back. I was dressed up and put on display. I was trained to look pretty and keep my mouth shut, at least as far as my uncle knew. I was rich and pampered and trapped—like a bird with no wings kept in a crystal cage. And I was brought up to hate the elf lords. They had what my uncle and the other royals wanted, the prestige and power that comes with ruling Alfheim.

"When it was announced the elf lords were putting together a group to take Amma into Gunngar, it seemed like the perfect escape. My uncle couldn't reach me there—not if he didn't want to be trapped there himself. And I'd built up the elf lords to be everything the royals weren't—noble, open, my chance to be me.

"But I was wrong. They didn't want me to be me, they wanted me to be one of them. They were thrilled to have a 'princess' in their midst and under their control. They wanted word of my secession to spread through Alfheim. They thought it would help them gain the faith of the citizens who still followed the royals. I was a pawn, again. But this time I had a whole new act to follow if I didn't want to wind up with a dagger in my back. Because while a princess working with them was great, one working against them…well, there'd be no reason to keep her around.

"I was trapped and if I wanted to survive I had to play along. I had to play at being their most fervent believer."

And she'd embraced the act, Raf reminded himself. The witch she'd burned was proof of that. A snarl threatened to curl his lip. He firmed his jaw, kept his emotions hidden. She could play the victim all she wanted, but he wasn't buying it. She didn't have to do any of the things she'd done. She had made a choice, and now he would, too.

Chapter 4

Marina held her breath, waiting for Raf's response. She'd told him everything, a lot of it at least. She'd certainly been more upfront with him, shared more of her history with him than she'd ever shared with anyone.

He walked to a pile of bags that lay in the corner. Started shuffling through them.

Marina frowned.

After only a few seconds, he stood. His hand was curled around something, an object she couldn't see. He walked within six feet of her, held out his open palm. A silver case, the size and shape of a lipstick lay on top of it. Then he closed his hand around it again and slowly, his gaze on her the entire time, pressed the top with his thumb.

She didn't respond, wouldn't. She knew what he'd done, what he was saying. He didn't believe her or cared so little for her it didn't matter. The object was elfin. A caller, a locator. He'd just signaled Alfheim.

After Raf had called the elf lords to let them know Marina was caught and ready for their representative to retrieve, he had turned his back on her. There was nothing left to say. She'd tried to trick him...again. She had been convincing and he'd been tempted to believe her. But he wouldn't. Lies from beautiful lips were still lies.

He walked to the window and stared out, not really focusing on anything.

It would be a while until the elf lords arrived. He had time to follow through on the rest of his plan. The box he'd brought was still sitting against the wall, waiting for its occupant.

But after hearing her story, he'd lost interest in personal revenge. He was having a hard enough time clinging to the truths he knew of what she'd done in Gunngar, the truths that helped justify selling her to the elf lords. Past feelings and other truths kept intruding.

He *had* betrayed her; he had been working for the elf lords, spying on her. He hadn't seen it as bad at the time. What were a few reports back on what she was doing?

But hearing her side of things, he realized he would have reacted exactly as she had. No...he would have reacted worse.

Guilt clawed at him. He had to get rid of her as quickly as he could—turn her over to the elf lords before he completely backed out.

This wasn't just about Marina. This was about avenging his family. Raf had devoted his life to the task, had only slipped in his dedication once—when he met Marina.

Her betrayal had been a good thing, put him back
on task.

He couldn't let guilt or some twisted idea that he
might care for the elf princess cause him to be sidetracked again.

Marina waited what felt like hours. Raf had turned
his back on her, cut her off and she'd let him. She'd
known arguing, begging would do no good. He'd
already sent the call.

And she had more pride than that. Perhaps that
was her problem, perhaps if she had less pride she
would have confessed all this to someone long ago,
found an ally, the strength that came with knowing
you weren't alone.

But she hadn't. And apparently it was too late now.

So, she waited and wondered who Raf had called, her
uncle or the elf lords? Which would be worse?

She leaned her head against the wall and closed her
eyes. She was almost past caring, maybe she was meant
for life as a pawn.

There was a knock on the door.

Marina stiffened. Not the dragon. He wouldn't knock
and not another hellhound—they would shimmer inside
unannounced.

Funny how all of a sudden the idea of facing another
bounty hunter didn't seem like a bad thing.

Raf opened the door.

On the other side stood her uncle, Geir Sturlbok.

No, facing another bounty hunter didn't seem like a
bad thing at all. Marina closed her eyes and let out a
tired sigh.

He slid past Raf without even glancing at the hellhound. In Geir's world there were elves and nothing else. He had even fired his last wife's long-time house-keeper because she was a dwarf. Dwarves were highly valued as hired help in most worlds, but not in Alfheim.

His clear gaze locked on to Marina. She wrapped her hands around her upper arms and squeezed. He strode toward her.

"We've been worried about you." His eyes roamed her body, settled on the shackles connecting her ankles. "What are those?"

"Irons," Raf replied. He'd stayed by the door, was watching them with a hooded gaze.

Geir ignored the hellhound's comment, held up a hand to motion to four elves who were waiting just outside the door. They hurried inside. "Unlock her," he ordered.

The four elves stared at the dwarf-forged iron, then back at Geir. "How?" one of them finally asked.

"Perhaps with this?" Raf stepped closer; a black key was pinched between his fingers. The gesture was calm, indifferent, but there was a tautness to his muscles, a contained anger Marina recognized, but doubted her uncle saw.

Geir nodded and one of the elves, the one who had spoken, reached out to take the key. Raf snapped it back out of reach. "Who are you?" he asked, an edge of danger to his voice. "I need I.D. before I hand her over."

Geir moved next to Marina, ran his hand down her face, whispered in her ear. "What have you been up to, my niece?"

Marina stiffened.

"The royals aren't very happy with you, and thus me. Sneaking off like that to Gunngar. What were you thinking?" He pulled back, patted Marina lightly on the cheek. "We were almost ready to move on our plan, and you threw it all away. Risked everything." He placed his hand on his chin and studied her through narrowed eyes. "We have your sister, but she isn't the princess, not as long as you're alive. There were those...still are who think you are too...undependable. But with things in Alfheim beginning to—" He closed his lips over whatever he'd been about to say, reached for her again instead. His hand stroked her cheek, then stilled. "You're my sister's daughter. I would hate to have to make that choice."

She tried not to flinch. "Ky? How is she?" she asked. Her sister was younger, and thus not a princess by elf tradition—not as long as Marina, the eldest, was alive. Because of that, she'd never been at risk of being used as Marina had. Marina had envied that freedom.

Geir ignored her, asked a question of his own instead. "So, what happened in Gunngar? Were you working with the elf lords as they claimed?"

Raf stepped closer, so close Geir had no choice but to acknowledge him. The elf dropped his hand from Marina's face.

"The key," her uncle ordered.

Raf arched a brow. "I.D.?"

Geir paused. "You aren't the one I hired."

Raf's eyes flickered. "Which means you aren't the one who hired me."

Geir's gaze slid to Marina, then to the elves who had entered with him. "So, the elf lords want her, too. Not surprising, but also not a problem. Trust me when I say the royal coffers are every bit as full as the elf lords'. More so, in fact." He snapped his fingers. One of the elves jogged forward and pulled a card from his jacket. Geir gestured for him to hand it to Raf.

Raf glanced at it then back at Marina's uncle. Before he could reply, or take the money card, something knocked against the door.

Geir turned to Marina. "Yes. I almost forgot. In case you had been working with the elf lords, I found something I thought might interest them." He gestured, and an elf opened the door. A woman, dressed in a shredded dress that would in better days have reached her feet, fell to the floor. A fifth and sixth elf walked into the room behind her. Like Marina, she was shackled, but her ties were thin, made of the same elfin magic as the net Raf had used on Marina had been constructed of. There was only one reason Marina's uncle would use such binds. The woman had magic, was either a shape-shifter or a witch.

And as she looked up, Marina knew.

She sucked in a breath. She'd never thought to see the woman again. Marina had assumed the woman had escaped Gunngar with everyone else, had gone on to find her family. But obviously, she hadn't.

The woman lying on the floor before her was, as far as anyone in Alfheim knew, dead. She was supposed to have been burned alive back in Gunngar by the elf lords' orders and Marina's hand.

Geir walked over and pulled the woman to a stand by her hair. "Niece, do you know this female? Do you know this witch?" He jerked the witch's face toward Marina's. "We found her in Gunngar."

Marina bit her lip. There was nothing she could say to get the woman out of this. She was now a tool, just like Marina.

Geir took a step, pulling the woman behind him. She grimaced and clawed at his hand. He pulled back his other hand, spun as if to slap her, but Raf stepped forward and grabbed him by the wrist.

The two males stared at each other, but only for a second—a shocked second. Marina didn't think anyone had ever dared to challenge her uncle. Even in Alfheim where his royal blood no longer gained him political power, he was held in revered regard. He was one of the last few elves of royal blood. Even the elf lords danced around directly challenging him—afraid to do so might spark a civil war.

Raf's glower made it clear he wasn't concerned with Geir's elevated status. He pulled Geir's wrist higher.

All six of the other elves pounced on him. Raf shook them off like a dog shaking off rain. They flew to the floor; one slid past Marina on his back. Red-faced he flipped over and sprang back toward the hellhound, but Raf had moved too. He had Geir by the throat, shoved against a wall.

His eyes glimmered red.

Geir's guards paused to look at their leader.

"I don't think you were listening to me. You are not who hired me, and I'm not interested in making a new deal." Raf tightened his hold. Geir's skin bulged over the top line of his fingers. "If you want to live, you need to leave—without your niece." He glanced at the witch whose wrist Geir still held. "And without her." The hellhound jerked his head toward the witch.

Geir curled his lip. "She is none of your concern."

Raf stepped closer, so his nose was only inches from the elf's. "Maybe before you brought her into my domain." He gestured around the dingy room. "I know

it doesn't look like much, but it's mine, and so is she—"
he jerked his head toward Marina "—until I hand her
over to those who hired me."

"I am willing to pay double what they can," Geir
growled.

"I think I said I wasn't interested." Raf turned so his
side was to Geir. One hand was still wrapped around the
royal's neck. With the other Raf stroked his own chin.
"But tell you what, you let that one—" he slid his gaze
to the witch "—go, and I won't crush your windpipe."

"I don't have to pay you for the princess. We can just
take her." Even with Raf's hand clamped around his
throat, Geir managed to sound bored.

Raf laughed. "You think?"

"Yes, I do." Geir's gaze flickered, a blink so quick
Marina knew the hellhound couldn't have seen it.

One of the elves reached into his pocket.

Marina screamed, "Raf, behind you."

The hellhound turned, tossing her uncle across the
room as he did. The two elves who had entered with
the witch dropped her and dashed to grab the royal
before he collided with a wall. The other two rushed
forward, swords in their hands.

Marina lunged, forgetting her ankles were bound
and landed on her face. Her lip split, blood spilled into
her mouth. As she pushed herself up onto her palms,
steel flashed. One of the elves danced forward. His
blade sliced through Raf's shirt, into his skin, left a
zigzag trail of blood in its wake.

Steel sliced through his skin, but the pain barely reg-
istered. Raf was too focused on the battle, too lost in the
desire to change. Anger bubbled inside him. He bared

his teeth and let the rage take over. He fell to all fours;
fur sprouted from his skin and his teeth and nails length-
ened. His eyes glowed red; he could feel the fire there,
simmering, waiting to boil over.

Elves were trying to take Marina from him. He
wouldn't let them, couldn't wait to taste their blood.

The elf who had cut him froze, then moved a few
steps back. Silly little elf. He was no match for a hellhound, didn't he know that? Raf moved to the side, his
head low, his teeth flashing.

"Step away from her," he demanded in their heads.

The elves exchanged glances.

They were unsure, had probably never faced a hellhound before.

Behind them Marina moved. She had fallen to the
ground. Raf eyed the distance to her. He could leap, land
on her and shimmer them both away, but…he glanced
to the right…there was the witch, too. She stood where
the elves had left her, her eyes huge and her face pale.
He needed to reach both of them, get both of them
away, but he also needed to fight. The bloodlust was
growing inside him, triggered by what he wasn't sure,
but he was angry, as angry as he had been in a very long
time.

He didn't just want to get Marina and the witch
away. He wanted to destroy the elves who thought
they could take them.

He growled, tried to control the beast inside him.
Letting the bloodlust take over meant losing control,
possibly losing the prize.

Near the witch, there was movement—her guards
and Geir. Marina's uncle reached into his pocket and
pulled something out. Whatever he held fit in his palm.

He nodded to the elves closest to him. One drew his sword and thrust—his blade pointed at the witch's heart.

With a curse, Raf leapt. Below him, Geir dropped to the ground and rolled. Instantly, Raf knew he'd been tricked, but he had no choice. The threat to the witch was real. If Raf changed direction or shimmered to Marina, where Geir was headed, the witch would be dead. He knocked into her, shimmering as soon as his foot struck her side.

He immediately shimmered them back into the room, but farther away, in the opposite corner from where they had been, but it was too late. The elves had donned some kind of masks that covered their noses and mouths and the room was filled with frothy white gas.

Raf fell to his knees. The witch collapsed beside him. He tried to stand, to shimmer, anything, but he was too weak to do anything more than watch as the elves grabbed Marina by the arms and dragged her unconscious from the room.

He'd lost her.

Chapter 5

Raf came to. Still in dog form, he shook his head, tried to clear the fog that seemed to linger. *Fog. Marina. The elves.* He stood and swallowed the bitter taste that coated his mouth—the taste of the gas the elves had used.

He had failed, had let elves beat him. A growl built in his chest, changed to a roar as it escaped his throat. He changed to his human form. Naked and shaking with frustration, he slammed his fist into the cement wall. Pain rippled down his arm, into his frame; he embraced it, then pulled back his fist to strike again.

A gasp sounded from a few feet away. He spun. The witch he'd saved stared back at him. Her hair was stringy and her clothes were torn. It was obvious she had not been treated well and now after his performance, she looked as if she expected him to tear her into shreds.

He bit back a curse, forced the anger surging through him to mellow, and started pulling on his clothes.

When his pants covered his lower half, she looked a little more secure, at least she worked up the courage to ask, "Who are you?"

Dirty, in torn clothes and obviously shaken by being left alone with a raging hellhound, her voice was still strong. "What happened to the elf? The female. Did they take her?"

Thinking she was worried Marina was still near, might still be working for the elf lords, hunting witches, he replied, "She's gone, with her uncle. You don't have to worry about her, or them. I'll protect you." *Like he'd protected Marina?* a voice inside him scoffed. He shook his head, still unable to believe he'd been duped so easily—twice now, once by Marina and then by her uncle.

The witch took a step back, her gaze wary. "I knew her from Gunngar. She saved me."

His shirt halfway down his chest, Raf froze. "Aren't you a witch? Marina didn't save witches, she burned them."

The woman let out a soft snort. "Or made others think she did. I'd believed that's what she was going to do to me. I was tied to the pyre. I could smell the smoke. I thought it was over...my daughters..." She looked up. "I have daughters. I didn't want to leave them, but I had to. If I hadn't the elves would have found them, too. The elves caught me and took me to the city square. Then Marina, their leader, arrived with a torch in her hand. I thought it was over. The flames hit the wood and my world exploded in smoke, but while I was preparing for the pain, something happened. I moved. I wasn't in the square any longer. I was across the land…in a field. No explanation, nothing."

"You were the witch Marina burned in the square? But you're…you're not—" Raf jerked his shirt down the rest of the way. He didn't know what to say. He needed time to process what the woman was saying.

"It took months, but I made my way back to the city. By the time I got there, everything had changed. Gunngar was open, the elves were gone, most of them anyway. I was asking for help, looking for my daughters, and I asked the wrong person. Damn Svartalfar, dark elves." She spat on the floor. "Willing to trade their mothers for an ale. They took me to the ones who brought me here," she continued.

"So, Marina didn't kill you?" Raf asked, even though the evidence was staring back at him.

The witch smiled and ran her hands over her bodice. "I've looked better, but I'm definitely alive. A few months living off the land, followed by a week in an elfin prison… my daily beauty regime suffered. But none of that matters, what's important is finding my daughters." Her torn skirt balled in her fists, she took a step forward, her gaze was steady and determined. "Will you help me?"

Raf glanced around the room. The net, box and locator were still there, but Marina was gone. He'd spent months hunting her, and in the pass of a few moments he'd lost her. Without her, there was no hope of getting the seer stone from the elf lords, no hope of finding revenge against his family's killers.

And this witch wanted him to take time away from his hunt to help her. He crossed the room without answering, picked up the net and folded it until it would fit into his pocket.

When he glanced back, the witch was still there fidgeting with her skirt, but staring at him. Waiting.

He walked to the box and placed his hands on it. The clear material it was constructed of was cold and unyielding—as he'd thought Marina was. But this witch claimed Marina had saved her. His mind swirled. His plan, his justification for it, was slipping through his fingers like sand.

"Hellhound?" The witch took a step forward. She licked her lips, but there was determination in her eyes. "Will you help me?"

Raf pressed his hands onto the box's top until he thought, indestructible as he knew it to be, it might crack. This wasn't a damn mission of mercy. He had spent what felt like a lifetime hunting who had killed his family—the stone was his last hope.

The woman moved again, started to speak.

With a growl, he turned on her. "I'll take you to people who can, but that's it." Then his good deeds would be over—guilty or not, he would find Marina and sell her to the elf lords. He wouldn't be distracted again, by anything or anyone—especially Marina.

Marina sat in the back of her uncle's open-topped car, her hands folded calmly in her lap. Only she and the three elves sitting across from her knew the silk scarf artfully tossed across her wrists hid thin ties.

She was shackled again. Geir had wasted no time replacing the heavy dwarf shackles Raf had used with thin elfin ones. So much easier to hide. So much easier to continue his guise of the happy royal family. He'd already sent out press releases, announcing the information the elf lords had spread of her joining their ranks was "misinformed."

Marina had listened to her uncle's explanation of what he'd done with a hollow spirit. Raf hadn't believed her, or hadn't cared. Despite everything, she'd thought…she closed her eyes, willed the tears that threatened to form to disappear. She was alone. It was time she accepted that.

"Your sister will be happy to see you," one of the elves, Tahl, said, then shifted his gaze over the others in the car. "She has missed you."

Marina sighed. She should be haughty and cold; it was what her guards expected, what her uncle expected, but she was tired. Tired to the marrow of her bones. "I will be happy to see her, too."

At her answer, the three guards started. She turned from them, stared out into the faces that lined the streets. They seemed different from the crowds she remembered before her journey to Gunngar, a little ragtag perhaps. She didn't linger on the thought for long. Her mind quickly returned to her own situation. Now that she was on her own and trapped again, she needed to concentrate—think of an escape.

Not only had her uncle claimed the stories of her joining with the elf lords were false, he had also worked to turn her time in Gunngar to the royals' favor— claimed that she had been there as *their* representative, not the elf lords, set her up as some kind of heroine who had pursued Amma when the witch escaped, then been captured by a hellhound and taken to the human world against her will.

The citizens of Alfheim had gobbled it up. The elves who had come out for her procession stared at her as if she had walked through the fires of Muspelheim. To them surviving the human world had to be as bad.

The idiocy, the farce, all of it made Marina's head ache. She tilted her head back against the upholstery. Her mind drifted to Raf, how he'd looked as he'd lunged to save the witch....

Her uncle's sharp voice cut through her moment of recollection. "Smile. Wave. These are your people. Your destiny. Your hope. Give them what they want." He rode beside the car on a stallion.

He was beautiful and regal on his horse. His blond hair rippled in the wind and his body clung to the horse's back as if he was part of the beast. He was the perfect elf, and he knew it. Expected Marina to be one, too.

But she never had and never could be. She was tainted with her witch powers, weak though they were, and she'd never "fit" into the royal life, not like her sister had. Marina didn't share the royals' outlook on anything. She hated the importance pretense seemed to hold in their lives, and as a witch herself, she couldn't look down on non-elves. She had acted as if she did, though, for the royals and the elf lords—and she hated herself for it.

The car rounded a bend in the road and left the crowd of misguided citizens behind—or most of them. Perched in a tree twenty yards ahead Marina spotted a gleam of light reflecting off glass. A camera. One hard core member of the paparazzi looking for the shot no one else would get, the shot that would make him millions in currency and fame.

Marina tensed. Temptation flitted through her. She'd never shown any public sign of the true relationship between her and her uncle. While never described in detail, she'd always known there would be a price to be paid.

She glanced down at the scarf. One quick upward movement of her arms and the photographer would have his picture. All of Alfheim would have evidence that she wasn't committed to the royals as her uncle would have them think.

But she would still be in this car, on her way to the mansion. And once he found out, she'd be forced to pay that undescribed price.

They were only a few feet away now. She could hear the camera clicking. She was surprised no one else seemed to notice, but maybe it was because she'd been gone, had forgotten what it was like to be under the constant scrutiny.

They were almost there; he was almost past, her chance gone. Slowly, carefully she pinched the scarf between her fingers and pulled it lower, just enough that the unmistakable sheen of the ties could be seen peeking above the silk.

She held her breath and the smile that she'd had on her face since arriving back in Alfheim. And as the car rolled onward, out from under the tree, she prayed the photographer had just snapped the picture of his life.

Raf had never been in Alfheim, not this deep into it anyway. When he and the others had walked through Gunngar's portal they had landed in some part of the silvery land, but there had been no buildings there, no elves, and they had gone no farther. They had stayed by the portal until the garm figured out how to work the traveling device, then each had gone to their own land or land of their choice. In Raf's case he had gone to the human world to find Marina. His hunter's sense had told him that was where she would head. It was where most who wanted to get lost for a while headed.

But this time he'd chosen to land as square in the center of Alfheim as he could, in Alfheim's capital city, Fisby. Home of both Marina's uncle and the elf lords.

The portal he'd gone through opened into a small room. The unadorned space was a major departure from the portals he usually traveled through. In most of the nine worlds, portals were run and guarded by garm. The wolves tended to taverns and bars. A nice compliment to the weary realities of travel.

But here there was nothing but elves. Just seeing them made Raf's hair ruffle. He crossed his arms over his chest and waited. Minutes ticked by. The four elves who occupied the room didn't even acknowledge him; they kept their gazes attached to their computers instead.

Their obvious attempt to ignore whoever walked through the portal, to intimidate them and make them feel insignificant failed with Raf. He strolled forward and tapped one finger on the top of a pewter-colored monitor.

The elf behind the monitor let out an exasperated huff. "One mo—" He froze. His hand slipped to the elf beside him. One by one as if they were engaged in a football crowd's wave, the four looked up and stared. A shocked, appalled stare.

Finally, one slapped the device protruding from his ear and began jabbering into his mouthpiece. Raf smiled, showing some teeth.

A door behind the elves slid open. A fifth elf entered, a grim expression on his face and a small electronic pad of some sort wedged under his arm. The other four stepped out from behind their terminals, swords drawn.

Armed computer geeks. Alfheim was already a treasure trove of new discoveries.

Raf stepped forward, his shoulders brushing against the blade of the closest elf.

"Type of being?" The tablet bearer tilted his head up to meet Raf's gaze. He held the device in front of him as if ready to take notes, but his stance was wide. He was ready for a fight. How Raf wished he had the time to give it to him.

He leaned forward, so his nose almost brushed the elf's. "Forandre." Then waited to see how they would react to his announcement that he was a shape-shifter. Alfheim had a reputation for not being overly welcoming of other beings.

The elf tapped his stylus on the tablet and his gaze flickered to the elves holding the swords. The elves inched closer until all four blades were within an easy thrust of Raf's chest.

"Reason for this visit?"

Raf twisted his lips to the side. The elves were tense and nosey. Travel through the portals was usually casual. You paid a fee or provided a bounty and you got through. He'd never been questioned like this.

But then he'd never traveled to the heart of Alfheim before. There was no telling what surprises might be waiting for him.

He slid one foot over the floor beneath his feet, felt for a trapdoor or weakness in the boards. All seemed solid.

The elf waited.

"Business." Raf replied.

"And you are…?"

"Raf Dolg."

The elf tapped his notebook with a stylus. "A…?"

Obviously, forandre wasn't specific enough for the pencil pusher. "Hellhound," he replied.

He wasn't prepared for the response. All four elves shoved their blades into his throat, the one on the right with a tad too much enthusiasm; blood ran down Raf's neck.

"We don't get many hellhounds here," the elf replied, but not before Raf noticed his jaw tightening. "Who is your business with?"

Raf knew nothing about elf politics, few outside of Alfheim did. The light elves kept to themselves. Should he mention Geir or the elf lords? He had business with both—although the first might consider it more thievery.

He decided to stick with a hellhound standby—arrogance. "No one who wants their name tossed about casually."

"Really? Have you been to Gunngar recently, hellhound?" The elf tapped a few times on his digital notebook and pretended to read something there.

Raf let out a growl. In the best of times he had little patience with bureaucrats and with four swords pressed to his throat, what little he did have was quickly evaporating.

The elf looked up, but Raf wasn't looking at him. He was looking behind him at the door that had just flown open and the six elves pushed against it, ready to rush in.

Without hesitating, he shimmered, aimed for the tiny bit of green grass he could see over the heads of his would-be attackers.

Raf solidified quickly. It was a short trip, maybe one hundred yards. His feet were on grass. He'd landed in some kind of small park, but buildings towered around him. He spun and searched his surroundings for more elves, more attackers.

A small square building sat at the bottom of the hill. Rushing towards it were a dozen or so armed elves. The portal.

Raf moved to the side, leaned against a white brick wall and concentrated on blending. The elves knew nothing of hellhounds if they thought he'd be that easy to trap.

As he watched, the flow toward the building stopped. The sound of a whistle pierced the air. The elves turned and quickly formed two lines leading to the building. The elf with the notebook stepped into view. He was talking into a headset and scribbling as quickly as he could.

Raf almost laughed at their idiocy. They were too preoccupied lining up and chatting amongst themselves to realize he stood only a few feet away—within an arrow's reach. He was tempted to step forward and show them how misguided all their work was.

Unfortunately, while he had made it past them, he had no idea where to go from there. He could shimmer anywhere within the boundaries of a land, but only if he had an idea of his destination. Alfheim was kept uncharted—or at least any maps of the world weren't available to outsiders. If he stepped forward, he'd have nowhere to shimmer to when the arrows started flying. So, he was stuck for a while, until the elfin guards walked through their motions, got done convincing themselves they were actually doing something to find him.

Sooner or later one would wander away, come closer. Close enough Raf could grab him and force the location of Geir's home out of him.

Until then, he would wait.

Chapter 6

Marina's guards stepped from the car one by one. Her uncle had told them to escort her to his office while he groomed his horse and released it into the paddock.

The beast had twice as much freedom as Marina had ever enjoyed.

Tahl reached a hand in to assist her. She stared at it. In Gunngar she had been responsible for ruling an army of elves. She hadn't enjoyed the job because of the act she'd had to put on while doing it, but still it was hard to switch her brain from being the person in charge, feared even, to a helpless princess to be assisted and watched.

She lifted her bound hands and slapped his away.

The other three guards smiled. That angered her even more. They took her rebuff as a sign she was like her uncle, arrogant and privileged, the person she'd pretended to be before escaping to Gunngar. Everything she did was completely misunderstood, even her anger.

She stood, and Tahl was beside her instantly. "Princess, your scarf." He pressed the silk into her hands, slicing the binds that held her wrists together as he did.

Marina looked up, her gaze shifting from him to the other three. They hadn't known...only Tahl...she locked the information away. Later she'd consider how to use it. The more of her reality her uncle hid from others, the more he opened himself up to being damaged by the truth.

The ties disappeared, tucked into Tahl's coat, and Marina stepped from the car. Her uncle'd had her change before entering Fisby. She was wearing silk now, pants and a sleeveless top covered by a gauzy floor-length coat that hung open in the front. Her hair was piled on her head with a garden's worth of flowers peeking from the white mass.

She felt and looked ridiculous.

"You look wonderful." Ky met her at the door of the garage and covered Marina's hands with her own. Her fingers found the indentation that the ties had left in Marina's skin. They hesitated there for a second, but her sister's expression never changed.

Ky looked one-hundred-percent radiant. "You have to tell me everything. Kidnapped by a hellhound. How was that?"

She tugged Marina behind her, her chocolate brown hair bouncing with every step. Ky, not being the princess, was allowed to wear hers down.

Marina followed, feeling relieved and guilty at the same time. She'd given Ky no thought when she'd blended in with the crowd and walked through the portal into Gunngar. Selfishly, she'd left her sister behind, but Ky seemed to harbor no ill will for Marina's desertion.

Ky pulled Marina close and whispered in her ear. "I'm so happy you're home. I never believed all that stuff the elf lords were spreading about you. Hunting witches. Seriously. Crazy."

Her lips tight, Marina smiled. "And how have you been?"

A cloud passed over Ky's face, but she shook it off. "Fine. Happy, but I missed you. While you were gone, uncle was different. He's been going out more and coming back angry—especially after reading one of these." Ky stepped next to a small round table covered with a silver cloth. She lifted the covering. Underneath sat a stack of gossip magazines. "He banned me from reading them, but Tahl brings them to me." She dropped the cloth and plopped onto the sofa that sat beside it.

"So, tell me everything." Her eyes were huge and hungry.

Marina perched on the edge of the couch. She suddenly felt guilty, and for an entirely new reason. She'd never really talked with her sister, never let her in on what was going on in her life. Ky had seemed so much younger before Marina had left for Gunngar, but now she was grown up and had no clue of the realities of their existence. She was still a child inside.

Marina stared down at her hands, calloused from her work in the human world. Should she tell Ky the truth? Or let her stay happy in her false world?

Ky frowned and leaned closer. "You know, one thing I never understood is how you got to Gunngar in the first place. When you first disappeared, we all thought you'd been kidnapped, and you were, later, right, by the hell-hound?" Her eyes lit up, but then she frowned. "But at the very beginning, how'd you get there?"

If Marina told her she had run away, she'd have to explain everything else—overhearing the royals plotting, knowing they were planning a rebellion with Marina as a figurehead. She just wasn't sure her baby sister was ready to hear all of that, that she would understand what all of it meant—to Marina and Alfheim.

"It was a mistake," she murmured. "I was out shopping. The crowds were huge. I didn't realize the elf lords were sending the Jagers through to Gunngar that day, then shutting everything down." She glanced at Ky. Her sister's expression didn't change. Marina continued, "Elves were gathered by the portal. I stopped to watch and somehow I got caught up in everything. The next thing I knew I was in Gunngar and there was no way to get back."

Ky sighed. "That is *so* incredible. Such an adventure."

Marina lifted her gaze; her sister's face glowed. Again, Marina considered telling her all, explaining the "adventure" for what it was—dark and terrifying. But then she'd have to explain what she had done, too, how she'd been the one terrifying all those beings in Gunngar.

She couldn't say it, not to Ky. "Yes, it was... exciting."

Tahl walked into the room, and Marina let out a breath. "Your uncle would like you to wait for him in his office."

She muttered an apology to Ky and hurried out of the room, for once grateful for her uncle's interference. She fisted her hands as she walked, tried to concentrate on what she was going to say, what she was going to do.

She knew the royals hadn't given up on their plans

to stage a revolution and to shove her into the forefront. She'd ran away when she'd heard of their plans before. Now she was back, but she wasn't that princess anymore. She'd been through too much. She was smarter and more confident.

She could face down her uncle. She could tell him no. She would not be responsible for putting a group she didn't respect back into power. She would not be their puppet.

It was time to take a stand.

Marina was sitting in an upholstered chair her hands resting lightly on the chair's wooden arms when her uncle stormed into the room.

He stopped and pulled back as if surprised when he saw her. "What, no argument? No having to hunt you down and drag you in here?" He stalked around her chair; his riding gloves snapping against his palm. "Perhaps there is hope."

He paused then, "I'm not going to ask how you got to Gunngar. I'm not even going to ask if you were truly doing as the elf lords claimed—working as one of them." He threw his gloves onto his desk. "I'm simply going to tell you what I did while you were gone. You're a smart girl. I think that will be enough." He strode to his desk, jerked open a drawer and pulled a tiny box from inside. He handed it to her.

Marina stared at the box for a second. Her fingers tingled. Without even cracking the lid, she knew there was some kind of elf magic inside.

"Open it," he said.

Marina flipped open the lid.

Nestled inside was a tiny fleck of clear crystal.

"Your sister's was red, fitting her name. Tahl said you were speaking with her. Perhaps you noticed it?" He tilted his head.

Marina shook hers, but kept her gaze on the stone.

Ky was elfin for ruby. She'd always reminded Marina of the stone, intense and alive, filled with life and beauty—nothing at all like her cold older sister.

"It's…pretty," Marina replied. She lifted a finger to touch the thing, but paused. Something wasn't right. Her uncle didn't give gifts.

"It is, isn't it? I'd planned to give you this before you disappeared. The other royals thought it was wise. I argued with them. Told them, you were with us, that you understood how important our cause was. But you proved me wrong." His voice turned hard.

Marina's fingers tightened on the box. The crystal caught the light, winked at her. A chill traveled down her spine. She wanted to set the box down, but she didn't. She licked her lips and looked up, kept her gaze steady.

"Did you see your sister's? I had the surgeons place it right here." He tapped a spot on his neck under his right ear. "She'd been begging for one of these tacky insets for months. After you left, I realized I'd messed up, and I needed to rectify that."

Marina lowered the box to her lap. Her voice tense, she asked, "Rectify how?"

He took the box from her and pulled the sparkling crystal from inside, held it to the light. "It is pretty, isn't it? You're a very lucky girl, actually. If I'd listened to the royals and given you this before you left…" He tilted his head. "Well, you wouldn't be sitting here in front of me now. You would be dead, and your sister would be princess."

He stroked the crystal. "And that would have been okay then—before the elf lords built you up even more than you had been. You were popular with the masses before, but since leaving? You have an almost cult following." He walked to a cabinet and pulled open a door. Envelopes flowed out onto the floor. "Fan mail. You get fan mail." He turned to his desk and swept his arm over its top. Papers, statues, his computer, all went flying. From someone else the outburst would have been unexpected, but from Geir...Marina didn't even jump.

"No one, not even your parents, had the following you do. Which makes you and your cooperation crucial to the success of our plans." He walked around the desk and sat down.

His chest was heaving and his eyes glittered. He held up the crystal. "Which brings me back to this. This is a miracle of modern elf technology and magic. It had been meant for you. That had made sense at the time— it was just a little insurance. But then you ran off and became indispensable. So, we adjusted."

Marina's body was stiff, tense. She wanted to scream at him to tell her what he had done, what the crystal implanted in her sister's neck could do.

"Do you love your sister?" He twisted the clear crystal between his fingers, then glanced at Marina.

Marina bit her lip. Of course, she loved Ky. She'd never said it, but...

Geir walked around to the far side of the desk. "You will play the role we give you. You will pose for pictures. You will give speeches. You will ride at the head of our first attack. You will tell the people the royals are their future. And, once we are back in power, once every elf lord is dead, you will take the throne and go back to being the pretty little princess you were raised to be—one who smiles for cameras and does as she is told."

Marina sucked in a breath. This was the conversation she'd ran away from once before. Not this time. "And if I refuse?" she asked.

He smiled and retrieved his laptop from the floor. Marina stared at him when she saw it in his hand. Royals didn't do technology.

He sighed. "I know. See how desperate you have made me? I've even allowed elf lord 'improvements' into this house. I hate myself for it, but there you have it. What's a misplaced royal to do?" He tapped his fingers against the laptop's hard lid. "Actually, I've been rethinking the whole no technology thing. Technology does have its purpose, one the royals would do well to discover. But…" He placed the computer on his desk. "I'll never be convinced it's for the masses." He pressed the power button and met her gaze. "Technology, whatever comes of it, should be contained, available only to the ruling parties—which with your cooperation will soon be us." He spun the computer so it faced her.

A drawing, the floor plan of the mansion, appeared on the screen. There was little detail to it, just lines showing walls, breaks in the lines showing windows and doors, a very simple design. But in one room, the sitting room where Marina had left her sister, a light blinked, slow and steady like the beat of a heart.

"Ky," she murmured. "It's a tracker."

He arched a brow. "Of course, but it's more than that." He tapped another button and the light flickered.

From the floor below someone yelled, and Marina's uncle smiled.

Marina jumped to her feet.

Chapter 7

"A hellhound. How unusual."

Raf jumped at the words. He was still watching the portal, still blended with the wall behind him, hidden or should have been from anyone except another hellhound.

And the male facing him, most definitely was not a hellhound.

He smelled of fresh cut grass and sun-warmed earth. Happy smells. Raf found it ironic that they were associated with elves.

The elf was tall, only a few inches shorter than Raf, but much slimmer. He was dressed casually in a thin sweater and canvas pants, both gray, and on his face were a pair of extremely odd-looking goggles.

He nodded toward the portal building. "They called me, told me there was a hellhound on the loose. I'm wondering if you might be looking for me."

"Are you?" Raf kept his face blank. He had never met his contact with the elf lords. They had only corresponded electronically. This elf might be him, or he might not. Either way, Raf was in no hurry to identify himself.

The elf studied Raf through his goggles. Raf lowered his brows. Dealing with elves was bad enough, but add the goggles and it was clear this particular elf saw him as some kind of specimen.

The elf must have sensed Raf's reaction; he jerked the goggles off of his face.

"Sorry. I don't need them now anyway, not since I've found you. You know that, right? That once you have spotted a hellhound who is blending or realize he is there, the talent doesn't work?" The elf tilted his head as if truly interested in Raf's reply.

Confused by the strange male's behavior, Raf crossed his arms over his chest and nodded.

"I thought you did, but you never know. I encountered a troll once who refused to believe that our sun would turn him to stone." The elf shook his head. "If you want to see him, he's located in a park two blocks over. He's quite popular with the children."

Raf shoved himself away from the wall. This conversation was going nowhere.

A small object, round and cold, pressed against his temple.

"I'm sorry. I can't let you leave. As much as I like hellhounds, I'm afraid most of Alfheim fears your kind quite irrationally. It wouldn't be responsible of me to let you just wander the streets. Unfair, I know. I mean, you do have your talents. You are, for example, infamous for being difficult to kill." He paused, seemed to think for a second. "Perhaps now would be a good time to assure you that one pull on this trigger and your brain will explode inside your head. That is a very difficult injury from which to recover. Don't you agree?"

With the muzzle of whatever weapon the elf held pressed against his skull, Raf recognized the question for what it was—rhetorical.

"Now, that we have our realities established, what brings you to Alfheim? Are you here to see me?" The elf's voice had changed, grown deeper, not menacing so much as businesslike. Raf had no doubt the male would do as he'd claimed, splatter Raf's brains over the inside of his skull.

Raf suppressed the growl that formed in his chest. "Am I looking for you? You tell me."

The elf smiled. The gun still pressed against Raf's temple, he held out his unoccupied hand. "Sim, Lord Sim to be exact. And you are?"

The name of his contact. "Raf Dolg." Raf let out a disappointed breath. He'd begun to hope the elf wasn't his contact. The male and his toys had burrowed under Raf's skin. It would have been nice to have had no reason to "play nice."

The muzzle pressed against his temple moved. The elf stepped back, taking the weapon, which Raf could see now was little more than a pipe with a trigger attached, with him. The elf motioned with the barrel. "I assume you have evidence?"

Raf reached into his pocket and pulled out the elf lords' locator.

The elf took the cylinder, flipped it over and studied the script etched on its side. He looked up, his gaze steely. "You called us, and you didn't have her."

"I did at the time." Raf felt no need to explain further.

Sim tossed the cylinder in his hand. "Interesting. You're saying Geir stole her from you? Perhaps a hellhound wasn't the right choice for this job." He slipped the locator into his pocket. "I'll tell the portal guards to let you through."

Raf's eyes narrowed. "I'm here to get her back."

Sim twisted his lips to the side. "Are you? You realize you stand out here? How exactly do you plan to get her?"

Raf smiled. "As you said, I'm a hellhound. Hunting is what we do."

Sim snorted. "Bravado means nothing to me. The elf lords pay for results—nothing less."

Raf's jaw tightened. "Do you still have the stone?"

The Lord tapped his chin with one long finger. "Of course we do. What would make you think differently?"

"And it can answer whatever question I ask of it?"

"I'm not an expert on the artifacts of Alfheim."

Raf frowned. He had heard that in Alfheim there were three objects that could reveal past, present and future. Further research had unearthed the name of one—the stone of Ord. He needed the stone to look back in time for him, to tell him who attacked his family, who killed his wife, child and brother. "But the elf lords have it, and are willing to give it to me in exchange for Marina?"

"Getting Marina is no longer the issue. As you know she is back in Alfheim now."

Raf raised a brow. "But you don't have her. Her uncle does." He crossed his arms over his chest. "That bothers you."

Something in Sim's gaze flickered. "Alfheim is a strange mix of modern and ancient. While we, the

Lords, embrace technology, many cling to old super-stitions."

Raf didn't comment, knew he'd learn more by letting the man talk.

"There have been rumors for years that Marina is destined to sit on the throne of Alfheim. That the throne itself won't be satisfied until she does."

"The throne?" Raf asked.

Sim made a noise of disgust. "Ignorant peasants fed lies, by the royals I'm sure."

"So, this throne? It exists? Does a Lord sit on it now?"

Sim's gaze hardened. "It's myth. The day Marina's parents died, their throne disappeared. Obviously, it was stolen just so such a legend could be created."

He slid his mouth to the side. "However, legend still has power here—perhaps more than fact. And Marina's name is tied to this one."

Raf smiled. He got it now. The elf lords were afraid. If the citizens of Alfheim believed this legend, whoever had Marina on their side held a huge advantage. No wonder the elf lords had been so happy when she had appeared to be working with them in Gunngar. And less wonder why they wanted her back.

But Marina had betrayed the elf lords, been responsible for releasing Amma…. "What about Amma?" he asked.

"The witch?" Sim waved his hand in the air. "Her spirit escaped. It was disturbing, but we have bigger issues at the moment."

Bigger issues, like keeping control of Alfheim.

"I want the stone," Raf stated.

Sim tapped his chin. "I know you do, and it is still in play, but the job has changed."

Raf stepped forward, his hands automatically reaching for the elf lord's throat. Sim raised his gun.

"That is no way to get the prize."

With a growl, Raf stepped away.

Sim turned his back on Raf. Raf fisted his hands at his sides. The elf was arrogant. The move was obviously meant to remind Raf of his inferior position, but only made Raf want to snap the male's neck more.

"The problem we have now is that Marina is firmly affixed in her uncle's household. Geir is a master manipulator of the press, and he has, in a very short time, unraveled all the good we had done." Sim turned back. "We had Alfheim accepting Marina as a part of the elf lords. For a brief time all of the uprisings settled down. Alfheim needs the elf lords, but they want a princess. We plan to give them both."

"Very generous of you," Raf murmured.

Sim ignored him. "Now that Geir has her back with him, things are touchy. If we simply grab her…rumors will spread. We need Marina to join us willingly." He paused. "Or for it to appear that way."

"So, no grab and go?" Raf kept his expression bland. "Our deal was that I got her to you. I don't remember any details on how."

Sim's gaze was steady. "Our deal is done. You're here asking for a new one. Lucky for you, I think we can make one." He tapped his chin. "You weren't the only spy I had in Gunngar. You realize that don't you?"

Raf stared off toward the portal. If he didn't need the damned stone he would have left by now. The elf's manner of speaking was grating and his attitude condescending. Raf could not imagine the spirited Marina he knew mingling with him or others like him.

He jutted out his jaw; *Marina and these elves...they didn't go together.*

"These spies had some interesting stories—about a hellhound and the princess. If I hadn't known there was a hellhound in Gunngar, one I sent there, I would have thought the stories insane."

Raf turned his head back to Sim, barely stopping a snarl from curling his lip.

The elf continued. "This spy told me Marina was taken with this hellhound. He even suspected they were involved—sexually. What do you think?"

"I think your spy left out a big piece of the tale. Marina rejected me publicly. She had me locked in a box. What kind of involvement do you call that?"

Sim smiled. "One of a very smart princess. This spy, the one I mentioned? He wasn't our...best. I discovered he'd left evidence of his work lying around. I suspect Marina found it. I suspect that is why she rebuffed you." He took a step forward. "I suspect she is still taken with you—or could be, if the proper situation presented itself."

Raf shook his head. Marina had already told him her reasons for locking him in that box, but that didn't mean everything else Sim said was true. Still, Raf's mind wandered to their last time together, their kiss, her story. He swallowed, tried to shove down the guilt that surged inside him yet again.

Still standing close, Sim rubbed his finger over the barrel of his weapon. "Are you saying you can't do the job? Are you backing out? My offer of escort through the portal still holds."

Raf tensed, realized what he'd been doing. It didn't matter if Marina had been taken with him, cared for him or, as he suspected, completely despised him. What mattered was that he turn her over to the elf lords and be paid with the seer stone for doing so. He couldn't be swayed from why he was here. *Couldn't...*

He stared down the elf lord. "No, I can do the job. Just tell me your plan." He forced the words through his teeth.

With a smile, the elf lord shoved open a door behind them and gestured for Raf to step inside. Once seated in a small café, Sim laid out his plan.

He wanted Raf to pretend to have feelings for Marina, to convince her to trust him, to tell her he'd come to save her from her uncle. Sim seemed sure she wasn't with Geir of her own will, even without Raf confirming it. Then when Marina trusted Raf, he was to get her to walk away publicly, with Raf as her guard. Once she had declared her loyalty to the elf lords, Raf would get his payment and be free to go.

Raf leaned back and placed one hand on the table. "And how am I supposed to get close to her? I don't believe Geir will exactly open his doors to me."

Sim laughed. "You know nothing of elves, do you? Don't worry about Geir. We'll use his love of the media against him. He'll have no choice but to let you in." He reached in his pocket and pulled out a phone. "I'll make the calls now. In a few hours you will be sitting on a couch sipping tea with a princess."

Somehow Raf doubted he and Marina would ever sit idly and sip tea. When they were together, there was always something much more exciting to do.

His heart beat faster, but he kept his emotions masked, fisted his hands and concentrated on why he was here. He couldn't let guilt or doubt sidetrack him.

Couldn't let Marina sidetrack him. He had a job to do,
that was all. Marina meant nothing to him, was nothing
except a tool to get the stone.

He repeated the words in his mind, as if saying them
would trick his weakening heart into believing them.

Chapter 8

Geir held out the crystal as Marina leapt to her feet. "Something to help you remember what's at stake."

She grabbed the box without looking at him, then hurried down the stairs to the sitting room where she'd left Ky, where the light on Geir's computer had faltered.

Ky lay on the ground. Tahl leaned over her, his ear pressed to her heart.

"It's beating," he said, low, unaware Marina stood beside him.

She fell to her knees, and pushed him away. "Call someone," she yelled. She grabbed Ky's head, twisted it to the side, and shoved her hair away from her neck. The ruby fleck was there, shining at Marina, mocking her.

She held her hand above it unsure what to do. If she pried it out of her sister's skin would it save her...or kill her?

"It's never wise to mess with something you don't understand." Geir entered the room, carrying a cup in his hand. "Besides, my niece...your sister...is strong, and if how she conducts herself otherwise is any judge, stubbornly hard to kill."

Marina's hands balled into fists. She glared at her uncle. She hated him; she'd never thought that before. She hadn't loved him, but she'd accepted him for what he was—but right now, at this moment she hated him. She glanced down at Ky. Slight shallow breaths whispered from her sister's lips, kept Marina from throwing herself at her uncle and clawing at him with rage.

"Stubbornly hard, but not impossible," he continued.

Marina bit her lip until it bled. How she wished she still had her blade.

The doorbell rang. Tahl, who hadn't left Ky's side, glanced at Geir. Her uncle waved his hand and the younger elf walked from the room. Near the door he looked back, but Geir motioned again and the guard disappeared from view.

"She's been having these spells lately. Tahl has been a bit worried about her—although I assure him she's fine. And she is...will be...as long as everyone remembers their place." Geir walked toward Ky and tipped the cup's contents onto her face.

For a second there was no change, then her eyelids began to twitch and her heartbeat to grow stronger. Marina released a breath.

"Niece..." Geir tapped the bottom of the cup with one finger, held it over Ky's face and let the last few drops of liquid fall onto her face. "I feel the need to say that the inset...it wouldn't react well to being taken out of Alfheim. You might want to remember that."

Ky took a deep jolting breath. Marina forced the hatred for her uncle out of her eyes, and smiled down at her sister.

"Did I...I had another spell, didn't I?" Ky asked.

Marina brushed her hand over her sister's forehead. "You're fine. There's nothing to worry about. I'm here, and I'm not going anywhere."

"But—"

The doors to the sitting room flew open, cutting off Ky's response. Tahl and three other males entered the room.

"Cas Dwin from the daily news with a photographer and a...guest," Tahl said.

Marina's uncle started when Tahl made his announcement, but recovered, quickly taking two steps forward. As the second male stepped fully into the room, Geir froze, and all color raced from his face.

But Marina hardly noticed. She was too occupied with her own shock, too occupied with staring at the last being she'd expected to see again—Raf.

Her uncle recovered quickly. "Cas, I didn't expect you. Welcome."

The reporter who Marina had met a few times before leaving for Gunngar stood back a bit studying her, and her sister. Ky, realizing they weren't alone, attempted to sit up.

Marina grabbed her by the arm to keep her in a reclining position. "My sister isn't feeling well." She glanced at the reporter, kept her gaze studiously off Raf. She prayed the rapid beating of her heart wasn't audible to anyone besides herself, and tried desperately to crush the hope springing to life inside her. "I was just telling my uncle I thought time out of the mansion would do her some good, but he feels her health is better served staying here."

Despite not looking at the hellhound, Marina was aware of every move he made, even the slightest twitch of his fingers. He crossed his arms over his chest and openly stared at her, his gaze dark. He seemed to be absorbing the scene in front of him. It made Marina want to cover up, hide.

The reporter shifted his gaze over the group, studied every nuance of what was passing between each person. "Geir, I believe you know Raf." He gestured to the hellhound while keeping his gaze on Marina's uncle, then shifted his gaze again to Marina. "I understand Raf is responsible for saving her royal highness from a rogue hellhound, and returning her to her family." He frowned. "I wasn't happy when I realized you didn't give me the full story first time around. The princess, rescued by a hellhound.... Our readers will love this."

Geir muttered something, his gaze darting from the reporter to Raf and back again.

Raf walked forward and bent to hold a hand out to Ky. Marina's sister's eyes widened, but she slipped both hands into his. With a quick and graceful tug she was back on her feet.

Suddenly uncomfortable on the floor, Marina rose, too.

Ky stared at Raf as if he were a prince straight out of some human fairy tale. Remembering her sister's questions about what it had been like to be abducted by a hellhound, Marina slipped her arm around her sister's waist and pulled her against her side.

The reporter's gaze settled on them for a second, then he turned back to Geir. "After how well we've worked together over the years, I'm assuming you haven't told anyone else. Raf has agreed to give me an exclusive, but he wanted to clear it with you first. He was very concerned that you might not want the story to get out. That isn't true, is it?"

Geir's hands shook; the cup he held clattered to the floor. He didn't look down, didn't acknowledge the dropped item in any way. "Cas, you know that anything I deem important enough to share with the press, I share with you first. I just didn't think..." He waved his hand and stepped forward, his heel crushing a bit of the porcelain cup as he did.

"That Alfheim would want to know how their princess was rescued? To meet her prince?" Cas pulled a small recorder from his pocket. "Do you mind if I have a few moments with her royal highness? Some pictures perhaps? With Raf?"

Geir stuttered and paled. "Her prince... I hardly think— He is a hellhound. I know Alfheim has become more liberal, but seriously—"

Cas laughed. "Oh, I only meant that in the rescuing sense. It makes for a great headline, though, don't you think? Her hellhound prince..." He shook his head. "And with things the way they are in Alfheim right now—" he curled his lip "—nothing would surprise me. And it is unique. Hellhounds don't come to Alfheim. Readers will be glued to this story."

Ky's fingers slipped into Marina's, reminding Marina she was there. She squeezed. Marina squeezed back. She needed her sister now—was glad her desertion hadn't seemed to affect Ky.

Their uncle closed his eyes, then opened them. Resolve shone from behind his green gaze. Marina could see his intent—to blow a hole in Raf's tale, to get the hellhound expelled from Alfheim, or worse.

She stepped forward. "Yes, Raf saved me. I don't

know what I would have done without his assistance. The other hellhound, he…" She shivered.

Behind her, Ky let out a sigh, and Cas's eyes lit up. His fingers wrapped around the recorder, and he stepped closer. "Would you be willing to talk about it?"

Geir held up a hand. "Marina has been through so much. We didn't want to distress her by making her relive everything. I'm sure you understand."

Marina patted his arm. Her years playing the perfect princess were serving her well now. "My uncle is over-protective. Actually, I spoke with a doctor, and he suggested talking about everything might help me work through it." She lowered her voice as she said the last.

Nodding, Cas leaned closer. His eyes were huge and eager. She had him hooked. Keeping her gaze away from her uncle, she slipped her hand through the reporter's arm. "Would you like the photos first, or the interview?"

Geir bounced back and forth on his heels. His gaze when it hit Marina was steely, but when the reporter glanced his direction he was springtime and smiles.

Still the reporter seemed to sense the tension. "Photo I think. Then I can call you for the full interview."

"I think—" Geir started.

Marina interrupted. "No, let's do everything right now. I have no plans of talking to another reporter, but…well, the doctor did say I should talk to someone. Things can get out."

After that the reporter was locked on his mission. He lined Marina up next to Raf and the two posed for a multitude of shots. Ky, sitting on the couch, watched every move, seemed to suck in the scenes like they were part of a live play being acted out in front of her.

Marina was amazed at her sister's seemingly never-ending attention. If anything, Ky's focus on what was happening grew more intense with every pose. To the point Marina felt uncomfortable when her sister's gaze fell on her, as if she was doing something wrong, was guilty of some act Ky was about to call her on.

Catching Marina looking at her, Ky smiled—a smile so sincere and filled with joy, Marina felt silly for her discomfort. She returned her sister's smile, and put her all into playing her part.

But after what felt like hours, Marina didn't think she could play any longer. She was exhausted both by standing in the impractical shoes her uncle had provided and by the act.

When Cas told the photographer to head back to the paper, she couldn't help letting out a breath of relief. One glance at Raf assured her the hellhound wasn't faring any better. His smile had turned to more of a grimace, and even it looked pasted on.

While Cas walked the photographer to the door, Marina stole a second glance at the hellhound. She had no idea what had brought him here, or how he had managed to get an in with the reporter, but she couldn't deny she was glad to see him. His presence upset her uncle. That alone was enough to make her happy. But it was more than that. She and Raf might have a less-than-perfect history, but they had a history—and strange as it sounded, an honest one. Except for that one moment when she'd had him captured and locked up, she had always been herself with him. Standing here in her uncle's living room made her realize how important that was, how much she craved a relationship where she *could* be herself.

Geir, who had stayed in the room the entire time, glowering when the reporter's back was turned, glowing when the reporter looked at the royal, covered the space between them in quick angry steps. He stopped in front of Raf.

"What game are you playing, hellhound?"

Marina stiffened, tried not to show how intensely she wanted to hear his answer.

Raf tensed. "I don't play. That would be a good thing for you to remember."

Geir lifted his lip in a snarl, but at the sound of Cas's return he smoothed his expression and smiled. "I really do think Marina has had enough excitement. She only returned today."

If the reporter left, Raf would go with him. The thought of she and Ky being alone with her uncle... panic pierced Marina. She didn't give herself a chance to question her actions; she stepped forward. "I'm fine really, but if uncle is uncomfortable, perhaps we could continue this tomorrow." Geir's face relaxed.

She glanced at Raf. "You could interview us together. Raf will be staying here, of course."

Her uncle paled. "I'm sure Raf—"

Marina grabbed Raf's hand, put as much bubbly princess energy into her words as she could stomach. "We would be so honored if you would. It's the very least we can do to repay you for all of your help. I know I will never forget the accommodations you had prepared for me while we awaited my uncle." She dug a nail into the hellhound's palm, let him know she wasn't the fool she appeared.

His eyes flickered. He grabbed her hands back, squeezed until she thought the bones would pop.

She covered the pain with a smile.

"How could I turn down such an offer?" Raf murmured. His gaze was steady, but there was something in his eyes, something that made Marina feel like a hare about to be snared. She carefully pulled her hands free.

His face turning red, Geir swayed. For a second Marina thought he might lunge at them, but he got his reaction under control. He called for a servant and asked her to prepare a room for Raf.

"Near me, please," Marina called as the female started to leave. Marina smiled at Cas. "Just knowing Raf is close…I know I won't have the nightmares anymore." She covered her eyes with her hand and let out a tiny hiccup of a sob, then choked down the urge to retch at her own act.

Cas seemed to buy it. As did Ky; she floated from the couch to Marina's side and slipped her arm around Marina's waist. At her sister's touch, guilt rose up in Marina, causing her to tremble slightly. Ky stroked her back and murmured in her ear. "I had no idea…" The words were right, but something about the tone made Marina glance at her sister.

Ky stood quietly, her face composed and concerned. *Things were getting to her.* Marina forced herself to keep quiet, to keep up her act.

After one last glance at Marina, the reporter nodded and let Geir lead him to the door. At the threshold he stopped and turned. "I'll have the pictures on the Web site tonight, and in print in the morning. This is just too huge to wait on. I'll be back tomorrow for the full story."

With the door firmly closed behind the reporter, Geir spun. He gestured to Ky. "You need to lie down."

Ky opened her mouth to object, but Marina whispered in her ear. "I'm fine. You rest. I'll find you later. I'll tell you everything."

"Everything?" Ky glanced at Raf, her eyes glistening—no sign of the hardness Marina had thought she'd heard in her sister's voice moments earlier.

"Everything," Marina said, not sure how true the promise was—or how much she should or could tell her sister of what was going on around her.

With a sidelong glance at Marina and Raf, Ky walked from the room. After a nod from Geir, Tahl followed her.

The door closed behind them, Geir spoke. "Whatever you are thinking, it will not work."

Marina dropped her distraught act. "Whatever who is thinking, uncle? Who exactly are you accusing?"

Geir strode forward. "Both of you." He looked at Raf first. "Tell me what you want. As long as I have a guarantee you disappear after, it's yours."

Marina's breath caught. She was as curious as her uncle why Raf was there. Somewhere inside a tiny part of her wondered, hoped it was as he'd said... Could he possibly just be worried about her? Had what she said before her uncle arrived back in the human world made a difference? Or perhaps the witch...seeing that Marina hadn't burned her...could Raf now regret what he'd done? Could he... care?

Raf's gaze flickered. Marina could feel the tension flowing through him. It was almost tangible, like electricity shooting off a live wire. "I didn't come here for payment from you. You have nothing I want."

A band tightened around Marina's heart. Killed the spark of hope that she had almost allowed to flicker to life. Her uncle had her...

Geir's hand moved toward his pocket. Raf grabbed

him by the wrist. "Don't. It wouldn't look good if your houseguest died his first night under your roof—do you think?"

"First and last." Geir shook the hellhound's hand off and turned to Marina. "He's using you—you know that? I don't know what for, but he isn't here to check on you. He doesn't care for you. He had you in shackles, was waiting for payment from—" His gaze darted back to Raf. "*The elf lords.* They did this. Well it won't work. Whatever they have planned, it won't work. You might as well go back to them now and tell them that."

Raf crossed his arms over his chest.

With a hiss, Geir looked back at Marina. "Don't let down your guard. Remember what I said—he's using you for his own gain."

Despite the hurt that Raf's declaration had caused, a disgusted snort escaped Marina. "If there is one thing I'm good at, it's being used. Isn't that right, uncle?"

She didn't wait for a reply—didn't glance at either male, just strode from the room. She had nothing to say to either of them—not right now. When her anger subsided, though, she would have to find Raf, have to discover exactly why he was here.

If he was here to help her…she licked her lips and blew out a breath. She wouldn't allow herself to hope again. No, she'd lived long enough to know the odds of that were slim. No one had wanted to help Marina in a very long time. No, he was here for some other reason, for some personal gain.

Marina had to make sure she remembered that.

Raf watched as Marina left the room. She didn't look like the Marina he knew. Her hair was wound in

some elaborate mess on top of her head and her body
was covered in layers of impractical silk and gauze. She
looked like a doll someone had dressed up.

And he thought he knew who—Geir. For some reason
the idea that Marina's uncle was dressing her up and
putting her on display—using her like some kind of
puppet—rankled Raf. But even as the emotion hit, he
realized he was here with the same purpose. Geir just got
to her first. The realization made him sick. The act he'd
seen her put on for the reporter made him sick. This
wasn't Marina. Yes, the Marina he'd known had
appeared for a few moments when arguing with her
uncle—but five minutes out of how many? What had
happened to her? How could she act like someone she
wasn't?

An image of her as he'd known her in Gunngar, her
hair pulled back tight and utilitarian, popped into his
mind. Then another image of him with her, unwinding
her hair, letting it flow free over her shoulders…. Her
hair had smelled of flowers, had wound around him,
seemed to capture him, hold him…. He closed his eyes
and forced these new images from his mind.

He was here to get Marina on the elf lords' side; he
had to concentrate on that.

Still in the room, Geir glowered at him. "The elf
lords are paying you something. Why not tell me what
and see if I can beat it? You might be surprised what the
royals have at their disposal."

As little as he liked or trusted the royal, Raf hesitated.
Geir was right. Raf thought he needed the stone, but he
knew little of the magical riches the elves possessed.
There could easily be some other artifact that would help
him find his family's killer. Perhaps even more easily.

But for that to happen, he would have to trust Geir. And he didn't. And he wouldn't leave Marina with him to be dressed up and displayed.

No, he'd take her to the elf lords for that, a voice whispered in his mind. He gritted his teeth, pushed the thought away.

"I'm happy with my deal," he replied. He turned to leave.

"She won't betray us," Geir announced. "The elf lords may think they have something to offer her, to lure her, but they don't have the hold on her I do."

Raf turned back. "There has to be a trust for it to be betrayed. Do you honestly think your niece has any for you? Or your royals? She isn't even herself here."

"You know my niece so well? You've only spent months with her. I am her family. Whoever this Marina is you think you know—I assure you she is the act. The real one, the princess, you don't know at all."

Raf's blood pounded at the base of his throat. He took a step toward the royal, then hissed through closed teeth. He wanted to shake the elf like a dog would a rat, but that would accomplish nothing. Would actually complicate the job he'd been hired to do. For Sim's plan to work, everything had to appear smooth and happy. A dead royal would not go unnoticed.

A disappointing, but undeniable truth. Raf turned on his heel and stalked from the room.

Chapter 9

Marina sat on the edge of her bed, stared at the door, and tried to get her emotions under control. Seeing Raf had given her hope for a few minutes. Now she was struggling to keep her noncaring facade in place.

She heard footsteps outside her door, knew it had to be Raf. Hellhounds might be light on their feet, but they couldn't compare to an elf for silence.

All her good intentions, her plans to stay cold and distant fled. She flung open her door. Raf stood outside, staring at her. She grabbed him by the arm and pulled him into her room.

"What are you doing here?" she almost hissed at him.

Raf walked to her bed and pulled back the lace that hung from the canopy. After looking inside, he turned back. "Do you want me to leave?"

She tightened her jaw. "Perhaps I do."

His body started to shimmer. With a curse she jumped forward and grabbed him by the arm again. "Fine. I want you to stay, but I want to know why you are here. As my uncle asked, what game are you playing?"

Raf arched a brow. "You heard my answer. I'm not playing a game."

Marina huffed out a disbelieving breath. "Everyone in Alfheim is playing a game whether you realize it or not. Tell me yours."

His free arm, the one she wasn't holding moved, slipped behind her back. Before she realized what he was doing, she was pressed against his chest. Her heart beat faster. She could feel his, too, thumping slow but hard in his chest.

"What game are you playing then?" he asked. His gaze was dark and intense. The room seemed to draw in around them, until all she was aware of was Raf. She pressed her hand against his chest, felt his heart beating beneath her palm.

She licked her lips. She wanted to be angry, to force the truth out of him, but she was so tired, and damn it all, so happy to see him. Her body molded against his, before she remembered her promise to herself. He wasn't here to help her. He wanted to use her, like everyone else.

She pulled back as far as his grip would let her, shifted her hands to his arms. "I bared everything to you. Told you everything, and you were going to sell me to the highest bidder anyway."

Raf frowned. "I didn't."

"Not because you didn't want to." She shook her

head. "My uncle is right. You're working with the elf lords. What is it they've promised you? What do they even want?" Her fingers tightened on his biceps.

Anger and adrenaline poured through her. She balled her fist to strike him, then realized she couldn't...didn't want to hit Raf. Didn't know who she did want to hit, who she could blame for the reality of her life. All passion drained out of her, and she sagged against the hellhound.

He lowered her to the edge of the bed and kneeled down in front of her. There was concern in his eyes—real or false? It hurt Marina to look at him. Hurt to have to guess if the concern she saw on his face was true.

She pushed him away, or tried to. He caught her hand.

"What's happening?" he asked.

The struggle became too much, feeling alone became too much. She placed her hand along the side of his face and kissed him.

It was perhaps the stupidest thing she'd ever done. More stupid than sneaking into Gunngar, than thinking she could handle pretending to be a coldhearted witch burner, than forcing Amma into her body. Stupid. She had done so many stupid things...what was one more?

His lips were soft; reluctant, she realized. Hurt shot through her. She started to pull back, but he leaned forward and pulled her toward him until he was kneeling between her legs. Her thighs pressed against his sides. She straightened her legs, slipped them around him completely, until he was trapped, couldn't get away—not until she wanted him to.

Another realization: She wouldn't want to release him. Not ever.

"Why are you here?" she murmured, then kissed him again. "You shouldn't be here. You don't belong," she whispered the last against his lips, afraid if she said it too loud, he'd agree and shimmer away.

"Do you?" he asked. His gaze was steady, but there was something hidden behind his eyes—his real reason for being here. He hadn't told her what it was, not yet. Would he? Would it matter?

She ignored the voice in her head asking the questions, chose to answer his instead. "I'm the princess of Alfheim—the only princess of Alfheim. Where else would I belong?"

She knew what she wanted him to say…*with me.* It was all she wanted—to be with someone who wanted her for her, not what she could do for him. No, that wasn't true. She wanted something else, too. She wanted to relax, be herself—good and bad. Be accepted for both.

Afraid she wouldn't like his answer, she captured his lips again. Denial, pure and simple. But she needed the fantasy, needed to believe for just a while that he was there for her…just her.

She ran her hands down his arms, along his muscles. He was so different than elf males—she should probably have been repulsed by the thick muscles that seemed to cover almost every inch of him. But she wasn't. Touching him sent a thrill through her. She felt small, in the physical sense, when she was with him—which strangely enough made her feel safe. Safer than she had ever felt in her life.

She had liked playing the strong leader in Gunngar, and she *was* strong. She wouldn't have survived if she wasn't, but with Raf she didn't have to worry about any of that. She could let down her guard, relax in the knowledge that no one could harm her—not while Raf was by her side.

He was wearing human clothes—a cotton tee that clung to his chest and denim pants that molded to his thighs. Simple items only a peasant would wear in Alfheim, but they fit Raf, made him appear all the more masculine.

He ran his fingers up through her hair, and yanked at the pins that held the braids in place. In seconds the intricate design a maid had worked hours to create was gone. The perpetual tightness of Marina's scalp was gone with it. She sighed against Raf's lips. His fingers dug into her hair, massaging her scalp. She sighed again and moved her hands from his arms to his chest.

He pulled her closer, off of the bed so she straddled him on the floor. Her breasts were pressed against his chest and her sex against his. She could feel his hard length through the thin silk she wore. She moved to the side, rubbing against him. He growled and his hands moved from her scalp to her back. His fingers slipped up under her shirt, onto her bare skin.

She pulled his shirt off, too, greedy to have his skin against hers. His fingers moved to her spine, massaged the muscles that ran from its length. She arched her back and slid against him. The tips of her breasts brushed his chest and a tingle shot through her.

He lowered his head and caught a nub between his lips, suckling over and around the sensitive tip. Another tingle shot through her, causing her to rise. He pulled her back down so she was pressed against him again.

He was hot and hard. She slipped her hands to her pants, wanted to be free of them. He pulled her body up, so both he and she were on their knees, still touching from shoulder to waist, and slipped his hand down under the silk—found the part of her that was hot and wet. She shivered. His finger slid over the nub hidden between her folds and she shivered again, grabbed onto his shoulders. He stroked and swirled and she gasped.

She leaned down and nibbled her way along his throat. He tasted salty and smelled of smoke. Memories of their time together in Gunngar, the good time, flooded her mind.

His finger slipped inside her, and her body tightened. She pulled in a breath. She had missed him. She trailed her tongue up his neck and pulled his ear lobe between her teeth.

He tensed and she reached down for the zipper of his pants. His sex sprang free. She shoved his jeans down and grabbed his buttocks—strong and hard like all of him.

He murmured something against her lips, then pulled her up. Her pants fell.

Naked, she straddled him again, this time his sex was free and she guided it, positioned it beneath her. They both paused for a second and did nothing, just listened to the other breathe and prepared for what they knew was to come. Then inch by inch she lowered herself, let her body stretch as he filled her, until he was entirely inside and she was ready to scream with the need to move—to feel him move.

She stared into his eyes. The blue so dark and deep at that moment they almost appeared black. There was no anger there, only desire...for her. And hope, was there hope there? Or was it all in her mind?

Realizing she was slipping, letting reality take hold of her brain and pull her out of the moment, she closed her eyes and pulled her body up, let Raf slide out and then back in—over and over.

Her breasts began to tingle. Little charges shot through her each time they brushed over his chest. Her center clenched and tears formed behind her closed eyelids. Her body was rising, or seemed to be, she was rising, swirling—the tension so intense and filling her with such pleasure she thought she would explode. Beneath her, inside her, Raf's body tightened, too. His fingers dug into her hips as he helped her to move, until they could move no faster. Then her body found its release, and she fell, floated until she was lying against Raf's chest, breath falling from her lips as if she'd ran from a legion of hell-hounds rather than made love to just one.

Not one...Raf. She'd made love to Raf, again. How she had missed him.

Marina lay cradled against Raf's chest. They were both naked. The smell of sex filled the room. There were other smells, too, emotions he didn't want to recognize, to deal with. Hope, fear and maybe even a tiny tinge of love hung around them.

Marina's emotions or his? He didn't know and wouldn't allow himself to discover the truth. He couldn't think about what Marina's hopes might be or why she might fear him. And love? That couldn't be true...not for either of them.

He glanced down. Her hair was spread over his chest. He wanted to reach down and brush it back from her face, to gather it up in his hand and inhale the scent of her shampoo—violets and roses. A mixture made for an elf, a princess.

He wanted things to be simple between them, their past to be erased. Wanted his past gone, too, so all he had was a future to look forward to, a future with this female. But life wasn't that simple. Even if their past could somehow be overcome, forgotten, Marina's future could never be his. She was an elfin princess, and he was a homeless hellhound who had lived for nothing but revenge for over one hundred years. Neither belonged in the other's world.

Her fingers, which lay against his chest opened. She seemed to be staring at them, or his skin, he couldn't tell which. She closed them again, then curled them under, her nails scraping over his skin, but lightly, pleasantly. She let out a sigh and he knew she felt as he did, that she hated that the moment was about to pass, dreaded returning to the conversation they'd avoided by making love.

But he had to go back to it. Had to finish it. Every moment he spent here, being with Marina, was another moment his family's killer walked free, breathed. Was another moment he risked falling back under Marina's spell, and risked forgetting his family all together.

He placed his fingers over hers, carefully moved them from his chest onto the carpet beneath them. "Marina?" he murmured.

Eyes, green as new buds, glanced up at him, then down at her fingers. She scraped her nails over the wool. When she looked up sadness flickered behind her eyes, then the emotion, all emotion, was shuttered off.

Her face went blank, cold, prepared for whatever he had to say.

The moment was over.

Marina pushed herself away from Raf. She hadn't wanted to move, but he'd said her name and when he had looked at her she'd known he was ready to tell her the real reason he was here.

She walked naked to where her clothes lay and pulled them on. When she looked back, he was dressed, too, and standing.

She hardened her heart before returning to him. She'd been hurt before, and she was about to be hurt again. Funny how she could predict that now.

She retraced her steps until she was standing before him. Her spine straight, she stared up at him. "Are you ready to tell me why you're here? Or at least to tell me where you think I belong?"

She held her breath and waited for his reply, even, though, she knew it wouldn't be the one she wanted.

He stared over her head for a second as if gathering his thoughts, or resolve, then looked down at her. "With the elf lords."

Her facade cracked. She tensed, then shoved him. Caught off guard, he jumped backward. She whirled around in a circle not sure what she was searching for, but needing to release the anger that had exploded inside her. He was, as her uncle guessed, working for the elf lords. He had made love to her knowing he planned to turn her over to them.

She felt betrayed. She should be used to it—but she was tired of it, too. And coming from Raf when she had hoped…

The gleam of brass caught her eye. She twirled toward it—a metal letter opener. Her fingers wrapped around the handle and she held it up, the tip aimed at Raf's throat. Her hand shook; she steadied it, forced the hurt down, let anger fill the void inside her.

"I am an idiot, aren't I? I let you so close…why wait to take me to the elf lords? Why not just kill me yourself?"

The elf lords had to want her dead. That had to be

why they had sent Raf. Amma was free; Marina couldn't change that, or change that she was responsible for it, either.

Her hand was shaking again. She'd faced down so many beings who wanted her dead in Gunngar and hadn't blinked, but now facing Raf she was trembling. She hated that she couldn't stop her body from betraying her.

To cover, she took another step forward, pressed the metal against the vein that throbbed under the skin of his throat.

He wrapped his fingers around hers and stared at her. She could see in his gaze he knew the truth, knew she lacked the strength to shove the blade into his throat.

She closed her eyes, cursed herself and dropped the opener. Waited for him to do whatever the elf lords had hired him to do.

Seconds ticked past.

She opened her eyes. He hadn't moved. He didn't mean to kill her here then, perhaps something more public, more fitting for the media which her uncle and the elf lords seemed to incessantly court.

"Killing you will solve nothing. They will just send someone else," she muttered. She turned and walked toward her dresser. Inside was her wardrobe of silk and satin. Not practical for prison or the gallows.

"What are you doing?" Raf asked.

She dropped the handful of silk she held into the drawer. "You're right. This is silly. They will hardly want me to dress in silk, or have a new outfit for each day." She turned back and held out her wrists. She wasn't sure what she would do when he tried to slip the ties around her wrists again—didn't know if she could stand it or not. But she couldn't kill Raf; she'd accepted that. Not even to save herself.

He frowned. "The elf lords didn't send me to get you." He hesitated on the last. Marina tilted her head, suspicious.

"But they sent you. You didn't come on your own."

He closed his eyes, seemed to be making some kind of decision. "Not exactly."

His hesitance made Marina calm, something inside her click. Deny it as he might, he was playing games, and she knew games. "Exactly what then? Are you going to tell me why you're here? Did the elf lords send you? And if so, why? Are you here to help me or hurt me?"

Panic flickered deep in Raf's eyes. Marina knew then whatever he was about to say would be a lie.

"To help. I'm here to help you."

She sat down on the bed and stared at the mass of silk that was piled on her floor. She wished she could believe him, but she'd been trained in deception by the best. By elf standards, by her standards, Raf was a babe in training. And she was about to teach him how out of his league he was.

She smiled, made her body relax as if she did believe him, as if until this moment she'd been holding everything inside. "Thank you. It's a relief to have someone I can trust." Then she squeezed out a tear and waited for him to tell his next lie.

Chapter 10

Raf frowned. He'd never seen Marina cry. He had seen her happy and angry, known earlier she was afraid, but tears? He had never seen that—and she was forgetting something.

Hellhounds smelled emotions. She wasn't sad; she was angry. It made him angry, too.

He strode forward and grabbed her by the arm. "Don't."

She blinked, her eyes still huge and damp. "Don't what? I'm just so happy to have someone on my side, to not be alone. You don't know what it's been like."

He laughed. He knew plenty about being alone. Since losing his family, he'd kept to himself, not allowed himself to get close to anyone…until Marina.

And look how that had turned out.

Resisting the urge to shake her, he dropped her arm. "Quit the act. I don't buy it." Her pretense reminded him of his own, of the lies he'd told to get into her uncle's house, of his role as spy before that. But he'd told her the truth. He had decided while watching her with the reporter and her uncle that he would help her—by getting her out of here and taking her to the elf lords. Life with the elf lords had to be better than this....

Her tears disappeared. Her eyes hardened. "What do you expect from me? You think I don't know you're lying? You think I can't see through that—" she waved her hand in a dismissive manner "—act?"

Her anger freed him from his worry, freed him to be angry, too. He bared his teeth. "And yours was so great?"

She rubbed her fingers over the skin where he'd held her. Through the thin gauzy top she wore, he could see the white imprint of his fingers. He reached out, meaning to rub away their imprint. She stepped back.

"Don't, as you said. I'm fine." She walked to the other side of her room to her desk. She pulled out the chair and sat down. "Time to be honest. Tell me why you're here." Her emotions shut off; she was cold, distant.

Raf glanced around the room, his gaze moving from the floor where they had made love to the female watching him through suspicious eyes. He wanted to run his fingers through his hair and pull it out in frustration. He hardly recognized himself anymore.

"Tell me," Marina said again, her voice hard.

He let out a breath. "Before I came to Gunngar, I had a family—a wife, a child, and a brother. My brother came to stay with us one holiday. He was only a year younger than me, but he'd gone through a lot, screwed up a lot. He was working through that, was finally getting his life together." Raf swallowed. He hadn't told this story to anyone—ever.

"I was on a job, hunting an escaped prisoner. I was gone for two days. When I came back they were all dead."

Marina rolled her lips into her mouth; her eyes were moist again, but this time Raf could smell her emotion, knew it was real.

"What happened?" The question was soft.

Raf dropped his gaze; emotion clogged his throat. "I don't know. It wasn't other hellhounds. I could tell by how they were killed—swords. But there was no scent at all, not the killer's anyway." His brother, wife and child's scent had been everywhere, their fear and anger everywhere. Raf fisted his hands, tried to keep the image of their bodies, of their slit throats and the blood-stained floors from flashing through his mind. It didn't work. He saw, smelled, felt everything—just like he had that day. His knees buckled; he walked to the wall and slammed his fist into it. The noise and pain helped, brought him back to where he was.

Marina was quiet. She didn't need to speak; he could smell her distress, feel her support. He'd shouldered this feeling alone for so long....

He inclined his head and kept talking. Now that he had started, he needed to get it all out or he would freeze up, be unable to say any of it again. "I started searching that day, but I found nothing of use. There was no scent, no trail, nothing. It was as if whoever had done it had dropped in, then disappeared." He looked at her. "A trail is never dead, not for a hellhound. But this one was. I went crazy for a while, then I started researching all the legends and tales I'd ever heard of, concentrating on elves and Svartalfars."

"Because of the swords," Marina murmured.

"It is their choice of weapon," he said. "I didn't find

anything that explained how the killer had appeared and disappeared without leaving a trace, but I did find a tool to help me learn who that being was—the seer stone of Alfheim."

Marina shook her head. "I've heard of it, but I don't know anything about it. There are so many myths in Alfheim. It's impossible to know which are real and which aren't unless you have experience with them yourself."

"And you don't?" he asked.

She shook her head. "Should I?"

"You are the princess." He didn't say it as an accusation, just a statement of fact. Sim had admitted the stone was in the castle.

She seemed to realize what he was saying. "Is it supposed to be royal?" She frowned. "I've never seen it, not that I know of, but that doesn't mean it doesn't exist. I was a child when I left the castle, and not much into Alfheim lore."

Raf accepted her answer. The information he'd first found on the stone had been ancient—a diary from an elf who had heard tales of it from servants. Even that elf's account had indicated the stone wasn't common knowledge, that its very existence was kept hidden from the masses. Which, of course, made it all the more likely servants would speak of it.

He'd followed that lead, though, to the elf lords. After they claimed the stone was real and were willing to give it to him, he'd taken the job spying on Marina.

Marina looked down at her hands. "I'm sorry. I really am, but…" She looked up. "Do you expect me to turn myself over to the elf lords? What if they are lying to you?"

He stared at the canopy above her bed. "If they are, they will regret it."

Marina stood and paced across the room. Her scent flowed after her. Raf gritted his teeth and tried to ignore the warmth that surged through his veins. "I don't expect anything—" Then bit the words off.

He had expected her to follow the plan Sim had laid out, and if not, he'd meant to somehow force her. Now none of it seemed that simple. He relaxed his hands. "The elf lords don't know about Amma. I don't know that they'd even care. Right now, all they want is you to publicly support them."

"Why?" She stared him down, demanded with her eyes that he be honest with her.

He met her gaze, knew he had to tell her everything. "The legend, that the throne picked you to rule Alfheim."

She rolled her eyes to the side. "I knew the royals placed stock in that, but I didn't think the elf lords did."

Raf lifted one shoulder. "The citizens of Alfheim do."

Understanding passed over her face. "The elf lords want to use me to court Alfheim."

"From what I was told, there have been uprisings."

Marina's brows lowered almost imperceptibly. "I hadn't heard." Her hand drifted to her throat. She turned. "I'm sorry. I can't help you."

Raf stared at her for a second. "You would benefit from this, too. You would be out from under your uncle's roof."

She shook her head. "And under the elf lords'."

"In the castle."

She laughed. "Gilding doesn't make the cage any more tolerable." Seeing his face, her expression softened. "I'm sorry. I know you want the stone. I even believe that you think pretending for them would be better than being here, but I've already dealt with the elf lords. I won't do it again."

Raf's world closed in around him. He blinked, confused. Her uncle had forced her to return here, held her now, he was sure, against her will. But Raf had offered her a choice, life at the castle, working with the elf lords who he knew she'd worked with before, and she had turned him down.

Was his suggestion that bad? How could life with her uncle be preferable to life with the elf lords?

Not knowing what else to say, he walked out of the room.

Marina fell back onto her bed and stared up at the white curtains. She wished she could roll up in them and disappear. She'd sounded cold and harsh when she had turned Raf down, but she had her sister to think of.

And no reason except Raf's misplaced trust in the elf lords to swing to the elf lords' side.

Elf lords or royals, a case of lesser evil. Not a choice she would ever have wanted to make. Lucky her, she didn't have to. Lucky her, the choice had been made for her by her uncle and the damned inset embedded in her sister's throat.

She closed her eyes and lay her arm over her face. Why couldn't Raf have been here for her, had a plan to save her sister and whisk Marina away? Why couldn't he be the prince Cas, the reporter, referred to him as?

She dropped her arm to the bed and opened her eyes. Because she was a commodity. Nothing else.

The room assigned to Raf was bigger and more luxurious than any room he'd ever occupied. The bed was piled high with cushions and his feet sunk into the thick pile of the rug. He ignored it all, strode into the room and snapped the door shut behind him.

His arms crossed over his chest, he scowled at the satin-covered bed. He'd shared his story with Marina, thought the reason he needed the stone would sway her, but it hadn't.

She refused to go, to leave her uncle's even though he treated her as he did. If she wouldn't help Raf, why wouldn't she help herself?

Raf picked up his bag that some servant had left on the mattress and tossed it to the side.

The bag flopped over. A white note fell out onto the blue comforter. He paused, suspicious.

He'd had no note in his bag, had nothing in there but the most basic of toiletries and a couple of changes of clothes.

He glanced around the room as if someone might still be there, then, sure he was alone and unmonitored, he picked up the note.

It was on common printer paper, and the words inside, when he unfolded the note, were typed—or more accurately printed—by a computer or similar device. A note from the elf lords; he knew it before he began reading.

It was a script, outlining his part for the next day— what to say, what to do. It was detailed and explicit, down to how he should smile and tilt his head at the appropriate moments.

He frowned. He didn't appreciate micromanagement. He took jobs of his choosing; the mission decided by the employer, the details decided by Raf.

Uneasiness crawled over him. Someone had been

in his room, gone through his belongings. What else had they done?

He dumped out the bag. Under his clothes was a package wrapped in brown paper. It was soft, obviously contained cloth. Inside was a bland gray tunic like the lords' minions wore.

Apparently the elf lords' spy had messed up, not realized the photos had already been taken. Or perhaps this was for Raf's appearance before the crowds after he convinced Marina to leave the royals, publicly declare her allegiance to the lords.

He stared at the tunic for a moment, thoughts whirling through his mind. What did the elf lords think he was? A brainless pup with no pride, no sense of self? That he would let them dress him, put words in his mouth, tell him when to smile and when to scowl?

A growl found its way past his lips. He tossed the package against the wall, then spun back toward the bed, shoved the bag off the bed and crumpled the note.

He reached for a pillow, meaning to toss the pair that decorated his bed onto the floor also.

The material was smooth—like the silk Marina wore. He paused, stared down at it.

The silk... If Marina did as he asked, if she chose the elf lords over the royals, she'd never wear silk again. Would never be bossed about by her uncle again...no, she'd have new bosses, new elves picking out her clothes and putting words in her mouth.

The cage...the castle...would be grander, but her life wouldn't be different. She'd still be a puppet, valued only for whatever part her owners forced her to play.

Did he really want that for her?

He thought about her story, what she'd told him back in the human world. Remembered their time together in Gunngar, holding her again here… His fingers dug into the down-filled pillow, creased the silk.

Did he really want her to pay the price for his revenge?

He forced the tension from his hands, flattened them and smoothed the wrinkles he had created.

Did he want her to pay a price at all?

The pillow smooth again, he stared at it….

No. He didn't. Not anymore.

The next morning Raf waited in the sitting room for Marina and the reporter. After finding the note and package, he'd prowled his bedroom, stopped himself a thousand times from shimmering into Marina's bedroom and shaking her, then pulling her to him and repeating what they'd done earlier, made love. Something about finding that clothing…thinking of what it meant to Marina, had broken through the shell of lies he'd built around himself.

He wanted revenge, but he wanted more than that now. He wanted Marina.

There had to be a way to have both.

Today he would figure out how.

Sitting on one of Geir's fancy couches, dressed in his own outfit of jeans and a dark T-shirt, he waited for Marina to arrive.

He was growing antsy when the reporter walked into the room, followed immediately by Marina. In her hand was a white sheet of paper—a script, he guessed, just like the one that he tossed aside last night.

She was dressed in silk again—yellow, and some kind of purple flowers were woven through her hair.

She looked every inch the princess, but, he realized, it was simply a costume.

Time to stop the play acting.

As she and the reporter went through social niceties that Raf didn't understand or like, he waited, his anger at the elf lords and the royals growing.

Marina turned, a smile on her face. It looked real, her eyes and skin glowed—but Raf knew it couldn't be. She had the script, knew her part. She probably thought he had slipped it under her door. She had to be angry. He was.

He stepped forward and pulled the paper from her hand. Startled, her eyes rounded. "Did you need my list for some reason?"

He glanced down; it wasn't the script as he'd thought, but a simple "to do" list of frivolous duties involving hair, nails and shoes. It angered him almost as much as the script. He balled it up, too and tossed it onto the floor.

Cas took a step back. "Is this a bad time?"

Marina's gaze flickered from Raf to the reporter, then with a smile, she placed a reassuring hand on the reporter's arm. "No, this is perfect. Raf is just…tired." She shot Raf a look that sizzled with warning. "He's not used to Alfheim's…weather."

"Oh." Cas looked confused, but Raf wasn't concerned with the reporter or what he believed. He was focused on Marina. The look…she hadn't given up, wasn't beaten. The strong female he'd known in Gunngar was still in there—just disguised in silk and flowers. He knew what he had to do. He had to bring her out.

With a smile, he slid onto the couch and waited to see what she would do next.

The reporter pulled out his recorder. He talked

mainly to Marina. When he did refer a question to Raf, Raf ignored him. He was done with the games—fed up to the point of exploding.

Marina spun a tale that combined what the elf lords had laid out on the script—how her time in Gunngar had been both fulfilling and exciting, how she had looked forward to coming back to Alfheim and working with them some more—and what he was sure her uncle wanted said—that she was equally excited to be back with her family.

She was playing both sides, offending neither. She was pretending, coloring every word and gesture to appease either the elf lords or the royals.

What she wasn't doing, was being honest, real, herself.

Raf's annoyance surged.

He cut her off midsentence. "What Marina didn't know was that I was working for the elf lords all along. They'd hired me to spy on her." He crossed his arms over his chest. "Just like they've hired someone in this household to spy on her now. When she found out, she had me locked up. A deserved punishment, although I wouldn't have been so generous, and I don't plan on being so generous now."

The reporter paused, sat there with his recorder going and his mouth hanging open. "Excuse me?"

Raf smiled. He could feel his eyes glittering, knew their normal blue had darkened. "What part did you miss? The part where the elf lords have spies in this house or the part where Marina locked me in a box?" He glanced at her and raised a brow—dared her to step up, *stand up* for herself.

She pursed her lips and sat back.

"The princess…?" Cas turned in his seat. "Locked you in a box? But I thought, Sim said…"

At Marina's refusal to respond, Raf growled. "Yes, a box. It's one of the reasons I decided to hunt her down. She wasn't easy to catch, but I had a net and a dragon. It worked out."

He stared at Marina. She stared back. Her eyes were sparkling with anger, but her lips were pressed together in a tight thin line.

He leaned forward, elbows on his knees. "There was a witch, too. More than one actually. The one Marina burned...or didn't. And the one she forced into her body. That one was tricky, but we dealt with it." He glanced at the reporter. "Have you met Amma? From what I hear, she can be quite the bitch, but then again so can our princess."

Marina's nostrils flared and her hands formed fists in her lap. *She didn't know what to do, how to react— which personality to pull from.*

Raf smiled and leaned back against the couch cushion.

The reporter flipped off his recorder and pulled a paper from his pocket. He glanced around the room, then leaned forward. His voice tense, he addressed Marina. "I don't know what's going on here, and I don't want to. I have a story to run and I'm not letting some *hellhound* get in my way." His lip turned up. "This is the version of events I had heard. Can you confirm them?"

Raf grabbed the reporter by the back of his collar and jerked him backward.

Words, or what would have been words, gurgled from the reporter's throat. Raf reached for the paper, but Marina beat him to it. She glanced over the sheet quickly as if she already knew what was written there, then nodded, folded it in two and shoved the paper into the reporter's jacket pocket.

Raf lifted the reporter higher, until he had to stand on his toes to keep from strangling.

"Does it matter if I can confirm it?" she asked. Her gaze darted behind Cas to Raf, as if the question was for him...or perhaps the reporter's answer. Raf loosened his grip, let the reporter croak out a reply.

"No."

She nodded, then pressed a button on the table beside her. As if he'd been standing just outside the door, Tahl appeared.

The guard's gaze slid over the three of them, took in the reporter's awkward position and Raf's grip on his collar. He didn't hesitate, kept his face blank and respectful.

Marina waved one hand. "Mr. Dwin is ready to leave. Would you see him out?" Then she turned on her heel and floated from the room.

With a snarl, Raf threw the reporter to the ground and stalked after her.

Marina waited for Raf outside in the hall. When the doors to the sitting room exploded open, she headed for the garden. She knew he'd follow. At the fountain, she stopped. She'd risked a lot playing the interview as she had. While she hadn't betrayed the royals, she hadn't denounced the elf lords, either. Geir wouldn't be pleased.

But she understood Raf's pain, and wanted to help him. She'd lost her parents, too, and while two elves had been caught and tried for their murders—no one really believed they were their killers. Like everything in

Alfheim, it had all been pretense, an act for the populace.

Besides, she'd guessed the interview was a set up, that the elf lords had already paid Cas to get the story they wanted. What she said didn't matter. Meeting with her and Raf was just window dressing.

Her uncle was experienced enough in the ways of Alfheim to know it, too, she hoped.

But Raf wasn't. And for some reason now, he was angry with the way she'd played things. Which made her angry, too.

She crossed her arms over her chest and waited for him to storm forward.

Barely aware of where Marina had led him, Raf ground to a stop in front of her. "What were you doing in there?" He couldn't explain his anger, wasn't sure if he was angry at her or himself—but the note, her performance, spending the last day in a world full of pretense…it was more than he could take. He was done.

"What you wanted me to do, what everyone wants me to do. I was playing my part." Her face was pale.

"There's a spy here," he said.

She shrugged, cold, uncaring. "More than one, probably."

"Doesn't that bother you?"

She took a step toward him. Her chest almost touching his, she stared up at him. "In Gunngar it bothered me because it was you, because I let you get close and see the real me. Here? What are they going to see or hear? Just what I want them to. I won't make the mistake I made with you again."

He grabbed her by the forearms and pulled her up

onto her toes, just as he had the reporter, except his intentions for Marina were far different. What had happened between them was real. He accepted that now. Everything else— He cut off the thought, and blurted out, "Was it a mistake? Or has everything we've done afterward, with the exception of what happened between us last night, been the mistake?"

He pulled her closer, kissed her.

Her body was stiff and he was angry. Angry at the mess he'd found himself in. He felt trapped by his need for the elf lord's seer stone, and he resented the hell out of it. He was angry that Marina didn't seem to resent it with him.

He ignored the rigidity of her body and pulled her against him anyway. She tried to turn away, but he deepened the kiss. Slowly his anger began to seep away, be forgotten. His senses, his reality were engulfed by the female in his arms.

As his anger ebbed, Marina's seemed to increase. Her hands shot from his chest to his neck, and she locked them behind his head. Began kissing him with the same angry energy he'd had only seconds before.

His hands cupped her buttocks and he pulled her even closer. She sighed into his mouth. He moved his lips to her throat and rained kisses down its ivory length.

In the distance, through a fog, something crashed. Marina jerked from his embrace.

Her eyes wary, she glanced around. He pulled her against his side and listened. Footsteps, soft, elf soft, pattered along the far side of the garden. Leaving Marina behind, he shimmered.

The garden was plopped down in the center of the mansion—like a hole in the middle of a doughnut.

There was no way out without going through the house.
Whoever was listening wasn't some stranger who had
wandered upon them from the street. It was someone
from inside Geir's household. Geir himself?

Raf doubted it. Geir didn't seem the kind to spy. He
would hire spies. More likely it was the person who had
left the note in Raf's room.

What had he seen? The kiss? The interview?

What the spy had seen didn't matter. What did matter
was that someone *was* spying. Hypocritical as it was—
Raf had no patience for spies, had no intention of putting
up with one.

Fed up with everything as he was, he didn't stop to
think any more. He shifted.

Within seconds, he was in his canine form. He shook
himself free of his clothes and padded forward, searching for a scent. The smell of elf was everywhere. He
listened, heard material brushing against plants and soft
breaths no louder than a moth's wings as it drifted
through moonlight. He turned his head, caught a flash
of blue among the plants.

He had spotted his prey. His lips pulled back and leapt.

Chapter 11

Marina braced a hand on the fountain to keep from falling. Raf's abrupt shimmer had left her surprised and unsteady. She'd barely regained her balance when she heard him materialize on the far side of the garden. Magic flowed toward her—into her. She blinked, startled by the strange sensation.

She'd noticed magic around her before, but never felt it this way...as if it was streaming into her. She opened her hands, felt it surging through her veins. She spread her fingers, tried to do as she had when Amma had been inside her, to send power shooting from her palms. There was a pressure, like something building, preparing to escape. Her muscles tensed; she held her breath. Then nothing. The feeling was gone as quickly as it had come.

Her shoulders dropping, she let out a breath.

There was a crash. She spun. She'd forgotten where she was for a second, forgotten about Raf and what he was doing.

She hurried toward the noise, across the grass and stone floor of the garden. Through the plants she saw golden fur flying through the air—Raf leaping. He had caught someone—or was about to.

Marina's heart thumped. The spy he'd mentioned. What would Raf do with him? What would Marina do with him? She hadn't lied, it had never occurred to her to call out the spies she knew followed her everywhere.

Spies were a part of royal life. She'd been stupid to think they wouldn't follow her to Gunngar, but here...they were so expected...to hunt one down? Challenge him?

Raf roared and landed. A body fell, knocking more plants to the ground. Marina raced forward, eager to see the spy's face, eager to face at least one pretense head on.

She shoved ferns and flowers out of her way, stepped over broken pottery and heaps of dirt. Then before her, blocking any other steps she might have taken, stood Raf, in his hellhound form. His head was low and his back was rigid. He growled.

Marina stepped to the side to see who lay trapped under him, to see whose neck was wedged between his jaws.

Her sister's stormy blue eyes, wide and filled with terror, stared back at her.

"Raf. Stop!" Marina pulled on his fur. Caught up in the heat of his hunt, he didn't lift his head, didn't move his jaws from around his prey's throat, he simply snarled.

"Raf." Marina squatted next to him, stared him in the eyes. "It's Ky. It's my sister. Let her go."

Slowly, the blood lust receded. He came back to himself, realized the scent he'd caught right before leaping was familiar, that it belonged to Marina's sister, the female he'd helped from the floor when he first arrived. Still…

"She was spying," he said in Marina's head.

Marina pressed her lips together. "Let her go."

Every instinct he had screamed that he shouldn't, that while he held the quivering elf female he should question her, find out exactly why she'd been lurking behind the plants, but Marina's gaze was determined, and he could smell her worry.

He opened his jaws and stepped back.

Ky grabbed her neck where his jaws had been, but otherwise didn't move. She seemed unable to.

Without looking at Raf, acknowledging that he'd done as she asked in any way, Marina sat next to her and slipped an arm around her waist. "Are you okay?"

Raf padded back to his clothing, changed into human form, then jerked on his clothes. He wasn't sorry for jumping on Ky or pinning her to the ground. She had been spying. He wouldn't let her walk away without answering for that, but he would give Marina a few moments with her first.

Dressed, he went back to where the two females sat on the floor.

"I just…I saw you two come in here, and I was curious. I've never met a hellhound—" Ky glanced at Raf, and her hand automatically moved back to her neck. There was no mark there; he'd had no intention of killing her, just holding her, intimidating her.

She licked her lips and swiveled her gaze, eyes round and huge, back to Marina.

He'd succeeded in that at least. Planning to keep the advantage, he crossed his arms over his chest and stared down at the small woman.

Marina frowned at him, but kept talking to Ky. "Raf thought you were spying on us."

"She was," he said.

Ky's gaze moved between the two of them. "I just… well…" Her hand tightened on her throat. "You could have killed me."

He shrugged. "Could have, didn't." He wasn't going to be taken in by female hysterics.

Marina's eyes narrowed. "Raf's an expert on spies. I had no idea he was so…sensitive to them."

Ky's brows lowered. "Why do you keep talking about spies? I was watching you, but that's just because…I was nosey." She threw her hands into the air as if the declaration was a huge admission.

Raf cursed under his breath.

Marina pulled her sister's hand into her lap. "Don't worry about it. It has nothing to do with you, and next time—just announce yourself. As you've seen Raf can be a bit quick to react."

"It tends to keep me alive," Raf replied, but Marina ignored him. She helped her sister to her feet. Ky wandered from the room, glancing back over her shoulder twice before finally disappearing through the door.

Marina turned on him. "What was all that?"

His hands on his hips, he kept his face bland. "She was watching us. She could be the spy. How well do you know your sister? Gunngar was cut off for a hundred years. You don't know what may have happened to her since then. What she wants."

Marina's lips parted, her face paled then flushed.

"My sister isn't a spy. She has nothing to do with any of this." Her hands opened and closed. She pulled in a breath and stepped closer. "And just when did you decide you didn't like spies? And what happened to the Raf who talked to me last night, asked me to change allegiances, go with the elf lords? When I went for the interview, he'd disappeared. I need some kind of cheat sheet to know which side you're playing from one meeting to the next."

Raf tightened his jaw. She was right; he had been moving back and forth, switching from what he thought he needed, the stone, and what he wanted, Marina. He still wasn't sure he could have them both—but suddenly he was determined to try.

"I don't understand elf politics. Before I decided I needed the stone, I hadn't even heard of the royals or the elf lords. And even now, I don't care who rules Alfheim. Hellhounds don't have a government, we rule ourselves."

Marina's eyes flickered. "Alfheim is a lot more—"

"I'm not comparing the two, just explaining where I've come from."

Marina closed her lips over whatever she'd been about to say.

Raf continued. "In all of this I only care about a very few things. The first hasn't changed. I want the stone and I intend to get it, but the second has. I want you, too."

Her eyes rounded.

He waited.

She blew out a breath. "Well, get in line. The royals and the elf lords have already staked a claim." She turned on her heel and walked toward the door, head high and gait steady—every inch the princess.

"And you're going to let them have a go at it? Without a fight?" He called. "You can't trust anyone here. The place is built on deceit. Do you want to live like that?"

She stopped. "I do live like that. I have my entire life. It's the only reality I know. And you know what? It's safer this way. It's safer trusting no one, than someone who's working against you. You tell me I can't trust Ky, and you're right, I'd be foolish if I did. But, as much as I'd like to, I can't trust you, either." She turned back toward the door and disappeared.

This time he let her leave.

How could he ask someone who'd been raised surrounded by intrigue to trust him? Especially when he kept agreeing to work with one of the groups determined to use her?

It was time to get his stone and cut off his connection to the elf lords. Maybe then Marina would trust him. Maybe then she'd see what they'd had in the past was real.

Raf materialized in front of Cinderella's castle. It was the only description he could think of, a castle with pointed spires and shiny stones that seemed to change from purple to gray to a silvery blue, then back again.

He stepped onto the drawbridge and glanced around, expecting knights in armor to rush toward him. Instead an unusually thin and pale elf in a black and gray uniform jogged from the outer gate blowing a whistle. "Stop," he yelled.

Raf kept walking.

"Stop," the elf yelled again, this time producing a short blade.

Raf turned and strode directly toward the smaller

male. The elf held his ground. Short sword raised, he stared up at Raf. "The castle is closed to visitors." He pointed at a sign that hung on a pole protruding from the drawbridge. "It opens again tomorrow."

"I'm not a tourist," Raf replied.

"And you're not an elf."

Raf felt no need to argue the point. He turned back toward the castle. "I'm here to see Lord Sim," he replied over his shoulder. He planned to demand to see the stone, to make sure the elf lord wasn't lying when he said it existed and the elf lords had it. Then when he knew where it was kept, he'd borrow it. He had no intention of keeping it. He only had one question to ask.

There was a rustle of noise and the elf landed in front of him, his sword still drawn. This time he pressed it against Raf's chest.

"What type of being are you?"

Raf frowned, annoyed. He would like to get past the elf and on to what he came here to do, but obviously that wasn't going to happen without either bloodshed or niceties. His preferred choice was bloodshed, but he suspected Sim would frown on a dead guard left lying across his drawbridge—and right now Raf wanted the elf lord to help him.

He smiled, his lips feeling tight across his teeth. "Hellhound."

The elf bared his own teeth then snapped them together in a faux bite. "Impossible. There are no hellhounds in Alfheim."

Raf's nostrils flared. "There is now." He held out his arms making his case.

The elf lunged. Raf shimmered, but the elf's blade struck, pierced Raf's skin.

Materializing behind the elf, Raf growled. The elf spun. He slashed his blade. Raf jumped backward, his mind darting. Instinct told him to kill the elf, but logic told him the guard worked for the elf lords, that he needed to stay calm, assure the guard he was no threat— that if he killed the elf, Raf's chances of being invited into the castle would disappear.

It was a tough choice, kill the elf and alienate the elf lords, or let him live and keep his relationship protected, for now. His strong desire was to snap the small male's neck.

The elf whirled to the side, light flashing from his blade. Raf dropped and rolled, his goal to knock the elf to the earth, pin and disarm him. But the elf leapt and landed easily on his feet. His chest barely moving with the exertion, the elf faced him. "Leave, hellhound." His eyes glittered with warning.

Raf frowned. Alfheim had a history of being intolerant of non-elves, but the guard's reaction seemed extreme, and Raf's patience were about used up.

"I'm here to see Lord Sim," he replied, keeping his voice low and steady, the same tone he would use to speak to a crazed dog.

"I said to—"

His blade held high, the guard started to attack again, but before he could complete his obvious intent, a voice called, "Guard! Halt!"

The elf paused.

Sim appeared and barked out a command in elfin, the words sounding like water rushing over rocks. The elf didn't look at him, and didn't lower his blade. Deciding now was not the time to teach the guard manners, Raf shimmered, materializing next to the elf lord.

Sim bit out another command, but the guard only turned, his forest green gaze focused on Raf.

Sim yelled another phrase in elfin, then gestured for Raf to precede him through the barbican.

"He's old-school," Sim commented striding at a quick pace. "He came with the castle."

"Does he hate all outsiders, or just hellhounds?" Raf asked.

Sim glanced at him, his gaze appraising. "I can't say. You're the first of either that I know of who has tried to enter the castle."

Raf raised a brow, and didn't reply. But as he followed Sim across a second drawbridge and into the lower bailey, he could feel eyes on him, knew the guard had followed them, was watching him. He angled his body so he could scan the structure they'd left, kept his eyes open for the flash of steel or the glint of an arrow.

Sim, either unconcerned or unaware of the guard stalking them, led Raf to a grassy area filled with picnic benches and barbecue pits. He motioned around the park-like grounds. "This area of the castle is open eight to five. Many elves have celebrations here."

Raf stared around. Sim made everything sound so positive, but if that were true, if everyone was happy under the elf lords, why did they need Marina to keep the citizens behind them?

Sim stopped next to a statue of two elf children, one wearing a crown, the other carrying a sword. "This symbolizes the old and the new Alfheim. Before rulers were chosen by heredity, now it's by fitness to rule."

"The sword?" Raf raised a brow. Make it a fist and it would fit with the hellhound way of doing things, but hellhounds lived alone or in packs. There was no hellhound world, no one hellhound or group of hellhounds that decided things for all. "Is that why you need Marina?" he asked.

Sim frowned. "We need Marina because the citizens believe we need Marina—in reality we don't."

Raf had visited too many places where constant force wasn't needed to keep the peace to believe what Sim said. However, he let it drop. The elf lords were delusional. It wasn't his problem.

"We met with the reporter. I want to see the stone," he replied.

"Already?" Geir frowned. He gestured to one of the tables. Raf waited for Sim to sit then followed his lead. "Is Marina cooperating?"

"Have you talked with the reporter?" Raf asked. Evading questions was not a natural hellhound talent. His time in Alfheim was beginning to affect him.

Sim stared toward the barbican. There was noise outside the gates. Yelling.

He glanced back at Raf and smiled. "Someone who doesn't respect our hours. No matter what, you can't please everyone."

The yells didn't sound like an unhappy family looking for a picnic—more like an angry crowd with torches and hay forks.

"The reporter, no, but the paper should be out soon." Sim pulled a slim box from his pocket, glanced at it, then spoke into it—asked someone on the other end to bring him that day's news.

Raf bit the inside of his cheek. He didn't like waiting, especially since he had no idea what the reporter might have chosen to print. "While we wait, why don't we see the stone?"

Sim leaned back. "Is there a problem?"

Raf placed his hands on the table. "I've done what you've asked so far. I need assurance that what you've promised me in return is still available."

"Are you questioning my honesty?"

There was a crash near the gate, then another. Sim tensed, but didn't look. Raf smiled.

"Yes," he replied. "I am."

Sim fiddled with the box he'd used to call for the paper, then stood. "Fine. I can show you, but you won't be able to touch it."

He lead Raf past the picnic tables and the statues, to the back part of the inner bailey and finally into the keep. There were no obvious signs of guards or locks, but as Sim walked through each doorway in front of him Raf heard a sizzle, like some kind of field being disabled. Magical or technological? The elves had skills with both.

They climbed a set of stone stairs, simple and un-adorned. In fact the entire interior was bare, stark even, with only a few pieces of furniture dotting the halls. Sim noticed Raf glancing at a wall where a large lighter square of stone shone against the darker stone surrounding it.

"A tapestry. They were all sold," Sim offered, and kept walking.

Finally after climbing two flights they came to a narrow hall and at the end of it, a small doorway. Sim went through first. This time there was no missing the sizzle. It was more than a sound; it sent every hair on Raf's body to a stand. He pretended not to notice.

Inside sat a plain round wooden table and on it, a box.

"The stone?" Raf asked. There were no windows in the room, but aside from the sizzle as Sim had crossed the threshold, there were no signs of security to guard the artifact. There was nothing Raf could see that would stop him from grabbing the box and shimmering. He stepped forward and reached for the box.

Chapter 12

"I wouldn't do that if I were you." Sim slid his hands into his pockets. There was no expression on his face, no threat, no warning, nothing.

Raf paused. "I can't see the stone. Does the box open?"

Sim walked a few feet to the right of where he'd entered from and pressed a place on the wall.

There was a creak and Raf spun. The lid on the box slowly opened. As it rose, Raf held his breath. The legends said the stone had a phosphorescent green glow, showing its power was strong and ready to be used.

The lid fell back. Nestled inside on a bed of white silk lay a stone—dead and gray in color.

Disappointment clutched at Raf; he spun. "It's not it."

Sim smiled. "You really do need to know what you're working for." He moved back to the doorway and slammed the door shut.

Raf lunged forward, determined to grab the elf before he could spring whatever trap he'd laid out in the small room, but the eerie green glow that filled the space brought him to a stop. He turned back. Rays of green light shot from the stone, as if something wanted to explode from within it.

Raf tried to move forward again, but the light was blinding and painful. He placed his arm over his face and staggered a couple of steps before stopping again.

"It won't let you any closer," Sim murmured. "Not with the lid open. And if you took the box, and tried to open it by hand...standing close." He made an exploding noise. "Your brain would explode—just like with the gun I held to your head when you first arrived. The stone would be much more thorough."

"How do you...?" Legends, you couldn't always trust them. Although looking at the stone, or trying to, Raf could understand how this one had been created.

"We lost a lord. It wasn't pretty." Sim jerked open the door, then walked back to push the button that lowered the box's lid.

"So, you're saying the stone is of no use to me? That I can't ask it a question?" Rage pounded at the back of Raf's head. As he should have known, he'd been tricked.

"You asked for access to the stone and permission to ask it a question. We are willing to give you both."

"But knowing how to ask the question, to hold the stone...that's my problem?" Raf asked.

Sim stepped back out into the hall. "Exactly. You get the princess on our side and we fulfill our part of the bargain. We give you the stone—getting it to work wasn't part of the deal."

Raf clenched his fists, and worked to calm the anger that was flooding his body. The stone existed. He knew that now. There had to be a way to use it. He'd just have to find out how to do it.

Sim was already moving down the stairs ahead of him. Raf followed.

He knew where the stone was now. He'd come back later to get it. Then he'd denounce the elf lords, and convince Marina to do the same, convince her she didn't belong in Alfheim—she belonged with him.

Marina had sat at her desk for hours trying to concentrate on the multitude of invitations she'd received since returning to Alfheim. None of them were from friends. She had no friends. As she'd told Raf, she'd always known she could trust no one, and she'd always kept everyone, even her sister, an arm's length away.

Everyone except Raf.

She dropped her forehead to the palm of her hand. She'd told him she didn't trust him—because she knew she shouldn't. But despite knowing he had come to Alfheim for the stone, and his admitting that he had been working for the elf lords—not just in Gunngar, but every day since—she wanted to trust him.

Trusting him was insanity; it would get her trapped. She had to remember that, and not to weaken. When Raf returned, she had to look at him as if he meant nothing to her—make him mean nothing to her.

It had been hours since she'd walked out on him. A servant had told her he'd left the mansion. For good?

The thought should make her happy—one less person

to betray her, but hot tears formed in her eyes. She bent her head, hiding them from anyone who might wander by her open door.

If only she could hide them from herself, too.

"Princess?" A servant, one of the many new additions to Geir's household since Marina had left for Gunngar, appeared in her doorway. She held a paper-wrapped box in her hands. "I found this sitting in the front hall. It has the hellhound's name on it." The elf slid it onto a small table not far from the door.

Marina flattened her hands and tried to hide the wrinkled mess her fingers had made of the invitations. "For Raf?" Marina frowned.

The package was clearly marked with Raf's name. It was meant for him, not her. She should instruct the servant to deliver it to his room.

She touched the rough paper. "Is there a note?"

The other elf shook her head.

"A gift?" Marina mused out loud, but from whom?

The servant tilted her head in question.

Marina sighed. There was no elf word for gift or present. Elves didn't give gifts; elves gave nothing without an expectation of return.

Marina did her best to interpret.

The servant's brows rose.

Marina gestured for the servant to place the box on a table that stood at the foot of her bed. "It's a human thing."

"Oh." The servant eyed the box expectantly, then glanced at Marina.

The servant wanted to see what was inside the box, and so did Marina. Raf was a guest in her home, by elf rules he had no rights to privacy.

A simple cord kept the paper-wrapping in place. One tug on the string and the bow came undone. It unraveled with a hiss. Marina blinked, thinking for a moment the falling paper had made the sound. Then the noise sounded again—louder.

The box moved.

Marina jumped back, shoving the servant behind her as she did. She had let go of the cord, but the tie continued to fall; the sides of the box fell, too. Until it lay completely flat on the polished wood.

Inside there was straw—moldy dirty straw that filled Marina's bedroom with the stench of the stables. She pressed the back of her hand to her nose, but kept her gaze on the box. The straw moved. Marina reached for her blade, but her knife holster was missing, had been tossed aside by her uncle before they left the human world.

Unarmed and afraid to turn her back, she waited for whatever was inside the box to appear.

Before she could do anything else, even warn the servant to step back, the flat, brown and white speckled head of a snake sprang into sight.

The snake bobbed up and down, its head spreading flat and its mouth opening wide, revealing fangs dripping with venom. Marina pressed her arm against the servant's chest, warning her to stay back. The other elf stood stiff and pale, her gaze glued on the snake.

The serpent was rare in Alfheim, but well known. Its venom was paralytic; its bite deadly. It stalked its victims, first splattering them with its venom, then moving in to finish them off with its bite.

She nudged the servant backwards, tried to edge them

both toward the door, but as she did, the servant came out of her stupor, opened her mouth and screamed.

The snake jerked to the side, venom flying from its fangs.

Raf shimmered into the front entryway of Geir's mansion. He'd been gone for hours. The place was quiet. A piece of straw lay on the marble floor. He picked it up and twirled it between his fingers. The bit of debris reeked, at least to his sensitive nose, of old barns, mice and other creatures. It was a strange thing to find on Geir's otherwise pristine floors.

The thought had barely formed when a scream echoed down the hallway. Raf dropped the straw and shimmered again.

A female elf stood in the center of Marina's room, her mouth open, a scream hurtling from her throat. Marina shoved her to the side, moving the opposite direction as she did. On the table in front of them a huge snake wove and bobbed. Its head darted forward in a strike, liquid flew from its fangs.

Marina swore and grabbed a lamp to swing in front of the snake, seemed more interested in blocking the barrage of venom than striking the serpent.

Raf quickly stored the thought and shimmered again. Solidifying behind the two females, he placed a hand on each and shimmered them into the hall, out of the serpent's reach.

Marina's eyes were huge and wild. Her hair had come loose from the elaborate braids that had held it back from her face and energy crackled around her. She shoved against him and tried to move toward the door.

He stepped in front of her. "What the hell was that?"

"A snake. It's deadly. I have to catch it before it gets loose." She tried to reach around him.

"I don't think so. Stay here." He crossed his arms over his chest and shimmered back into the room.

The snake had disappeared from the table. Raf spun in a circle, inhaling, searching. The smell of serpent reached out to him, obvious in the small room filled with Marina—sunshine and flowers, and lead him to the far corner where a basket full of clothing sat waiting to be unpacked and placed in Marina's dresser.

Something in the basket moved.

He glanced around the room for a weapon or trap. There was nothing more dangerous than the lamp and nothing more secure than an open-topped woven trash can. He considered shimmering back out to look for something else, but Marina was right, the snake could easily escape the room while he did.

The door to the bedroom creaked, and Marina slipped inside.

"Get out," he growled.

"Where is it?" she asked.

He growled again.

Following his gaze, she focused on the basket. "We need to trap him." She pulled a blanket off of her bed, and took a step forward.

Raf pulled the blanket from her hands.

She frowned, but let him.

He reached into his pocket and pulled out the folded-up net. "The weave is too open." He frowned and started twisting the blanket around his hand instead. If he could get the snake to latch on to the cloth, he could shimmer the creature somewhere else—an ocean, a volcano, somewhere.

Marina's gaze moved to the net. "It's elfin. It will adapt. Let me help."

The contents of the basket shifted again. A flash of brown scales slithered over a piece of turquoise silk, then disappeared somewhere deeper in the stack.

"Raf, please," Her gaze and stance were strong, but her voice was soft. She was asking him to trust her. In the garden she'd said she didn't trust him. He hoped that wasn't true, but either way, he knew how important trust was between them. They'd lost it so many times; he'd thought it could never be regained by either of them.

He reached into his pocket and pulled out the net.

Her eyes shone. Her expression was happy and alive; a bystander would have thought he'd given her some elaborate gift, not a net to snare a snake. Her fingers brushed his. They stared into each other's eyes.

He felt the energy again, crackling through her, around her. He glanced down at her fingers…saw it there…green and unmistakable, magic. It flowed from her to him, wrapped around his fingers where they touched like blue wires.

Marina glanced down, too. Her eyes rounded. "It's—"

An explosion sounded from the street below and the snake jumped.

Raf leapt forward, his arm in front of him. At the same moment, Marina spun, energy dancing from her fingers. The snake's fangs sank into the blanket. Raf grabbed Marina by the hand. "Shoot it," he said.

She hesitated; he could feel her doubt.

"Now," he said.

She took a breath. He could see her resolve harden and smell her confidence returning. She hesitated, but only for a second. Then she opened her palms. A stream of magic flowed from her body and into the snake.

At first nothing happened, or didn't seem to. Marina tensed. A shadow passed over her face. Raf prepared to shimmer, where to he didn't know....

The snake stiffened and its mouth opened. Before it could fall to the ground, it began to spin, faster and faster. It ceased to look like a snake, was just a whirl of brown and cream. Its body curled, its head reaching toward its tail, until it formed a perfect circle. With a snap, its fangs sank into its flesh.

Raf reached for Marina's hand, but she took a step back. Folded and unfolded her hands, cutting off the flow of magic. The snake froze and then hung in midair as if held there by a string dangling from the ceiling.

Raf couldn't remove his gaze from the snake. He'd seen the symbol of a serpent latched onto its own tail before, knew it meant something—he just wasn't sure what.

Marina's eyes were huge, her face pale. Unsure whether to comfort her or reach for the snake, Raf stood frozen.

Without warning the snake fell.

Raf stared down at it. "You're a witch." It was more than that, the symbol...it had to mean something, couldn't be coincidence. He waited for Marina to explain.

Marina fisted her hands. "I've never done anything like that before, not on my own...with Amma...but not—"

He nudged the snake with his toe. It held its position, seemed frozen with its fangs embedded into its tail.

"It's a symbol," he murmured.

Marina nodded. "Usually, but—" the nod changed to a shake "—this is a coincidence. Maybe it's about the magic. It affected the snake strangely."

Raf wasn't convinced. "What does it mean?"

"It's the eternal circle—something that seems to have an end—" she pointed at the snake's tail "—simply starts again."

"Why would it appear here?" he asked.

She smiled. "It didn't. I told you. The snake just reacted to the magic."

Raf stared at her, not sure if she believed her words or not, then decided it didn't matter. She was safe. He pulled her into his arms and lowered his mouth to hers.

Despite what she'd said to him at their last meeting, she didn't fight, didn't object all. Her body fell against his, her fingers curled against his shirt, and she kissed him back.

Raf smelled good, felt good. Marina smoothed her fingers over his chest. Then raised up on her toes and wrapped her arms around his neck. He was warm and strong and she had thought he was gone. But he'd come back…again.

His lips parted and his tongue found its way into her mouth, stroked over the inside of her cheek. Something inside her tightened and fluttered. Her heart was beating hard and fast.

She shouldn't be doing this, kissing him. He'd helped her fight one snake, a snake in a box labeled for him. It could have been a trick….

Even as her mind struggled to form reasons for her to step away, her hands locked around his neck, and her body melted against his.

The snake, the circle, she could tell Raf didn't believe her when she said it was coincidence—but what could it mean? It had to be coincidence. The snake hadn't been sent to her, and she didn't think whoever sent it planned on it being killed. No, the thing was meant to eliminate whoever opened that box.

Raf. Someone wanted the hellhound dead.

She stiffened, started to pull away to tell him. But his lips were against her neck, and he growled when she moved. She lowered her hands and let her fingers trail down his chest. Hard, broad and padded with muscle. She found the end of his shirt and shoved it up, baring his skin. She would never get tired of touching him.

She would tell him the snake was meant for him, later.

Her fingers danced over his bare skin and he growled into her mouth, encouraging her now. The sound fed her on, made her bolder.

His hands found her hips, and he pulled her against him. He was hard. The feel of him excited her more, reminded her how special she had felt when they'd been together before the shadow of the elf lords and the spying had fallen over them.

He took a step forward, causing her to take a step back. Her leg collided with the bed. Raf bent and she let him, let him lean down, carry her down with him until they both lay flat on the sheets, panting and staring into each other's eyes.

She reached her hand to his face…the door knob rattled, and before Marina could move or think, Raf had shimmered.

She was left alone, her heart hammering in her chest, her body throbbing with longing. She bunched the bed clothes in her hands. He was gone, again.

Her eyes flew open. And she hadn't warned him about the snake, that it hadn't been sent to him. He didn't know someone wanted him dead.

Chapter 13

"**M**arina!" Ky rushed into the room, the guard Tahl close on her heels. "Dae, she said—" Marina shot upward to a stand. Her hands and legs shook.

Tahl leaped in front of Ky, his sword drawn. He sprang forward and drove his blade into the floor...the snake, Marina realized. He'd seen the snake's body and attacked.

"Oh, gods, she was right." Ky stepped back, eyeing the reptile's now limp corpse.

Marina's heart still raced, from her realization that Raf had left unwarned, and the surprise arrival of her sister. She stood stupidly staring at the pair, her gaze moving from Ky's shocked face to the dangling dead body of the snake.

"It's nothing," she said finally, her heart slowing and her brain coming to grips with what was happening. "I killed it."

"It's biting its tail…." Ky stepped forward her hand held out as if to touch the serpent.

Marina slapped her sister's arm upward, away from the snake. "It's poisonous. Even dead its venom is still there."

Her sister blinked at the snake, her blue eyes narrowing. Marina couldn't tell what Ky was thinking, but the silence made Marina want to move, do something to change the mood in the room.

She jerked the sword from Tahl's hand and shook the snake off into the trash. Then she shoved the basket into Tahl's arms.

"Have someone get rid of it, burn it." She turned away and stared at her mussed bed.

Her mind instantly returned to Raf. She wrapped her hands around her arms, wondered if her sister sensed her discomfort.

"Where did it come from?" Ky asked.

Marina turned back. Her sister had risen onto her toes in an attempt to see inside the basket. Marina hesitated.

"A box," she murmured, keeping her gaze from going to the table where the unfolded box with its tag still lay.

"Dae said something about your hellhound." Ky glanced around the bedroom. "Is this what it came in?" She tapped the box with one finger.

Instantly worried that there might be another threat attached to the box, Marina grabbed her sister by the arm and pulled her away.

Ky frowned. Marina slowly loosened her grip and stepped away.

Ky's expression returned to normal, but misgiving settled around Marina. Suddenly, she wanted her sister to leave. She pressed a hand to her forehead. "I'm not feeling well. I think I need time alone."

Ky glanced at Tahl, who still held the basket, then nodded at Marina. "You've been through a lot. We should leave. Tahl will take care of the snake, and I'll get rid of this." Before Marina could stop her, she'd gathered up the box, cord and card. Realizing objecting would seem odd, Marina let her.

Without another word, the pair strode from the room.

Marina waited until the door clicked behind her, then dropped onto her bed and stared at the ceiling.

What was going on? And what exactly should she do about it?

Raf shimmered to the street outside the house. He hadn't known who was entering Marina's room, but hadn't wanted to be found there. His relationship with Marina was growing, whether she knew it or not, and he didn't want to tip off any spies to the fact.

He placed a hand against the wall that surrounded the house. The brick was cold and rough. He concentrated on that for a second, let his heart slow and his mind focus.

There was a story that went with that snake. He needed to get back to Marina and discover what it was.

Suddenly the ground shook and a group of elves raced by. Frowning, Raf moved out of their way, then grabbed the next elf who ran past. "What's wrong?"

The elf tried to pull away, but Raf held strong. "Subversives," the elf yelled. "They bombed a storefront." He jerked his arm. Raf let go, watched the elf disappear into the crowd.

Subversives. Another group loose in Alfheim. The land of light and plenty was spotted with darkness and desperation. Raf wanted nothing more than to get the stone and Marina, and leave.

He turned, ready to shimmer back to her. Another explosion rocked the street. A female screamed, something about her child.

Raf glanced over his shoulder at Geir's mansion.

Another scream, a female elf, her face drawn and her clothes stained, shuffled toward him mumbling. "My son...he's in there...trapped."

Raf closed his eyes, tried to ignore the voice inside his head urging him to help, tried to remember Alfheim's problems weren't his own.

The female stumbled and fell. Another wave of crazed elves ran past, trampled over her.

With a curse, Raf shimmered and grabbed the female by the arm...shimmered her to safety. "Where is he?"

Leaving Alfheim would have to wait.

Hours had passed since Raf left. Marina paced back and forth in her bedroom, not sure what she should be doing, but feeling she should be doing *something*.

She stopped at the table and flattened her palms against its top. The snake. Who had sent it? The only being she knew in Alfheim with reason to want Raf dead was her uncle, but a snake packaged up like some twisted Jack-in-the-box did not seem her uncle's style.

"Someone tried to kill you." Raf spoke from behind her, his voice gruff.

She spun. His clothes were stained and there was a gash over his eye. She stepped forward and touched the raw flesh. He didn't move, just stared down at her, his gaze dark and troubled.

"What happened?" she asked.

He captured her fingers with his, pulled them from his brow. "Nothing."

She pursed her lips. "Don't lie to me. If you want me to trust you, you can't lie, not anymore."

He squeezed her fingers and nodded, told her about being on the street, about explosions and families being separated. "Things are ugly here," he finished. "You should leave. We should leave—together."

Marina hesitated. She hadn't told him about Ky, about her uncle's hold on her. "What do they want?" she asked. "The subversives?"

He shook his head. "No one seems to know. I don't think they've made any demands. It's as if everyone has gone mad."

"Someone should stop it," she said.

"If the elf lords could, they would have. No rulers like uprisings." Raf ran a hand over his face. "The citizens seem to hate them, and the royals, too. I couldn't find anyone willing to stand behind either group."

Marina nodded. It didn't surprise her. If the royals had thought they had enough influence to take Alfheim from the elf lords, they would have done it a century ago. Which was why they wanted her to trick the citizens of Alfheim into accepting them—as if she being back in the castle would change anything. It was just another elfin trick.

Raf seemed to be thinking the same thing. "Could you change things?"

She shook her head. "Change what? What are the citizens objecting to? How would I know which group to support? The elf lords are pushing Alfheim toward technology and away from magic, the royals would do the opposite. But I don't believe either is any better or worse than the other—just different."

He rubbed her knuckles with his thumb. "How would you do things?"

She started. She'd never thought of that before; no one had ever asked, because it hadn't mattered. Neither group really wanted her input. They only wanted her name and image.

"Somewhere in the middle I think. The elf lords are right—Alfheim needs to change and grow. But the royals are right, too—we can't forget who or what we are." She shook her head again and turned a little to the side. "What I'd do doesn't matter, anyway. Neither group would listen to me." Her words sounded bleak, even to her own ears, but they were true. She couldn't help Alfheim, couldn't save her world from itself, not even if she wanted to.

Raf grabbed her by the arms and pulled her back around. "Then leave with me." He stared into her eyes.

She wanted to tell him yes, to tell him to shimmer her away right then, but she had Ky to think of, to protect.

At her hesitation, he growled and pulled her against his chest. His body was hard, but his touches were soft. His chin as it brushed over her face and neck was rough with stubble. She knew it would leave a mark, a mark she'd have to hide or repair, but she didn't care... couldn't care...

She was with Raf, and they weren't yelling at each other, weren't accusing each other...they just were. It was everything she longed for.

She cupped his chin in her hands and pressed her lips against his, tiny nibbling kisses that grew in speed until he groaned and moved his mouth away from hers, trailed kisses down her throat.

Her head fell back and his lips moved lower, to her breasts which pushed up against the top of her blouse. He jerked the gauzy coat from her body and tossed it onto the ground. It wound around their feet and they stepped on it, giving it no more thought than what it represented—the pretense that had always been her life.

He backed against the bed and fell onto the soft mattress, pulling her with him. She landed on top of his chest and smiled. The move was almost playful, something else she'd missed. Princesses didn't play; elf lord minions didn't play.

He smiled, too, then wove his fingers into her hair and pulled what remained of the elaborate hairdo loose. It fell down around her shoulders framing her face. She started to brush it aside, but he stopped her, ran his fingers through it instead, then wound them through its length and used it to pull her mouth to his.

She met his kisses, harder now. The time for tiny love bites was past. She wanted him, needed him, had missed him. Tears leaked from the corners of her eyes, surprising her. She brushed them aside then shoved him down on the bed when he noticed and started to rise.

"No," she murmured. "Don't stop. We can't stop. I need this."

He lay back down, his arm around her back hard and firm. He was angry; she could feel it, but not at her. Not this time. This time he understood, and was on her side.

She sighed and shoved his shirt up, baring his chest. He pulled the shirt from his body and they fell back down together. She pressed her lips to his nipple, swirled her tongue around it as her hand drifted lower, to the front of his jeans. He was hard beneath the denim. Excitement shot through her. She slipped the button free and slowly pulled down the zipper.

He caught her lower lip between his teeth and growled. She smiled and stroked him, reveled as he growled again.

He murmured something she didn't understand; she murmured back, telling him in elfin that she loved him, needed him. He didn't understand, but that was for the best. Trust him or not, they couldn't be together, even in the middle of their passion she knew that. A hellhound and an elfin princess—it was insane.

She pulled her top over her head. Her breasts hung free. He pulled the tip of one into his mouth. She groaned and squirmed against him. His lips still covering her, he slipped his hands under the waist of her pants and edged the material down her hips until she was naked on top of him.

They were both naked. Their bodies seemed to cling to each other, as if a static charge attached them. She pulled back, felt a zing sizzle across her skin, then lay back down and did it again.

"Your magic," he murmured. "It's growing."

Marina had never felt energy like this before. She wiggled her fingers. Tiny bolts of electricity zinged from her fingers, zapped over his chest and stomach. He sucked in a breath and she did it again, moving her hand lower each time. Finally, her hand hovered over his sex. She stared down at him, daring him to give her a nod, an okay.

He grabbed her by the back of her head and jerked her body down onto his. She groaned. His skin was hot; they seemed to meld together. Her legs parted and his erection nudged against her. She wiggled until the tip inched inside her, held her breath, then rose up and plunged her weight down. He filled and stretched her; she had to fight back a scream.

He flipped over and pressed her down into the mattress. Then he rose up above her and stared down at her. His eyes glimmered. She reached up and ran her hand down his chest. He braced his arms beside her head and pulled back, almost out of her. Her hips angled toward him, her body searching for him. Then he tilted his hips and moved forward again until his length was fully sheathed inside her.

Her breath caught in her chest. She ran her hands down his sides, dug her fingers into his muscle and held on as he continued his movements, in and out. Her body tightened and her mind separated. She was floating overhead, but feeling every movement his body made against hers, smelling the wood smoke scent of him. He murmured again. She struggled to make sense of what he said…love…mine…words that made no sense… words she couldn't believe he would say, mean, not about her.

She blocked them from her mind, lost herself instead in the physical reaction her body was having to his, in the warmth of his touch and the passion of his kisses.

His pace increased and her breath came out in tiny pants. Her world swirled and her body tightened. He grabbed her and held her closer still, his length pounded in and out of her body one more time, then he tensed, too, and together they fell over the edge. The bedclothes, her hair, their breath all tangled together, tying them together as he collapsed next to her and tugged her into his arms.

Raf's heart pounded. He pulled Marina closer and pressed a kiss against her ear. He hadn't come here with the intention of this happening. There were too many things for them to discuss, resolve—what he'd seen in Alfheim, what he'd learned about the stone, the snake. All of it added up to a gigantic mess.

But he didn't regret what had passed between them, either.

She was his and he wasn't giving her up. That he was sure of.

Still they needed to talk. He forced his mind away from the feel of her snuggled against him.

"Tell me about the snake. Who do you think sent it? Who wants you dead?"

"The snake wasn't meant for me. The box had your name on it."

Raf digested that. He imagined many elves might want him dead, especially if they saw him with their princess right now, but not many…any…knew his true feelings for her, that he had completely turned his mind again, realized she had just been a pawn…loved her. Still, someone stood out.

"Would your uncle have left it?"

Marina rolled over and stared up at the ceiling. "I don't think so. It isn't his style."

Raf considered this. Geir was the only being in Alfheim who could have a personal grudge against him. The guard at the castle certainly hadn't held any love for him, but Raf had never met the male before, couldn't believe he would go so far as to track Raf—the guard had gone home by the time Raf left the castle. He hadn't even waited around to see that Raf did leave.

"Are you sure it was meant for me?" he asked. It wasn't that he couldn't believe some elf might prefer him dead, but the snake, the box…it seemed like such an effort to get him that way. His death couldn't be that important to anyone in Alfheim.

"The box had your name on it," Marina repeated.

"Still..." He laced his fingers through hers. "Perhaps the royals heard the elf lords were courting you. Perhaps putting my name on the box was just a trick." He paused. "How did the snake get in your room, if my name was on the box?"

She dropped her gaze. "A servant brought it. I wanted to know what was inside."

He nodded. "They would probably have suspected that."

"But they wouldn't know. You could have been here and opened the package."

He shrugged. "If I had and the snake had killed me, would they have cared?"

"No." She shook her head, but didn't look convinced.

Raf sat up. "So, we don't know who sent the snake. It doesn't matter. Someone could be trying to kill you. That's enough. I will get you out of Alfheim." It was his fault she was here, in danger. He had to make that right. He stood and pulled on his clothes.

Marina stood beside him. She clutched onto the blanket which was still wrapped around her. "I can't leave."

He stopped.

"My uncle has Ky booby trapped. If I try to leave Alfheim he'll hurt her, maybe kill her."

Raf shoved a shirt into her hands. "Then we take her, too." He was sick of the issues of Alfheim, sick of not knowing who to trust—not knowing if he and Marina could trust anyone.

Marina shook her head. "We can't. My uncle told me the trap will go off if she goes through the portal."

"He could be lying."

Marina smiled, a sad tilt of her lips. "He could be, but then again, he might not be. I'm not willing to take the chance."

Frustration caused Raf to growl. "So, you're going to stay here instead? Let him and the elf lords fight over you like a battered bone? There's no winning for you. You realize that, don't you? No one here cares what happens to you. They just want to use you."

Her eyes snapped with anger, but only for a second. She let out a breath. "I've known that most of my life." She walked back to the bed and sat down, looked as if she had no intention of moving.

Raf picked up the shirt she'd dropped and held it out to her. "Get dressed. I don't believe you are stuck here. I won't let you be."

Chapter 14

Marina wanted to believe Raf, but he didn't know Alfheim as she did. She was the princess; the only escape from the job was death.

She pulled on the shirt he'd handed her and reached for her pants. "I'll help you find the stone. Then you can leave."

"I'm not leaving you here."

"You have to. I know all this seems crazy to you, but I'll survive it."

He walked to the table where the snake's box had lain. Straw, like what he'd seen in the front hall, was scattered over the floor. He pushed it into a pile with his toe. "What about this?"

A shiver ran over her body, but she hid it, shrugged instead. "Just another day in the life of a princess. Besides, I told you, you were the target."

Raf tapped his fingers against his leg, then stood. She stepped in front of him. "Where are you going?"

"To see your uncle."

"You can't."

Raf crossed his arms over his chest. "Why can't I?"

"Because, I just told you. He can kill Ky. I'll talk to him, I'll see if he knows anything about the snake."

"I'm the reason you're here, in this mess. I'll fix it." He walked past her, headed toward the door.

"Raf!" She reached for him, not sure what she was going to say, what else she could say, but her hand hit glimmering air. He had shimmered.

As soon as Raf left, Marina knew what she had to do. She had to get her sister out of the middle.

Carrying the tiny box that contained the inset Geir had given her, Marina wandered into the sitting room. She hadn't spoken to Ky about it. If her sister's life truly was at risk, she deserved to know.

The sitting room was empty; Marina moved on through the house. No one was around, except servants, of course. And Marina barely noticed them. She stopped when she realized this. Old habits were returning. Old habits she wasn't proud of.

She walked back down the hall where she'd seen a female servant polishing a table. "Hello," she called.

The servant continued her work. Marina moved closer until she was standing only inches away. "Hello."

The servant jumped.

"Have you seen my sister?" Marina said.

The servant licked her lips and glanced back at her cleaning rag.

When it became obvious the female wasn't going to

answer, Marina decided to try another tactic. "How about Dae, have you seen her?" The servant who had delivered the box with the snake was the only other person besides Tahl whose name Marina knew, and that was only because Ky had used it.

"I'm Dae," the servant responded.

Marina frowned. "Your name is Dae, too?"

The female darted her gaze to the side then back at Marina. "We are all Dae. All the female servants. Jarl Geir felt it would be less confusing."

"He calls you all by the same name?" And her sister did, too. This was new to Marina; she was fairly certain before she left for Gunngar each servant had a unique name...or did they? It horrified her to realize she didn't remember.

"Yes." The servant glanced nervously back at her cloth.

"Marina?" Ky appeared at the end of the hall, near an open door that led to the back garden. "Were you looking for me?"

Marina hesitated, but the servant had already gone back to her cleaning. Feeling uncomfortable in her own skin, Marina clasped the box tighter against her palm and moved down the hall toward Ky.

"Her name isn't Dae," she announced as they walked out the door into the noon sun.

"Whose?" Ky picked up a knife and began scraping thorns off a rose bush.

"That servant, any of the servants probably. Geir just has you call them that."

"So?" Ky ran her finger down the now bare stem. Satisfied it was smooth, she picked up the knife and started to work on another bush.

"So, you call them that, but it isn't their name."

Ky held out a hand and gestured to a basket lying near Marina's feet. "Could you hand me the wax?"

Marina frowned, but retrieved the small pot and plopped it onto her sister's palm. "Doesn't that bother you?"

Ky looked up. There was a line between her eyes. "Should it?"

Yes, damn it, it should. Marina wondered if she knew her sister. Had she left her alone with Geir too long?

She took a breath. "They are elves, like you, like me."

"Of course they are, Geir won't hire anyone else. The elf lords use dwarf and half-dwarf servants, but none of the royals do. We're an all elf household, except for your hellhound."

"He isn't *my* hellhound," Marina replied.

Ky dipped her finger into the wax then held the pot back out for Marina. "I don't know why you're getting snippy. No one else in Alfheim has a hellhound to show off. Everyone will be jealous."

As Marina watched her sister buff away even the tiniest sign of the thorns she'd snipped off, her stomach clinched. Ky didn't get it; didn't get any of it. Her life had been nothing but pretty dresses and parties for too long.

Marina squatted down in the dirt and pulled her sister's hand into hers...she glanced at the ruby set into her sister's neck. "When did you get that?" she asked.

Ky lay a hand over the jewel. "Only a few months ago."

Marina opened the box she'd been holding and placed it on her sister's hand. "Geir had one made for me, too."

A question appeared in Ky's eyes. "It's pretty."

"You don't know what this is, do you?" Marina

asked. She kept her voice low and calm. She didn't want to frighten Ky, but she had a right to know.

Ky's finger danced over the ruby set in her own neck. "It's a decoration. They're popular now."

"It's more than that. How long have you been having your spells?"

Ky's hand stilled. "Why are you asking that?"

"Did you have them before?" Marina moved her gaze to the ruby.

Ky pulled back. "What are you saying?"

"When I was in Geir's office, when I first arrived, he showed me this." She shook the box with the crystal. "Then he told me about yours. It isn't just a decoration. It's causing your spells. That last one. He did that to show me he had control of you."

Ky shook her head. "Don't be silly. Geir doesn't need to control me. I'm nothing. You're the princess." Something flickered behind her gaze. Anger?

Marina plucked the box from her sister's palm. "I said it wrong. He's controlling me, by threatening you."

"Because you care what happens to me?" The question was soft.

Marina's gaze shot to her sister's face. "Of course, you're my sister."

Ky sighed. "And Geir is our uncle. He's controlling, but he wouldn't do that. We're royal, even without the throne, that means something."

"It means we're tools." Marina sat back on her heels and snapped the box shut. "He and the other royals want to overthrow the elf lords, use me to get and keep Alfheim on their side."

"What's wrong with that? We are supposed to be living in the castle. The elf lords have no right to it." Ky cupped her hand around her neck. It was an unconscious gesture. Marina wondered if her sister even realized she'd done it.

Marina faltered. The look in her sister's eyes…it was dead. Thinking it was the realization they *couldn't* trust their uncle, Marina pulled Ky's hand away from her neck. "That isn't what I wanted to talk about…. We need to learn more about the inset. Maybe we can figure out a way to get rid of it."

Ky lifted the knife to her own throat. "We'll cut it out."

Marina stared at her sister, shocked at how she held the knife, at how cold the intent in her eyes was. She placed her hand on Ky's. "Geir said it would explode if we messed with it, or if you left Alfheim."

Ky shrugged and dropped the knife. "Since I have no intention of leaving Alfheim, the last doesn't matter. So far as the first…I'll leave it in. I like it, anyway."

Marina's eyes widened with concern. She touched her sister on the chin. "It could kill you. It gives Geir total control over you. Doesn't that bother you?"

Ky tilted her head. "Are you saying you don't mean to work with the royals? Are you planning something I should know about? Something that might cause our uncle to feel the need to threaten me?"

Marina pulled back, her hands and heart cold. The conversation wasn't going as she'd thought it would. Ky was different, but then what Marina had just told her, it had to have shaken her sister more than she was letting on.

Marina placed her hands in her lap and forced her voice to stay steady and reassuring. "I don't want you to be threatened. That's why I'm here. Together maybe we can figure out a way to get rid of the inset."

Ky smiled, a flash of the little sister who'd greeted

Marina on her return from the human world. "If it bothers you, I'll have it removed. It isn't a big deal, elves reverse them all the time."

Not the answer Marina was looking for, but maybe Ky was right. She'd lived with Geir while Marina was gone. Maybe what he'd told Marina wasn't true, maybe there was another explanation to what had happened to Ky while Marina watched the flashing light from their uncle's computer.

But she didn't think so.

Marina stood. She'd done what she'd come to do, she'd told her sister. If Geir allowed Ky to have the inset removed, the issue would be over, if not…she'd know that Marina had told the truth, that Ky couldn't trust their uncle. That would at least be a start to saving them both.

Ky picked up a pair of shears and began clipping. Every few seconds she reached up and brushed her fingers over the ruby.

Marina shoved the box into the pocket of her pants. Maybe it was time to talk to the elf lords. They created the technology. They would know a way to free her sister from the inset. It was that or let Geir use her and Ky forever.

Her sister was right. She wasn't the princess and she shouldn't have to pay the price for Marina having the title.

Raf found Geir in his office. He didn't knock. He walked forward and grabbed the smaller male by the neck, shoved him up against the wall. "Let Marina go."

The royal didn't object, made no reaction at all to Raf's attack, simply lifted his eyebrows. "I didn't realize I was holding her prisoner."

"Are you saying the inset in her sister's neck isn't real?"

Geir smiled. "Of course it's real. I wouldn't let my niece walk around with a fake."

Raf moved his fingers, pressed one and then another into Geir's neck, until a raspy squeak escaped the royal's throat. "Is it a booby trap? Did you cause her spell?"

Marina's uncle stared back at him, anger shining from his eyes. Raf moved closer, so his body was inches from the elf's. He whispered in his ear. "I want it removed." He released his hold and let the elf fall to the ground.

Geir landed on his feet, jumped without falling. Rubbing his neck, he stared back at Raf and laughed. "So, you're worried about Ky now? That is rich." He shook his head, laughed again, then held up one hand. "You want the inset disarmed?" He reached past Raf to the lap drawer of his desk.

When Raf moved to cut him off, he held up both hands. "I can't do as you ask if you get in my way."

Raf hesitated, but stepped back. This was all too easy, too simple. He knew it, and he was prepared for the elf's trickery.

Geir pulled open the drawer and slipped his hand inside. Raf froze, ready to attack if the elf pulled out a weapon. When the royal's hand reappeared, it turned out he was holding a computer storage device. He held it up, showed Raf, then slipped the small device into his laptop. A screen loaded with a flashing light appeared, just as Marina had described. Geir clicked on the light, and a small box opened over the current window.

He paused, his hand poised above the mouse. "Are you sure you want it disarmed? Here—" he moved the mouse so the cursor changed to an arrow and pointed to a box that said something in elfin "—and the princess's sister has another attack. Here—" he slid the arrow down one line "—she's dead, and here—" the arrow slid lower, to the last line "—the inset is disarmed, becomes nothing more than a harmless, tacky adornment."

Raf stared at the royal, unsure what to make of his apparent invitation to kill Ky. "Disarm it," he replied.

Geir smiled and shrugged, then clicked on the last line. A word Raf couldn't read appeared on the screen and the light quit flashing. Geir pulled the device out of his computer and handed it to Raf. "Without this, no one can activate Ky's inset. You might want to keep it. You might find use for it later."

Raf stared at the tiny rectangle, no bigger than his thumbnail. "What happens if I destroy it?" Geir's demeanor and willingness to hand over the computer drive was sending prickles of unease over the hellhound.

Geir had sat down at his computer, seemed to be reading e-mail. He looked up as if surprised that Raf was still there. "Nothing, but you would lose control over Ky." His attention moved back to the screen.

Raf closed his fingers over the drive. Still confused, he moved toward the door.

Geir called after him. "I'd keep it, if I were you."

Raf stared at him, waited for him to say more, but Geir, typing, seemed to have shut Raf out completely.

Raf slipped the drive into his pocket. He knew Marina would want him to destroy it, but he couldn't, not yet.

Ky was Marina's sister—in Alfheim did that make her a more likely friend or villain?

Chapter 15

Tahl stood by the front door, blocked it actually. Marina walked up, pretended she didn't know he was there to stop her from leaving. "I'm going out for a while, to do some shopping. Will you tell Geir if you see him?" She reached for the handle. Tahl moved to the side, stymieing her attempt.

"There's trouble in Fisby, princess. Your uncle has requested you stay in today."

And every day, Marina added mentally. He didn't want her communicating with the outside world. The phones were shut off and she had no access to a computer, either. The reporter and Raf were the only beings from outside this house she'd seen since her arrival. "I'm sure my uncle is just being overprotective. I did survive on my own in Gunngar."

Tahl didn't move.

Marina pressed her lips together. She could force Tahl out of her way, but that would be an obvious move of revolt—too obvious until she'd spoken with the elf lords and knew they could help save Ky. She smiled. "Have you seen Raf? I'm sure my uncle would feel I was safe with a hellhound with me." If she could find Raf, he could shimmer her to the elf lords, or take a message to them himself, but she had searched the house and found no sign of him.

"He met with your uncle earlier, but he's been gone for some time. As I said, the streets are dangerous now. He may have ran into...difficulties."

The way he said it... "Do you know something? Has something happened to Raf?" Marina leaned forward, forgetting her role for a moment.

Tahl shook his head. "Of course not. I'm just pointing out there is a reason your uncle wished for you to stay here."

Marina pressed her hands against her sides, to keep from doing something that would make her and Ky's situation worse. Magic leaked from her palms, warmed her legs. She took a breath and tried to force it down. No one but Raf knew this secret. She wanted to keep it that way.

The door to the garden banged. Marina turned, thinking Ky would appear, but a servant slid through the door instead and disappeared down the hall.

Marina glanced back at Tahl, ready to argue. His gaze was directed at the garden, and the expression in his eyes....

"Tahl?" Marina waited for him to look back at her. "You wouldn't want my sister to be in danger would you?"

He started, and Marina knew she'd guessed right.

She stepped closer, murmured in a low voice, "I don't need to go out to go shopping. I need to go out to save Ky."

He frowned. "Ky is fine. She's in the garden."

Marina stared at the guard, hoped she wasn't misjudging him. "It's about the spells she's been having. Our uncle is causing them." She paused until she saw his reaction, shock and concern, then hurried, told him everything she'd told Ky and Raf about her sister's inset.

When she was done, Tahl paled. "Does Ky know?"

Marina nodded. "I told her, but she doesn't seem concerned." She brushed her fingers over the guard's arm. "She's my sister. I don't want to see her harmed."

"Of course." Tahl's gaze darted behind her, to the garden. He seemed to think for a moment, then finally, he looked at her. "I can't let you leave. Geir would know, but if you write a message, I can get it to the elf lords."

A written message. It was dangerous. Marina committed very little to writing. In Alfheim, it just wasn't wise. But she wanted to save Ky.

She nodded.

In the sitting room was a writing desk, stocked with heavy vellum, pens and sealing wax. She scribbled out a note, asking the elf lords to send a representative to her uncle's home. She didn't get specific in the note, but still if her uncle found it, it would be damning.

Knowing the risk was huge, she lit a stub of sealing wax and watched bright red splashes fall onto the envelope. She held it for a second, pinched between her finger and thumb. Tahl watched, waited.

She shook her head. Writing the note was foolhardy,

but what choice did she have? And risk, though, it might be, she was willing to take it to save Ky.

She handed the note to Tahl. A servant entered the room carrying a bucket filled with cleaning supplies. Tahl slipped the note inside his jacket and nodded for her to leave.

She walked away, praying she'd judged Tahl correctly— that he loved her sister as much as she thought he did.

Still no Raf, and no word from Tahl. Marina had stayed in her bedroom as long as she could stand, then came into the sitting room and flipped through an old magazine. It happened to be one filled with stories of her in Gunngar.

She set it down, feeling a bit sick.

The doorbell rang. Marina tensed, hoping the elf lords had sent someone. One of the Daes walked toward the door, but Ky cut her off and pulled it open first.

Marina stood.

Five elves dressed in the finest silk waited on the other side of the door. One by one they walked inside, kissing Ky on the cheek as they passed. The last one had two newspapers folded under his arm.

Marina's stomach clenched. Royals. She sat down and tried to look pleased.

Ky lead their guests into the sitting area.

"You remember my sister, the princess?"

There was something about Ky's tone, an edge, that made Marina sit straighter. She nodded and held out her hand. The royals walked up to her one by one, but none took her hand. She curled her fingers toward her wrist and slowly lowered her hand onto her lap.

This couldn't be good.

"Yes, the princess." The royal with the newspapers arched a brow. Marina returned his stare. He looked familiar. She searched her memory and came up with a name—Anton. He and her uncle had been friends and rivals. The two things tended to go together in Alfheim.

"I see you've been reading." He glanced at the magazine she'd dropped onto the couch cushion beside her. "So have I." He unfolded the paper and held it up. An image of Raf and she dominated the page.

"Geir had assured us when you returned from Gunngar, you'd understand your position better. But it doesn't appear that you do." He dropped the paper onto her lap.

She didn't glance down, just held his gaze. "I'm not responsible for what my uncle says."

He laughed. "But you are responsible for what you do, aren't you?"

She bowed her head in cool recognition of what he'd said. "Of course. We all are."

"What about this? Do you know anything about this?" He threw the second paper on top of the first. This time she glanced down.

Another picture, this one older by a few days. Marina riding in the car next to Tahl and the other guards when she'd first arrived back in Alfheim. At first glance the photo was innocent enough, but the headline couldn't be missed. "Princess Held Against Her Will by Royals."

Marina's gaze darted back to the photo—this time she saw the circle highlighting her hands in her lap, bound with ties.

She tossed the paper to the side and stood. "Who knew the media in Alfheim would print the truth?" It was a stupid move, but the mere presence of the royals reminded Marina why she had run away from Alfheim in the first place.

Anton turned his gaze to the royals behind him. As one they stared at her. Hardly the explosive shocked reaction she'd hoped for.

Behind them there was movement—Ky. Marina's ire turned to dismay. She'd forgotten her sister, forgotten Geir's threat.

Fisting her hands at her sides, she forced herself to be calm. "What do you want? My uncle told me your plans. I won't endanger Ky. If you want me to retract all of that—" she motioned to the newspapers that had fallen on the floor "—I will." As she said it, she thought of Raf. This could cost Raf the stone. Marina hoped he could forgive her.

Anton motioned for Ky to move forward. "Did you hear that? Your sister doesn't want to endanger you. A bit late for that, don't you think?" He reached into his jacket.

Marina lunged, but Ky stepped in front of her. "Don't. Don't make it any worse."

Her heart pounding Marina stepped back. Her hair had fallen from its design. She could feel its weight on her shoulders.

Anton's hand crept into view. Instead of the weapon Marina had expected, he held an envelope—an envelope sealed with red wax.

She closed her eyes, then opened them and gazed at her sister. "I'm sorry."

Tahl and three other guards moved into the room.

Ky stared back, her midnight eyes dark and cold. "Are you? I'm not. This is exactly the proof I needed to convince the royals you are not fit to be princess, that you will never be fit. Our uncle, who you insisted on hating, was the only one who believed in you, the only one who kept me from the position I deserved. But then you came home and handed me the crown. I should thank you, and I will. When I cry at your funeral, I'll thank you for being too conceited to realize who your greatest threat was."

Her sister turned on her heel and walked toward the door. "Let me know when it's done. Until then, I'll be in my room picking out my mourning outfit."

Anton stepped back and the other royals parted. Tahl and the guards moved closer. Marina stared at all of them for a second, not understanding what had just happened.

Her sister who she'd thought she was protecting was ordering her killed—eliminated so she could have the role Marina had never asked for or wanted.

Only in Alfheim could something this twisted happen. And only to Marina, because like a fool, she'd trusted again.

The guards were close now, all with swords drawn. Marina swallowed, forcing down the hurt. She was going to die, but she was going to do it on her terms.

Power surged through her body. It was time to reveal her secret to the elves.

She looked forward to the surprise.

Alfheim had gone mad. Elves ran down the streets, and store doors slammed shut. In the distance there were explosions and screams.

And Raf forced himself to ignore it all. As he and Marina had discussed, there was no saving Alfheim, nothing he or Marina could do. Instead he had to concentrate on saving the two he could—Marina and her sister.

He pulled out the computer drive Geir had given him and stared at it. He might hold the key in his hand, but there had been something off with Geir's reactions. Raf couldn't risk believing him. He had to know for sure the drive was what Geir had said, that by destroying it Raf would disarm the inset, and the only being he could think of that might be able to tell was Sim.

He was outside the castle; the drawbridge was closed. It was the middle of the day—during the time Sim had bragged the grounds were open for picnics and weddings.

Another explosion sounded; this one closer.

Raf blew out a breath. He needed to see the elf lord and he didn't feel like waiting. Seemed a good time to check the castle's defense against shimmering.

He relaxed and pictured where he wanted to be—in the inner bailey, next to the statues. Within seconds that is where he stood, but everything looked very different.

Picnic tables were overturned. The statue of the children with the crown and the sword was on its side. An arm had broken off. Raf picked it up; the child's hand still grasped its sword.

Raf tossed it back down.

Looked like someone had decided to challenge the elf lords' claim, but who? The bailey was empty.

His gaze moved to the keep. *The stone.* If the elf lords had left, where was the stone? His heels digging into the dirt, he stalked toward the door.

He was only a few feet away, when someone landed in front of him. Raf stopped. His head lowering and his stance widening, he glared at the threat—the elf who'd challenged him the last time he'd visited.

"The elf lords are gone." The guard held a short sword in each hand.

There was something about how he stood, how he lowered his body instead of springing forward as another elf might... Raf paused, considered.

"You're different than other elves. Had different training," he announced.

The guard bared his teeth. "I'm better. You have issue with that?"

Raf shrugged. "Just means I'll have to shake a little harder before I snap through your neck."

"Shake away, hellhound." The guard shifted his blades so one was held above his head and one at his waist—both were pointed at Raf. "Things are peaking. Time for you to disappear." His eyes were wild; he bounced forward.

Raf shimmered, appeared behind him. "What things?"

The elf growled. "None of your business. Alfheim is none of your business. You don't belong here—never will."

His vehemence surprised Raf. It felt personal.

"I never said I did. Never thought I did."

The elf cursed. "I saw the papers—you with the princess, siding with the elf lords. You'll ruin everything."

"The papers?" Raf froze. The article had run, and it sounded as if the reporter had pushed the story to the elf lords' side.

Which meant Geir would think Marina had betrayed him.

He had to get back to her.

The guard, one sword held high, the other low, charged.

Raf barely gave him a glance. Marina and her sister were in danger. He shimmered.

Chapter 16

Raf materialized in Marina's bedroom. It was empty. He shimmered again, to Geir's office. It was empty, too, but things were not as he'd last seen them. The desk was upside down and Geir's laptop was smashed into pieces on the floor.

A residue of anger and shock hung in the air.

Raf pulled it into his lungs, let it feed the hellhound bloodlust that always lurked inside him.

His gaze swept the room, looking for a clue as to what had happened. A shoe lay behind the door. He picked it up—a loafer, shiny and expensive—Geir's.

A crash sounded from the main part of the house, a thud actually, like a body hitting a wall. Still holding the shoe, Raf shimmered again.

An elf flew toward Raf; he dropped to the ground. The elf, one of Geir's guards based on his clothing, hit the wall. A lamp crashed onto the marble floor.

Raf sprang to his feet, his gaze darting around the sitting room, looking for the attackers.

There was a crowd in front of him, all dressed in colorful silk—royals. He roared and they parted. Their faces were white and drawn. Shock flowed from them.

At first he thought it was from seeing him, realizing a hellhound had shimmered into the room.

But then he saw Marina. Her arms were stretched in front of her and her long platinum hair flowed behind her as if lifted by a wind—magic.

It surrounded her, surged from her.

She was stark, terrifying and beautiful.

Without pausing, Raf strode forward, grabbed the first royal he reached—an older elf dressed in gold silk—and tossed him out of his way. A second seemed to come out of his shock, lunged at Raf with some kind of snapping device. Raf spun and kicked, knocking the weapon from the elf's hand.

Two more raced forward swords drawn. Raf growled, let them almost reach him before shimmering. He moved six feet to one side where he watched them collide with a table before they realized he no longer stood before them.

There was another crash. He spun. One of the guards Marina had thrown against the wall rose to his feet, had shoved a chair over as he did. The elf, his stance unsteady but his gaze locked on Marina, pulled a knife from his boot. Raf leapt across the space, hitting the smaller male in the side.

The elf slashed with the blade; the metal tore through Raf's pants and into his thigh. He ignored the pain, concentrated on the guard instead. He picked the elf up, placing a hand at his throat and crotch. He held him overhead for a second, then tossed the struggling male like an empty ale barrel across the room.

The elf spun as he flew, trying to twist and land on his feet, but the wall came too quickly. He smashed into it, fell atop a marble table and lay there, his arms and head dangling.

Raf turned back to Marina. Her arms still extended, she held the royals at bay, but no magic coursed from her palms. Unsure whether she was reluctant to harm them or her magic had played out, Raf shimmered behind her, wrapped his arm around her waist and shimmered them both away—to the other wing of the house, to Geir's destroyed office.

They stood there a moment, saying nothing, adjusting to the change. Raf inhaled Marina's scent, and let the excitement of the fight subside. Her breathing ragged, she leaned her head back against his chest and bared her neck. Adrenaline coursed through him. Part of him wanted to shimmer back to the fight, but another...

He kissed the vulnerable spot below her ear, nibbled her ear lobe, inhaled again. Her scent was addictive, flowers and spring, seasoned with courage and determination. Feminine, but strong. She wasn't the elf leader who had hunted witches in Gunngar, or the princess who only wore silk and gauze—she was both, the best parts of both. How could he ever have doubted they were meant to be together?

He ran one hand up her arm, while the other cupped her breast. Kissed her again.

She moved against him, murmuring something...then spun in his arms, laced her fingers behind his head and pulled his mouth down to hers.

Her kiss was urgent and sad. He understood that. The royals had turned on her, attacked her in her home. She nestled against him, soft and warm. He didn't want to let her go, wanted to stay here—keep her safe, but he knew they had things to discuss—what had happened at the castle, and here.

When she pulled back, he let her, dropped his forehead to hers and just stood still for a second, letting both of their hearts slow and their minds come to grips with what was happening—what they had to do next.

"Ky…" Marina murmured, her eyes wide and worried.

He ran his hand down her cheek. "She's safe—at least from the inset. Geir gave me what he claimed was the control. We should find her, though. If the royals attacked you, they will probably be looking for her next."

"No, no." Marina stepped back and placed her hands on Raf's forearms. "It was Ky. She betrayed me. She wants to be princess, and stupidly, I handed her the weapons she needed to turn the royals against me." She laughed. "My uncle…he wasn't the bad guy after all."

Raf reached into his pocket and pulled out the computer drive he'd taken from Geir. "Well, then, what should we do with this?"

Marina stared at his open palm, made a move as if to take the drive, then pulled her hand back and fisted her fingers. "Nothing. Are you sure it controls the inset?"

Raf glanced at the drive. "I'm not sure of much here, but it certainly appeared that he deactivated the program from his computer. We could test it." Raf walked around Geir's desk, searching for his laptop. He found it in pieces on the floor.

He held up two of the bigger chunks. "What happened here?"

Marina shook her head. "Based on what Ky said, I'd guess nothing good."

"Would she have him killed?" Raf asked.

Marina's eyes showed hesitation. "My sister isn't who I remember. I have no idea what she would try to do—but, do I think she *did* kill our uncle?" Marina's gaze dropped to the debris that covered the floor. She bent and picked up a thin tie. "No. I told you, my uncle is tough. Besides, I think she'd be afraid to—killing me, well, she needs me dead to become the princess. But Geir has a lot of connections, and she probably thinks that once I'm dead he'll come around to her way of thinking—support her." She held the tie over her wrist, stared at it as if it were studded with diamonds and she was trying to choose between it and another adornment. She looked up; her gaze was hard. "And she'd probably be right. My uncle may not have supported eliminating me, but that doesn't mean he supports me, either."

Raf ran his fingers down her arm until her hand lay inside his. "What do you want to do?"

Marina glanced around the room, then blew out a breath. "As long as I'm alive, Ky can't be princess. She won't like that. If she really wants the throne with the royals behind her, she'll keep trying to have me killed."

Raf held up the drive. "We can take care of that. You don't even have to face her."

Kill Ky? Marina turned cold at the thought. Ky was her sister; she loved her…but her sister had ordered Marina killed, was probably sitting in her room waiting for news that she, Ky, was now princess.

Marina touched the tiny black box that Raf held. All they'd have to do was find a computer and press a few buttons. It would be faceless, bloodless. Ky's heart would just stop beating.

She jerked her hand back. "I won't do it. Not like that. I won't do it at all unless I have no choice. Right now, I do. I'm ready to leave Alfheim." She stared up at Raf. She would need his help. She had no way to travel from here to the portal, not without being spotted by the royals.

Once at the portal she hoped she'd be able to get through—hoped the royals didn't have spies there and that the elf lords hadn't sent out orders for her to be kept in Alfheim. "Can you take me to the portal?"

Raf shook his head. "If you leave, it will be like it was when I found you. They won't leave you alone. Your sister, maybe the elf lords if they still exist, will send bounty hunters."

At mention of the elf lords, Marina frowned. "If the elf lords still exist?"

Raf explained that he'd gone to the castle and found it deserted, except for one lone guard. "The subversives have killed them or driven them out."

"Who has the throne?" Marina asked.

Raf's gaze was blank.

"In Alfheim the throne isn't just something we say— it's reality. Whoever has possession of the throne has control of Alfheim. The elf lords have never sat on it, as far as I know, but they controlled it by keeping it hidden."

"My dear niece, there is a reason the elf lords didn't sit on the throne" a voice announced from the shadows.

Marina and Raf spun. Geir stepped forward. He smiled. "Your hellhound senses are no match for elf

magic." He waved his hand down his body. He was
wearing a body suit of reflective material. "After you
left—" he glanced at Raf "—I decided it was time to
take precautions. I was right. When Tahl and the royals
my younger niece had convinced into following her
arrived, I was already suited up and ready to…what's
the hellhound term? Blend. They had no idea I was
here—which didn't stop them from looking and—" he
took piece of his laptop and sighed "—destroying."

When her uncle had appeared, Marina had tensed,
but it was Raf who moved forward to grab him.

"What are you plotting, Geir?"

The royal smiled. He glanced down at the Raf's hand
around his biceps. "Is that necessary? Surely you don't
think I'm going to turn you over to Ky, do you? She did
try to have me killed, too."

Raf didn't comment, didn't move.

Marina slid forward. "Tell us what is going on,
Uncle, and maybe Raf won't tear you into pieces. You
know he's wanted to since he met you." She held the
plastic tie out then snapped it against her wrist. "You
do have that effect on beings."

Geir held himself erect and proud, tried to appear that
he wasn't shaken—but he was. Marina knew it,
probably more by the fact that he had underestimated
Ky all this time than by the threat of an attack by Raf.
Still, his world was off kilter. She would use what she
could.

"Ky has convinced a small but influential group of
the royals to follow her—which means to kill you.
Alfheim has been…uneasy for years. Your arrival seems
to have brought things to a head. The subversives have
become more active, the royals restless and the elf lords

jumpy." He paused, smiled. "You, my dear niece, have sent Alfheim into chaos without even leaving this house."

Marina narrowed her lips. She had no desire to be the cause of unrest in Alfheim. She had no desire to be involved in Alfheim's politics at all.

"There's a storm unleashed in the land of light, and you are in its eye. You *are* the eye." He looked at Raf. "She's the only one who can bring things under control quickly. There are pieces of each group who will follow her. She can steal the foundation of all three groups. She can put the royals back on the throne."

"I don't want the royals back on the throne. My parents were the only royals who ever thought past their own interests."

"So, you'd step back and let your sister rule? Let her kill you? Or leave it to the elf lords? No one *chose* them. How about the subversives? They are no more than a group of dirty thugs. Besides, my guess is none of them can sit on the throne. My guess is you are the only one. Why do you think I've supported you? It certainly wasn't because you were easy to lead."

Tired of all of it, Marina turned her back on her uncle. She strode toward the door. She was leaving. Let Alfheim take care of itself.

Raf gave Geir a shake. "Should I kill him?" The hellhound's face showed no emotion. Marina had no doubt if she asked him, he'd do as she'd asked. The thought both terrified and thrilled her. Raf was on her side, willing to fight this battle beside her, whatever that meant.

Which reminded her that she was thinking only of what she wanted, had forgotten that Raf had an interest in Alfheim, too. "The stone. Did you find it?" she asked.

Raf glanced at her uncle. "I did. But no one can get close to it, not even the elf lords. They've tried."

At mention of the stone, Geir's gaze flickered.

Raf nodded at him. "Does he know something?"

Marina stared at her uncle. He stared back, his gaze hooded. "He could. Alfheim artifacts are a hobby of his."

Geir smiled. "Of course I know about the stone. I know about all the artifacts of Alfheim—more than almost anyone. And I'll help you—if you set me free, if you do as I asked."

Marina slapped the tie against her palm again and took a step forward. "I do respect your self-confidence, Uncle. Always thinking you have the upper hand, even when it is so obvious you don't." She shook her head. "But, I'm afraid, this time I will have to point out you don't." She turned as if to leave, let her uncle think for a second she would. Then she let out a sigh and turned back, slapped the tie against her hand again. "So, we're clear…we are keeping you around because you may be of use. If you aren't…" She shrugged. "Well, you better hope you are."

Chapter 17

After a few minutes of discussion, Marina and Raf decided it was too risky to take Geir with them, that he would be too difficult to control. Which meant they needed somewhere to store him.

Raf reached into his pocket and pulled out the net that he'd taken to carrying with him. "I think it's time your uncle shared a bit of what you've experienced."

Marina stared at the net, then her uncle's sullen face. "I've been the only one to stand by you," he said. "You would trust this hellhound over me?"

Marina didn't hesitate. "I would trust this hellhound over anyone and anything, over myself. He's seen every side of me, but he keeps coming back." She took a step forward, unrolling the net. "And he wants nothing from me, but me. Can you imagine that? It's taken me a long time to believe it."

Marina looked at Raf and her eyes glowed. He knew his did, too, could feel the heat building inside him. She was right, he did want her...every aspect of her, and he would have her, keep her, and no one was going to take her away.

Geir's legs curled into his chest and his hand reached into his boot. A zigzag of power shot from a silver tube he now held. Raf shoved the royal toward the wall. The blue energy sizzled against the plaster a few feet away, leaving a black singed swirl of a stain.

Angry that he had slipped, Raf knocked the weapon from the royal's hand and pressed up against him. He whispered into Geir's ear, "Any more weapons and I'll forget Marina hasn't asked me to kill you, forget I need you to work the stone."

The royal's gaze glimmered, but he didn't reply, didn't struggle, either.

Marina snapped the net open. With Raf's help, she dropped it over her uncle. Raf pushed the royal toward the floor and patted him down. The older elf had nothing more in his pockets. With Geir glaring at them, they tied the ends of the net into a knot.

"Now what?" Marina asked.

"We need to put him somewhere safe. Somewhere no one will happen upon him while I take you to the portal."

A crease formed between her eyes. "What about the stone?"

Raf grabbed her by the chin and stared into her eyes. "After you're out of Alfheim, I'll come back for it. I'm sure I can convince your uncle to help me."

For the first time since entering the room, Marina looked indecisive. "Once we leave Alfheim, you may not be able to get back in, and even if you can, by then my uncle may be free or dead. My sister could be in power. The stone could be gone. Everything could be different." She shook her head. "I'm not leaving without you. We'll go together. We don't know who has control of the keep. Maybe they'll be one of the elves my uncle claims are loyal to me. Maybe I can help you get the stone."

Raf wanted her out of Alfheim, wanted her safe, but he knew she wouldn't leave him. He held out his hand. "We'll go together, but if things look dangerous—if it looks like your sister's circle is larger than we think, we take you to the portal immediately."

Marina stared at him a second. He could see wheels turning inside her head. "If we're faced with something we can't handle, we'll leave for the portal." She slid her hand into his.

He grinned. In other words, if all the fires of Muspelheim roared down on them...maybe they'd run for the portal. He tugged her to his chest and covered her mouth with his, felt her smile against his lips.

They were in this together.

Geir kicked his feet against the wall. The interruption was annoying, but good. Raf pulled his lips from Marina's. "This will work. I'll have the stone, and you'll be free of Alfheim."

Marina nodded, but dropped her gaze. She bent down and murmured to her uncle in elfin. At Raf's raised brow she interpreted. "I was reminding him that he can't trust anyone, that his best bet is to wait for us to come back for him."

Geir's eyes were like emerald chips, hard and glossy. "Leaving Alfheim is a mistake. If your sister thinks you're still alive, she'll hunt you. You'll be running forever."

Marina sighed. "It's the only choice I have—or that I'm willing to make." She gestured for Raf to pick him up. "I know a place. No one uses it anymore, hasn't for years. I can't imagine a reason anyone would go there."

With Geir wrapped in the net and flung over his shoulder, Raf followed her out of the room. She walked up two flights of stairs and down a hallway he hadn't been down before. At the end she flung open a door.

At first, in the semidarkness, he thought they were standing in a small room, then she flipped on the lights. A huge silver and crystal chandelier blazed to life. They were in a balcony, overlooking a ballroom.

"There." She pointed to the chandelier.

The decorative light hung two stories above the dance floor below.

"When my parents were still alive, there were parties here. I used to sneak up to watch." She walked to the right and reached behind a curtain. There was the sound of machinery grinding. The chandelier began to move toward them.

"Once a year the servants would take the chandelier down and clean it. I used to watch that, too."

The light stopped at the edge of the balcony.

Marina leaned over and stared at the ground below. "It's a long way down. Even an elf wouldn't try to jump."

Finally understanding what his niece meant to do with him, Geir began to complain. Raf lifted the netted elf from his shoulder and began hooking the silver arms of the chandelier through the holes. Once Geir was dangling like a cocoon from a branch, he stepped back. Geir kicked out, but Raf had twisted the net well. The chandelier began to sway, but the elf was unable to find an opening big enough for more than his fingers.

He looped them through the weave and yelled, "There are other ways. I should have listened to the others. If you are dead, Ky will be princess. I shouldn't have held to the legend. I should have—"

Raf cut off the rest of his tirade with a kick. The net swayed violently. Geir's face paled. "This chandelier is an antique; it can't take movement like that," he muttered.

Standing by the curtain, Marina flipped the switch. The chandelier began its journey back to the center of the ballroom. "Then you'd better hold perfectly still."

She turned on the heel of her foot and stalked from the balcony. With a grin, Raf followed.

This was the Marina he loved.

After leaving the ballroom, Marina lead Raf to Ky's room. She placed her hand flat against the door.

Raf didn't say anything, just watched her.

She was having a hard time accepting that her sister wanted her dead, felt deep inside if they could sit down and talk they could work all this out.

Raf placed his hand next to hers. "Forget her."

"Could you forget your brother?"

His jaw tightened. "My brother didn't betray me, didn't bring people into my home to kill me. He didn't fail me—I failed him."

Marina nodded. She knew he was right, but still... "Maybe I failed Ky, too. Growing up I didn't give her much thought. She was just a kid who lived in the same house as me, and then when things started going bad, I got so caught up in my own world, I practically forgot she existed. When I left for Gunngar, left her here with my uncle, I didn't consider her or her feelings. I wasn't a sister to her, not really."

Raf slipped an arm around her waist. The weight of it was reassuring, so was the smooth baritone of his voice. "That's what being young is about, being wrapped up in yourself. It's only when you're older that you get past that."

She licked her lips. "Ky is young. She's never left Alfheim."

He didn't say anything, but she could feel his doubt.

Marina sighed. He didn't understand. "It doesn't matter now, anyway. She's left hasn't she?" she asked.

He paused, listened, then nodded. "I don't think anyone is in the house. I don't hear anyone. Of course, your uncle fooled us—someone else could, too."

They should leave. He didn't say that, either, but it was true.

Marina pulled her hand away from the door and leaned against him. "Let's go. After we get the stone, and you get your answer, there will time to face Ky."

They solidified on the street outside the castle. Marina stiffened against Raf's chest. He waited, realized the place would mean something to her.

"I haven't been here in years. Before I went to Gunngar, I walked by, but I never went inside. I tried not to even look at it…" Her lips curved into a self-mocking smile. "It's pretty hard to ignore, but I tried."

He stared at the giant structure he'd thought of as Cinderella's castle when he first saw it. The stone glistened, shifting between pink and sea foam green. "Did your uncle come here, or your sister?" he asked.

She wrapped her hands around her arms as if she felt a chill. "I don't know. I doubt the elf lords would have let Geir inside. They probably wouldn't have let me or

Ky in, either." She laughed. "Funny, I hadn't thought about that before—that I wouldn't have been able to go inside even if I'd wanted to. I just knew I couldn't handle being in there...remembering."

He ran his hand down her spine, a light touch just to remind her he was there, that she wasn't alone.

"The last time...the day my parents died. I was playing in the bailey, and there was an explosion outside the walls...."

Raf pulled her to his chest. "You don't have to tell me."

She nodded, but kept talking. "Someone, a servant I guess, got Ky and me out of the castle and took us to Geir. He wasn't happy about it. I guess if we'd stayed here, we'd still have technically had the throne, but the elf lords were already here. My parents had hired them to investigate using technology. The royals weren't organized, and the elf lords were."

"There was an opening and they filled it," Raf added.

Marina nodded. "If I had stayed here, I'm sure Geir and the royals would have claimed my position, but everything got very complicated."

"Are you sorry?" Raf asked.

Marina's brows rose. "Sorry? I'm sorry my parents died, but the rest of it? What's there to regret? It's not like if I'd grown up here my life would have been any better. I still would have been a puppet with the royals in control of my strings." She glanced at the castle, then as if a thought had just hit her, back at Raf. "No, that isn't true. I'm happy that servant took me away from here—because if I'd grown up here as reigning princess rather than princess in name only, I never would have gone to Gunngar. I never would have met you."

Raf squeezed her against his chest. "Are you ready to go inside then?" He murmured.

She nodded and he shimmered them into the bailey.

Marina's heart thumped, and her knees bent. If Raf hadn't been beside her, holding her up, she would have fallen.

She was in the castle, almost on the spot where she'd heard the explosion that had ultimately killed her parents and changed her life.

Things were very different. There were picnic tables and statues, all scattered and broken. Where her mother had grown wildflowers, there were rows of ordered decorative grasses—and even those were trampled.

"What happened?" she asked. "Who did this?"

Raf shook his head. "The subversives, I think. Unless there's another group. The royals were busy attacking you."

Marina spun in a circle taking everything in. The sorrow she'd expected to hit, didn't. It had been so long ago, it was almost surreal now. It was time to let it go, let it all go…her past, her family, Alfheim.

She looked at Raf. "The stone. Let's get it."

He clasped her hand in his. Her body began to tingle—the shimmer coming—movement followed, then a jolt and they landed right back where they had started.

"What happened?" she asked.

Raf stared at the keep. "I can't shimmer inside. I thought I'd be able to…I shimmered here." He gestured, indicating the castle walls they stood behind. "But the buildings must be protected." He frowned.

Marina glanced at him. "So we walk." Ignoring a

stone path that wove through the grounds, she cut across the grass. She was halfway to the keep when a spear thunked into the ground beside her. Instantly Raf was there. His arm around her waist, he started to shimmer.

She pushed against his chest. "Wait." She wanted to know who had taken over the castle and why. From above there was a glint of sunlight on metal.

"Thank you for coming back, hellhound. Saves me the search" a voice called.

"The guard," Raf mumbled.

Another spear flew toward them. Raf took a step back. The metal head sunk into the ground an inch from his foot.

"I have plenty more," the guard called.

Marina could see him clearly now. He was thin and pale, and on his back was a pack loaded with weapons. He reached behind and pulled out two throwing knives. "Don't think I'm alone," he yelled.

Marina glanced around, but saw no signs of anyone else.

Raf growled low in his chest. "Don't think you can threaten us."

Marina licked her lips. There was something about the guard…she stepped forward, from behind Raf, into full view of the guard perched up above. "We have need of something in the keep. Nothing you'll miss, I'm sure. Let us retrieve it and we'll leave. We'll never return here again. I swear it." She held up her hand in a sign she hadn't used since childhood, a sign her mother had taught her in her cradle.

There was a clatter of dropped knives. "Princess? Is that you?" The guard scampered over the keep's inclined roof.

Raf reached for her, but she stepped farther away. She needed to see this elf.

When he reached the edge of the roof, he dropped his pack and jumped, hit the ground in a roll. Within seconds he was standing before her, his eyes huge and solemn. "You came back. It's time. Follow me." He didn't wait; he spun on his heel and scurried toward the keep.

Marina glanced at Raf. He arched his brows, seemed to say, "We wanted inside…"

Marina agreed; she followed the guard.

He held the door open for her, then hurried ahead. She waited for Raf, had to take time to adjust again. The pain she'd expected when she'd found herself in the bailey finally hit.

The keep smelled of old stone and wood, spice and magic. Her family had spent most of their time here. She could hear her father's laugh and see her mother sitting in front of the fire weaving magic into cloth. Ky, too. She'd learned to walk here, had pulled herself up by using Marina's leg as a crutch.

A tear crept into Marina's eye. She left it there, afraid Raf or the elf would notice if she wiped it away.

The guard had barreled ahead, stood in front of another door now. This one Marina didn't remember because it wasn't a door at all, not at first glance. It was a panel in the wall flung open to reveal a secret room.

Raf stepped into the keep behind her. She started to move ahead, but saw Raf glance to the left at stairs she knew lead to the tower. "Up there?" she mouthed.

He nodded.

She hesitated. They were here for the stone, but now that she was inside the keep she didn't want to leave, not yet, not until she'd seen whatever it was the guard seemed so eager to show her.

It was likely another mistake, could be a trap even, but she couldn't help herself. She needed to see.

Raf seemed to sense her thoughts. He pointed toward the elf. Marina walked forward and ducked inside the small door.

Raf followed Marina to the tiny door. It was small by even elf or dwarf standards, and had obviously been built to be kept hidden. He didn't feel good about following the guard, but Marina seemed determined, and it was her home, her past she was facing.

She ducked her head and stepped through the doorway. Raf closed the few feet between them in seconds, bent his own neck to follow her through, but when his hand brushed the wood, magic zapped through him, sent him flying. He landed on the floor, more startled than hurt and leapt to his feet. In front of him the tiny door snapped closed.

With a curse, he lunged toward it, but the door was gone. And there was zero sign of where it had been. He ran his fingers over the wood, searching for even a hairline crack—but there was nothing. It was as if the door hadn't existed at all.

He slammed his fist into the wood, then kicked, pulled back and kicked again. Nothing, not a splinter or creak. He walked through the keep until he found an old stone bust. He battered the thing over and over against the wall. The stone cracked; hunks of the bust fell off onto the floor—but the wall didn't change.

Raf dropped the now headless bust onto the floor and stalked outside into the bailey, circled the keep looking for some sign of a window or opening that might lead to a hidden room. Again nothing.

Rage and panic surged inside him. Marina was in there, but he couldn't get to her, had no idea what was happening to her. He picked up a statue and flung it at the keep's wall. The statue broke into chunks just like the bust had.

He paced up and down, wearing a path in the bailey's lawn. They had been so close. If he had just gone up the stairs, made Marina come with him...they'd have had the stone and been on their way.

But he hadn't. They hadn't. He stopped, fisted his hand and smashed it into the wall again, felt the pain, forced himself to calm down and think.

The guard had seemed excited when he saw Marina, eager to show her whatever lay inside that damn room. Yes, the elf had attacked Raf on each of their encounters, but he'd shown no animosity toward Marina.

Raf couldn't see or hear her, but that didn't mean she was in danger.

He concentrated on the thought, waited for calm to come.

It didn't.

Fury still coursed through Raf's body. He picked up the pile of knives and spears that had fallen from the roof, from the elf's pack and carried them inside. If he had to dismantle the keep splinter by splinter, he would get inside that room.

Chapter 18

The room was bigger than Marina would have guessed based on the door's size. Open and airy. The walls, floor and ceiling were all white. Dressed in his brown pants and tunic, the guard stood out against the background.

He stood across the room, next to a box. It reminded Marina of the box she'd used in Gunngar to hold Raf—except instead of a hellhound or garm, this one held a throne.

The throne.

The throne of Alfheim.

She wanted nothing to do with it.

She turned on the ball of her foot, back toward the door. Except the door was gone. There was nothing but uninterrupted white where the opening had been. She threw her body against the wall and ran her arms over the surface. There were no bumps or cracks. It was smooth as glass.

She pressed her ear against the wall, and strained to hear Raf.

Nothing. Either the walls were too thick or Raf had left when the door closed behind her.

No. She shook her head. He wouldn't. He wouldn't leave without knowing what had happened to her. She wouldn't believe that.

She laid her palm against the wall and prayed he was there.

Raf fell exhausted against the wall. He'd battered at the wooden paneling until his hands were bloody, and there wasn't a weapon, stone or piece of furniture left that he could smash against it. His fingers no longer bent and his legs no longer held his weight.

He'd lost track of how long he'd been here. The sun had set hours ago, and was rising again. He could see it through the door to the bailey which he'd left open.

He tried to stand, but his legs gave way. He fell to his knees. He had only felt this lost once before in his life—when he'd found his wife, son and brother dead.

But somehow this was even worse. They had been gone, lost to him forever, but Marina was close—so close, and he couldn't reach her. He turned and smashed his fist into the wall again. He didn't feel a thing, no pain, not even the vibration of his hand hitting the wood. His body was numb. He was numb. He didn't know what to do.

Yells sounded past the drawbridge. It was up—no one should be able to get inside. Still, he forced himself to stand...placed a hand against the wall he'd been battling to steady himself.

More yells, followed by smoke—thick and black billowing from where the drawbridge would be. The smell of burning tar tore at Raf's lungs.

The castle was under siege.

Elf lords, subversives or royals with Ky? Did it matter?

He glanced back at the damned wall and the door that was no more. Despite the guard's claim, Raf seemed to be the only living being inside the castle walls.

His instinct was to fight; as a hellhound it was always his first reaction. But for what? He had no interest in who took the castle. He did however have an interest in keeping Marina safe—but he had tried everything to get to her, and sitting here was wasting precious time.

If he stayed and fought, he'd buy some time. He could hold them off for a while. But if they pulled down the keep around him…he had his limits. He wasn't worried about himself, he could shimmer away—but Marina…what if the door chose to open just as he lost the fight? What would greet her?

The drawbridge was burning; the beings on the other side would be inside soon. He had to get Marina out—but he had no idea how.

His gaze shot to the stairs. The stone could tell him. He could use its vision to free Marina from the room.

The sound of heated wood and metal creaking gave him new strength. He turned and pulled himself up the stairs. Halfway up he realized while he couldn't shimmer into the keep, perhaps he could shimmer inside it. He tried and found himself standing outside the door that held the stone.

Now he just had to pray Sim hadn't left any little tidbits out—that he could grab the stone in its box and leave. His hand on the doorway, he started to step inside, but remembered the sizzle.

When he'd come here with Sim there had been some kind of force field on each doorway. Raf was fairly certain Sim just walking through before him had deactivated it, but today he hadn't heard a thing.

Had the elf lords turned it off before they left?

Prepared for whatever might happen, he held his hand toward the opening. No sound. No pain. He squared his shoulders and steeled himself for whatever might happen. Then he stepped forward.

The room was silent—no sizzle, no zap. And the box was still sitting on its table, the lid closed.

His gaze focused and his stride determined, he walked forward. Again nothing.

It was all so simple...so easy. *Too easy.* Raf paused with his hands over the box. If the stone killed him, he'd be of no use to Marina, but without it, he would fail her.

He grabbed the box. It was smooth and cold, like what it was, a wooden box that had been sitting in a chilly, damp tower for centuries. There was no shock, no slice of pain, no ground opening him and swallowing him whole.

Again, too simple.

There had to be more. Raf knew it, but he tucked the box under his arm and strode to the door. Once through, he shimmered to the bottom of the stairs and paused by the wall where Marina had disappeared. There was still no sign of her.

He hesitated. He didn't want to leave. Questions began to build in his head... Where had she gone? Would she come back?

At first the questions seemed normal, made sense,

but as he stood there they grew, became strange…questions he knew weren't from his brain. *How do you kill a draugr? Would Lord Alfred's wife cheat on him?* Names, places, things Raf had never heard of—but suddenly needed more information on, had questions on…. Questions that burned inside his brain.

He pressed the heel of his hand to his head and tried to stop the pounding.

More questions, just as intense, just as nonsensical. He glanced at the box….

With a curse, he placed it on the floor and stepped back.

The latest stream of insanity broke off midthought.

The stone. It was doing something to him—even holding it through the box. The questions, were they ones asked of it through the years, or ones that had gone unanswered?

More questions. He shook his head, afraid for a moment the stone was still tinkering with his brain—but no, these ideas were his own.

Outside there was a crash and a new puff of black smoke. The ground shook. Raf pressed his hand against the wall to keep from falling.

The drawbridge was down.

With one last glance at the door that was no more, he picked up the box, dashed into the bailey and shimmered back to Geir's ballroom.

The royal was about to find out how determined a hellhound could be.

"Princess?" The guard took a step forward, his face eager and concerned at the same time.

Marina glanced around the all white room one last

time, looking for an exit she had missed, before answering. "Who are you working with? Elf lords, royals, subversives?" She'd lost track of who wanted her for what, who might think her sitting on the throne would be in their best interest.

Surprise creased his face. "The throne, I'm working for the throne and for Alfheim. I'm the Paladin. The elf lords refused to let the throne do its job—to choose Alfheim's leader. Then when it wouldn't recognize them, they tried to destroy it. But as long as Alfheim exists, the throne exists. There is no magic, technology or combination of the two that can undo it. It is Alfheim."

Marina stared at the guard, unsure if he believed what he said. She'd never heard such tales or of the position of Paladin. Although she realized now the elf was familiar, was someone she'd seen in her childhood, she couldn't believe him. The throne was tradition in Alfheim, a strong tradition with the citizens, but as far as she knew that was all.

"The throne knows what is best for Alfheim, and the elf lords weren't." The guard...Paladin...scowled. "They thought they could take the seat, but no one sits on the throne without its approval. When the throne refused each and every one of them, and they were unable to destroy it, I hid it away, and they pretended possession of it was enough. But owning the throne doesn't give you its power. Alfheim knew, and unrest grew."

He raised his hand; an image appeared on the wall behind him. It showed the bailey overrun by elves. Elf lords dressed in their austere gray jogged for buildings as common workers spilled across the drawbridge, turned over picnic tables and knocked down statues.

"See the cost? Their actions, their refusal to let the throne choose led to this." He tilted his head to the side, studied her. "So, now you know why the elf lords courted you. You were their only hope. The stone had already said the throne would accept you. At first that was reason to keep you and your family away from it, but once you acted as if you would work with them—become one of them—they saw a new option. You would sit on the throne, appeasing it, and they would continue ruling as they saw fit."

Marina wandered to the left, away from him, surveying the room, trying to figure out where she was and if there was any escape. "And would that have worked? Could the throne be duped like that?"

He frowned. "The throne can't see the future. It chooses based on what is in the best interest of Alfheim at the time."

She raised a brow. "So, it wouldn't have worked?"

He shook his head, seemed annoyed by her questions. "If the throne had chosen you it would have been what was best for Alfheim, and the stone foresaw you on the throne."

She slid her eyes to the side. "Me?" Another believer in the legend.

He huffed. "The stone showed you on the throne. I was there. I saw it."

This stopped her. "The seer stone?" *The stone Raf needed…* "You saw it? What did you see? Were you alone?"

He let out a breath, spoke with obviously planned patience. "Your mother was there."

She blinked. She'd brushed the legend of her destiny aside for so long, but now…she was beginning to believe the strange elf.

"The stone is never wrong." He paused, glanced at the wall they'd entered through—where she'd last seen Raf. "There was more..."

Marina hesitated. What else he saw didn't matter, because she wasn't staying in Alfheim, she was leaving with Raf.

Without any encouragement, he kept talking. "The hellhound, he was there. He betrays you—tries to kill you."

"Raf?" She didn't believe him.

He nodded. "He's working for the elf lords, and has been all along. At first they wanted you to occupy the throne for them, but now they want you dead. The hellhound is supposed to get you out of Alfheim, kill you somewhere else—where no one here will know of it."

Marina shook her head. "How could the stone have known all that so long ago?"

The Paladin hesitated. "The stone saw a hellhound betraying you, the rest I learned from working here, spying."

Marina pressed her fingers to the bridge of her nose. Raf had betrayed her before, but he wouldn't again, not now. She wouldn't believe it.

"There was more, the stone said you would bring about a great change, be the most important ruler in Alfheim history."

"Pretty vague," Marina said.

He tilted his head in consideration. "Maybe, but the answer seems obvious now. You are to save Alfheim from this." He pointed back to the scene playing on the wall behind him.

Marina looked; she didn't want to show interest, but couldn't stop herself. "Who are they?"

"They call themselves subversives, but they are just a symptom of the throne being denied. As is this…" He waved his hand again and the scene changed, this time to the street outside the castle. Royals, dozens of them. All dressed in brightly colored silk and carrying some weapon. At their lead, sitting in the back of their uncle's convertible, was Ky. She murmured to Tahl who sat beside her. He stood and yelled something. The scene panned to a catapult. Balls of flame shot from it and flew toward the castle.

Marina pulled in a breath. "What is she doing?"

"Burning the drawbridge. Once it is charred through, they'll throw hooks and make their way across the ropes."

"For what?" Marina turned and stared at the boxed throne. "This?"

The Paladin's shoulders pulled back. "Yes, this. What could be more important than this?"

Freedom, love? Marina shook her head. "I'm not interested."

The elf turned red. "Not interested? You have to be interested. If you don't take the throne—you leave Alfheim to this." The scene behind him flashed from one ugly scene to another: fire, fights and destruction. It appeared every being in Alfheim was engaged in some kind of battle.

Marina swallowed. "None of that has anything to do with me. None of that was by my choice."

He stepped forward. "It wasn't. But it is now. You can stop it. You can take the throne and everything will settle down. Alfheim will return to what it was." He touched the box with two fingers; the sides fell away—

collapsed just like the box that held the cobra, and to Marina, what sat inside was just as scary and dangerous.

The throne—a simple seat of silver, no cushion, no jewels, just metal and magic.

"It only seats one," Marina said.

"You are only one." The Paladin clasped his hands together, watched her as if she might spring one way or another.

"When my parents sat on it, it was big enough for both of them."

He beamed as if she'd just solved a puzzle and he was ready to award her a gold star. "The throne recognized both of them." He turned to stare at the silver seat. "But you are alone. I told you the hellhound tries to betray you. If you don't believe me, ask the stone. You are destined for the throne. It will work for you."

Alone. Marina didn't want to be alone. She wanted to be with Raf. "Raf wouldn't betray me," she stated. "Not again. If the stone said he will, it's wrong."

The wall behind her creaked; the floor shook.

The Paladin's face paled and he threw himself toward the throne.

As he scrambled on the floor, tried to reconstruct the box that had protected the throne, Marina threw out her hands and tried to find her balance. The floor beneath her feet moved…slid as if being pushed. She fell onto her knees.

The Paladin, his face panicked, reached out to her, grabbed for her hand—to pull her toward the throne, Marina realized. She reached for him, too, unsure what else to do. What good would picking freedom be if she were dead? But Raf…if she let the Paladin drag her to that throne, what would happen to him…them? He hated Alfheim. He would never stay here, and Alfheim would never accept him.

She jerked her hand to her chest and rolled onto her back.

There was a rumble…of stone against stone. The white ceiling started to fade…to change. Speckles of brown shone through…wood beams. The floor vibrated; her head hit the ground. The ceiling changed again, seemed to be…falling.

Then nothing…darkness.

Raf materialized next to the curtain. He found the switch and flipped it. The box's questions were pounding through his head—so many, so important—he staggered under the weight of them.

Behind him the chandelier groaned as it moved. He turned to watch it approach. It seemed to inch forward. As it clicked to a stop, he set the box down next to his foot.

His gaze on the box, he flung his arm to the side. His fingers looped through the net's open weave. He glanced at it then, planning to warn Geir before freeing him, but the net was empty.

Raf shoved his hand up into his hair. He glanced at the box. Without Geir, he couldn't open it, couldn't discover how to get Marina out from behind the disappearing door.

He jerked the net off the chandelier. A segment of it had been cleanly sliced through. Damn the elf. He'd hidden a blade somehow—and not any blade. Only magic cut magic.

Raf tossed the net to the ground. No benefit in

berating himself. Now he had to choose whether to track the royal or return to the castle.

An explosion sounded from outside; plaster fell from the ceiling, landed in a gigantic crash onto the ballroom floor below.

Raf picked up the box.

If Geir was here, he wouldn't be long.

This part of the mansion was about to fall.

Chapter 19

Marina couldn't breathe. She coughed. There was a weight on her chest. She lifted her arms, or tried to—they seemed to be pinned down. Panicked, she opened her eyes. Dirt and grit fell into them, causing tears to flow down her cheeks. She couldn't reach to wipe either away. She just lay there, her eyes burning, her chest feeling tight and constricted.

"Did you find it?" A female voice—one she knew.

"We saw the Paladin leave. He wouldn't leave it un-guarded." Another familiar voice, this one male.

Marina blinked. Struggled to put names to the voices, to remember where she was, what had happened. Logic said to call out and ask for aid, but instinct told her to hold her tongue.

"Where else could it be? He couldn't carry it out in his pocket." The female's tone changed to a pout.

Ky. Her sister—looking for the throne.

"What about my sister? Geir said she and the hell-hound were coming here. Any sign of her?"

"In this mess? She could be six inches away and we wouldn't see her."

"Look. If she is here we can't just leave her lying under the rubble."

Marina's heart leapt. Ky had rethought her plan. Marina opened her mouth to call out.

"We will need her body or the citizens won't accept me as princess—even if I do have the throne. Which I don't." Ky kicked something.

Marina's jaws snapped closed. Something knocked against her side. The stones covering her shifted—still leaving her arms pinned, but she could breathe more easily. Then a face, the royal, Anton's, appeared in her line of view. He pursed his lips.

"Ky, why don't you wait outside? I'll let you know if I find anything."

Marina stiffened, wondered what the royal was plotting, but held her tongue. Her sister had made her plan very clear—and it wasn't one Marina wished to further.

Her sister grumbled, but Marina could hear her trudging from the room. Finally, Anton bent down over Marina again.

"Not a good place to find yourself, is it?" he asked.

Marina stared back. What was there to say?

"What about your witchy powers? Are they of no use to you with your hands trapped at your sides?" He tilted his head back and forth as if assessing her. "Your sister wants you dead, you know." He pulled a blade from his sleeve.

Marina pressed her lips together, let disdain pour from her eyes.

Anton laughed. "See, that is why your uncle insisted you sit on the throne. Your sister, lovely girl, though, she is, lacks a certain…spirit." He flicked the blade toward Marina's face, knocked a tiny piece of debris from her cheek. "Have you seen it, by the way? Shiny and silver? Holds the key to ruling Alfheim?"

She kept her mouth closed.

He laughed, then shook his head. "I really don't know what to do. The stone saw you on the throne. Despite your sister's cold hard belief that with you dead she will smoothly move into your position, I don't believe the throne or the stone will be that easily confused." He tapped the flat side of his blade against her cheek. "You could make things simple. Agree to take the throne and restore everything the elf lords stole from the royals. It really isn't that much to ask. It was all ours before your parents died." He rolled his eyes to the side, and sighed. "They really mucked up our lives." He pulled his hand back. Indecision shone from his eyes. Marina could see him weighing his options—kill her and hope the throne accepted Ky or save her and hope he or the other royals could convince her to see things their way.

The old Marina would have told him what he wanted to hear—promised her loyalty, then turned the knife once she was on the throne…if she intended to take the throne, which she didn't. But the new Marina? Somehow she couldn't force herself to form the words, to even pretend she might sympathize with his self-centered cause.

From outside Ky screamed, "The hellhound! Don't let him inside."

Raf materialized in the bailey facing the castle's entrance. The drawbridge was down and the grassy area was filled with royals. They had formed a circle in the center and were walking outward, their gazes downcast.

They were searching for something. Raf's mind instantly went to the stone, which he had hidden before coming here. He didn't know what would await him at the castle and he couldn't be sidetracked by the stone's constant pounding of questions.

After a quick assessment of the royals, he turned to enter the keep. What he saw stopped him cold. It had collapsed, or parts of it had.

He forgot the stone, the royals, everything except Marina and broke into a run. Halfway to the keep, he heard Ky scream.

He didn't slow his pace, shifted as he ran, shimmering as he did so his clothes fell to the ground below him.

In dog form he moved faster, was stronger, and he was more intimidating to the elves, who had probably never seen a hellhound in his canine form. Five elves dropped from the keep's roof. Swords in their hands, they blocked his entrance.

He cursed and kept moving, was determined to bowl them down, risk their swords. From the corner of his eye, he saw a flash—something flying toward him. He cut to the side, away from whatever had been launched his direction.

Air stirred his fur as the object fell to the ground, missing him by inches. He spun. A net, like the one he'd wrapped around Geir, glimmered from atop the grass. One hundred feet away a group of elves scurried around a portable trebuchet, loading another net into its basket.

He could easily get past the line of elves into the keep, but the fight would give other elves time to aim and shoot—to hit him with the net. Then he would be trapped, unable to help Marina.

He faced the elves and roared out his anger. A few paled and stepped back, but the ones near the keep held their position.

"Is my sister here, then?" Ky shoved her way past a crowd of guards. She glanced at the elves standing outside the keep. "Don't let him in." She motioned and Tahl appeared next to her. She whispered in his ear. The male nodded and ran toward one of the other buildings.

Tense, Raf watched, listened, looked for an opportunity.

Ky folded her arms over her chest and waited. No one moved.

A standoff. Raf wasn't big on standoffs. He was into action. He roared and pulled back in a squat to propel into a leap. As he did he saw another flash from above. This time it was steel—arrows.

Archers lined the walls around him.

His time was up. He catapulted himself forward, shimmered as the first arrows zinged toward him— through him. Solidified and sprang again. Until he was less than six feet from the keep's entrance, this time he stayed solid, saw the determination in the elves faces as he leaped at them. They moved forward leaving space between them and the building. He shimmered, aimed at that space. He solidified behind them in the air...still leaping and plowed through the door.

The floor was slick under his pads. He skidded and spun, barely let himself slow as he sighted the wall where he had last seen Marina. There was an opening now—a jagged gap in the stone. He bolted through. No one followed.

The room inside was nothing but rubble—stones and dust everywhere, but in the center of the space, bent low and holding a knife was the royal, Anton. His eyes rounded in horror when he saw Raf; fear poured from his body.

Marina. Raf could smell her, sense her, but he couldn't see her. Anton glanced down at the pile of rocks he knelt beside—and Raf realized the truth, realized what...who lay buried beneath those stones.

Fury hot and uncontrolled ripped through Raf's body. He roared and leapt.

Anton spun, tried to run, but the rubble got in his way. He tripped and Raf was on him. Raf could feel his eyes glowing, could feel the rage bubbling inside him.

Marina—his Marina, was buried and this elf was somehow responsible. He would tear him into bits, leave the remains strewn around for the rest to find, to learn from—except those outside. He'd hunt *them* down. Add them to his kill. Not a single one would walk away from this. Not a single one would live to celebrate his lover's death.

He stalked forward; his gaze glued on the elf. The fall had put the royal on edge, given Raf an advantage—not that he needed it. Still, the fear and insecurity streaming from the royal added to the fun, fed Raf's bloodlust, would make the kill quicker, give him more time to hunt the others.

"Raf?" A voice, muffled and rough.

Raf paused, his foot raised, ready to step forward.

"Raf, can you hear me?"

There was no mistaking it this time—a voice was coming from nearby. Lost in the bloodlust, Raf's hellhound brain couldn't process what it meant. He couldn't change course.

He growled; kept his gaze on the elf.

When the voice had spoken, the male had edged forward. At Raf's growl he pulled back.

"Raf. Get me out of here...please."

Raf blinked, the tone, the "please", broke through his fog. *Marina.* He turned to the pile of stone.

"I can't move my arms," she murmured. The words were soft, like a confession.

Raf found the space where her face was uncovered. Her eyes were dark, relieved, but alive—for a second—then they fluttered closed. He was losing her.

He pawed a pile of stones off her chest, then snapped his jaws together at his stupidity. He pressed his nose against her face again and shimmered her free of the rubble.

Once she lay atop the stones, he changed, gathered her into his arms and held her against his chest. She was breathing, but her eyes were still closed. He held her tighter, tilted her chin up so he could gaze into her face.

Anton moved. Raf looked up, but it was too late. The royal had already thrown his blade; Raf had already been hit.

Raf snarled and jerked the knife from his arm. Drove it tip first into the floor and started to stand. The room began to move and his vision to blur.

The smirking face of the elf grew closer. Raf reached out but swiped at empty air.

"Ky isn't completely stupid. It was her idea we make preparations for a hellhound. Of course, that doesn't mean the throne will accept her, and I am averse to getting rid of one option until I'm sure the second will work." Anton turned. "Don't you agree, Geir?"

Marina's uncle appeared beside Anton.

"You know I always have," Marina's uncle replied. He stepped forward and tapped Raf on the chest.

Raf lunged again, but this time he fell.

"Do we keep him?" Anton asked.

"I don't know..." Geir prodded Raf in the side with his foot. "If we don't my niece may be even more difficult, besides we might be able to use him. I think she actually cares for him."

"No. That can't be. The throne would never accept—"

"Of course not. There is no risk of that. But as long as we control him—she will be much easier to sway. It gives us a tool over her."

"Like Ky was?" Anton's tone was skeptical.

"Yes, well, that plan didn't work out, did it? But it doesn't mean this one won't." There was rustling, like another net being dragged.

Raf, his reality swimming, couldn't do anything but listen as the two elves stepped over him and started wrapping him up.

Marina sucked in a breath; her arms ached as if they were being pulled from their sockets. She fluttered her eyes, reluctant to open them, but she couldn't remember why. She could feel her body moving, being dragged... by her wrists, she realized.

"We'll hide them here until I've assured Ky that Marina wasn't here. Then come back and get them properly stored. Meanwhile, you find the Paladin. We need to talk to him, see what he knows *and* find the throne. If by some stroke the throne will accept Ky, then this—" something scuffed against her "—won't be necessary."

Whoever held her wrists gave another jerk. She barely suppressed a groan.

"We need to hurry. Ky and her elves know the hellhound came in here. They won't honor your order to stay out for long." Her uncle's voice, behind her. He was the one holding her wrists.

"I blocked the door. They won't get in without a struggle," Anton replied.

Geir grunted. "How are you going to explain the disappearance of the hellhound? And what if Marina wakes up while we are gone?"

Marina froze, didn't even breathe.

"I'll tell Ky the hellhound shimmered away. I don't know why he didn't. He had the chance. Proof the shapeshifters aren't that bright."

Geir huffed, didn't seem to agree with the other royal's assessment.

"And as to Marina, we'll wrap her in the net, too." Anton paused. "Once we get the hellhound over here. He's heavy. I'll need your help."

Her uncle muttered a complaint in elfin, but dropped Marina's wrists and stepped over her.

They had Raf—in a net she concluded—and they were going to drag him to wherever they had stashed her, wrap them both into the net and leave them.

Once under the net's magic, Marina would be helpless. She'd been there before—didn't like it.

She flexed her hands and felt for magic. The whole magic thing was new to her. She felt like she was blindfolded, groping around in the dark trying to find power inside her. Her mind knew it was there, knew she wanted to release it, but actually doing so...that was an issue.

The two times she had successfully used her powers

had been like explosions. She hadn't carefully drawn and fired. She'd been under some pressure that had caused the magic to bubble up. All she'd had to do was *not* control it.

But now, groggy and her body filled with a thousand pains, her physical state was much more apparent than any power hidden inside her.

She gritted her teeth and tried to locate some trigger....

"Why couldn't she have fallen for an elf?" Anton asked, his voice winded.

Marina cracked one eyelid open.

One end of the net was across Anton's shoulder. He leaned into it. Her uncle huffed a breath and picked up the other end. As they pulled, Raf jerked forward; his face pressed against the open weave.

Marina's jaw tensed. Anger crackled in her, and with it power. She focused on Raf, on how helpless he looked. He was unconscious; the net hadn't done that— Anton and her uncle had. What had they done to him?

As her concern grew, so did her fury...and her magic. She could feel it now coursing through her veins. She couldn't lie still. She had to move, so she wiggled her shoulders, her arms, her fingers until every bit of her body was filled with power.

Then she opened her eyes and stared the two royals down.

Both of them froze.

"Marina, you don't—" her uncle began.

Marina ignored him, opened her hands and let magic stream from her palms. She had no idea what she was doing, no idea if she was about to stun or kill the uncle she'd lived with most of her life, and at that moment, engulfed in her worry for Raf, she didn't care.

The power that flew from her was green, like her eyes. For a moment she wondered if there was a connection. Then as Anton turned, tried to flee, the thought disappeared—all thought except stopping his escape disappeared.

She opened her other hand, let magic stream from it, too. Two lines of power stretched from her body to the royals, rolled on the floor toward their feet like a vine grasping for sunlight. But this vine didn't want the sun—it was after the elves. It wrapped around their ankles and jerked them to the floor.

Marina smiled. She'd intended that—had seen it in her head right before it happened. She focused and tried again, envisioned the vines lengthening, coiling over and over around the royals' bodies like thread on a spool. The magic thinned, but didn't break. In unison, the lines snaked up and around their legs, pinning their calves together so they had to pull with their upper bodies to try and escape.

"Marina. We didn't harm him—or you. What are you doing?" Geir yelled. He grabbed a rock and jammed it at the power—as if the stream of magic *was* a vine and could be cut. Marina sent the magic higher, locking Geir's arms against his body and stopping his hacking with the stone. When he opened his mouth to cry out again, she urged the vine between his lips like a gag, did the same with Anton. They mumbled around it, their eyes huge. Anton's filled with uncertainty and Geir's with anger. She ignored both and walked toward them.

With the magic moving through her, her aches were gone, the tightness in her chest was gone. When she reached Raf, she stopped and kicked the net off of him.

She switched her gaze between the royals she held bound by magic and the net. She could use it to hold them, but she needed a free hand. The power felt and acted like independent lines, but both came from her body—if she didn't break the source, could she transfer it?

She brought her hands together and scraped one palm over the other. The line of magic moved, shifted from the palm she scraped to the one she held flat. She had two streams shooting from one hand now. She stared at it for a second, taking it in. She'd gone so long thinking her power was too weak to be of any use and now... She shook her head, prayed it would be able to do something for Raf—but first she had to take care of Geir and Anton.

More comfortable, she quickly tugged the two closer until she could throw the net over them. Unfortunately, the net cut off her magic. Both opened their mouths to yell. She picked up a knife that lay on the floor and slid the tip through an opening in the weave, pierced Anton's neck. Blood dribbled onto his silk tunic.

She stared at Geir. "Don't think I won't have the time or energy to slice your throat, too. It will take longer for them—" she jerked her head to the outside "—to hear you than it will for me to move."

Her uncle held her gaze—there was no fear in his eyes, but she hadn't expected any, didn't really want to see it there. Strange as it was, after everything he had put her through, she held no malice for him. It would be like hating the serpent. Both were snakes, both were just being true to those identities.

She slid her gaze to Raf. "What did you do to him?"

Geir arched a brow, and for a second she didn't think he would reply, then he blew out a bored breath.

"Nothing lasting, just at touch of canine sedative." He pointed to the side where a dozen or so arrows were scattered about.

"You poisoned him." Marina's hand jumped, drove the blade deeper into Anton's throat. The royal made a gurgling noise. Marina dropped her hold on him and reached for an arrow.

"Canine you say? Any idea how it works on elves?" She drove the arrow through an opening in the net and into Anton's thigh. His eyes widened and his mouth opened, but before any sound could escape his throat, his body locked up—like a convulsion had hit but hadn't released. Marina jerked out the arrow and prodded his chest. "Interesting. Looks like it's a bit rougher on elves." She selected a second arrow.

"I won't give you away—I can't. Only Anton was working with me. Your sister sees me as a threat—not as big of a threat as you, but still, given a choice, she would eliminate me."

Marina tapped the arrow against her palm. "You should be grateful then that I'm the sister who has you." She lurched forward and drove the arrow into his arm. Then sat back on her heels. Even frozen, her uncle managed to look superior.

She shook her head and shoved his immobilized form over onto its side. Then she turned her attention to Raf.

Poison had done this to him—how could she undo it? Could she?

She shook her head. She had to. There was no other choice. She couldn't shimmer and Raf was far too big for her to drag out of here—even with her newly found magic to help her with a battle.

Her magic. She stared at her fingers. Could she use it to revive him?

She rolled Raf onto his back and stared down at him, unlike her uncle and Anton his limbs weren't locked up, he only appeared to be asleep. She brushed his hair from his face and pressed a kiss to his lips.

Air moved in and out of his mouth, assuring her he was alive, but his heartbeat was faint. She placed her palm over his chest, felt the light tap that should have been a hearty thump.

Anger soared inside of her. She glanced at her uncle, rethinking the idea that she didn't hate him. She could. If Raf didn't survive, she would. He would wish Ky and her zealots had found him.

Power filled her. Her hair moved as if alive, rustling around her face. She tingled, and all doubt fled. She knew she could bring Raf back; she had to.

She covered his body with hers; ran her hands down his sides and breathed into his mouth. He lay still beneath her, lost in slumber. She pulled up her shirt and pressed her bare skin to his. Warmth built inside her. She willed it to move from her body to his, for his heart to beat louder, stronger, for him to breathe deeper. She placed her lips over his and blew gently into his mouth, filling his lungs.

His chest expanded, then froze. She froze, too, afraid the paralysis that had affected her uncle and Anton had struck Raf. Then in a rush, the air exploded from his lips, and he took one shuddering breath.

His arms wrapped around her and he cradled the back of her head with one hand; pulling her mouth more closely against his, he kissed her.

Chapter 20

Marina lay atop Raf—even with his eyes closed and his mind still half-lost in a fog, he recognized her. There was her springtime scent, but it was more than that....

A cocoon of warmth was wrapped around them, separating them from everyone and everything except each other.

He pulled her lips to his and slipped his tongue past her teeth, stroked the velvety inside of her mouth. Her hands and stomach pressed against his chest; warmth poured from them, excited him. His sex hardened and he wanted nothing except to be with her, inside her.

He moved his hands to her breasts, started to shove the silk she wore up and out of his way as he shifted his lips from her mouth to the side of her neck. Her hair wound around him, clung to him as if alive and part of their passion.

"Raf, Ky...the elves," Marina whispered.

He remembered then where they were, what had been happening when he'd fallen. He moved to get up, but she pressed her palm against him, keeping him from standing. "Anton and Geir...they're in the net, but we can't stay here. Take me somewhere...anywhere."

His gaze dashed around the room. The royals were on their sides under the net. He ran the back of his fingers down Marina's cheek. "You rescued me. The princess isn't supposed to do the rescuing."

She leaned forward and whispered against his ear. "Just get me out of here, take me away from Alfheim, keep me with you. That's all the rescue I need."

He wrapped his arms around her waist and ran his lips down her neck. "I will." But right now, at that moment, there was something else he needed, something he knew they both needed. He couldn't shimmer them out of the keep, but he could shimmer them somewhere else inside.

He pulled her to her knees and pressed chest to chest, thigh to thigh, he shimmered them to the tower.

His body still tingling from the move, he wove his fingers into her hair and pulled her mouth toward his. Inches from a kiss, he murmured. "Your rescue will have to wait, princess."

She looped her arms around his neck. "Princesses are used to waiting. We are good at it." Then she pulled his head down to hers.

Marina kissed Raf like she'd never kissed any other male. Her lips met his, demanding and filled with passion. She was strong; she had always known it inside, yet she'd had no power of her own, and had been forced to play so many parts. But now…because of Raf…because of her need to save him, she'd discovered what had lay hidden inside her.

She wouldn't forget. She knew he wouldn't let her. He believed in her and now she believed in herself.

They shouldn't be here, doing this. They should be running for the portal or bracing for a fight, but this was more important than anything to her right now. Without him, nothing else mattered.

She ran her hands down his chest and hips. His skin there was smooth, the muscle under it hard. A thrill shot through her, the same thrill she always experienced when she touched Raf, but this time there was more. This time she thought of him as hers. She had made the decision to leave Alfheim. In some other world she could be with Raf, they could be together…forever.

Raf stroked her back through her silk top. The expensive clothing seemed confining and cumbersome. She jerked her shirt over her head and reached for the waist of her pants. Raf stopped her, stared at her, then slowly reached out one hand and cupped her breast. His thumb wandered over its peak.

His eyes lit as if on fire. She'd seen the red glow hellhounds' eyes had when the bloodlust hit, but this was different—seductive rather than startling. She swayed toward him and he leaned down to catch her nipple between his teeth.

He rolled the sensitive tip between his lips, and laved it with his tongue. Marina grabbed him by the shoulders to keep from falling. She wanted to touch him, to make him squirm as she did, but she didn't want him to stop what he was doing, either.

Her body tensed—ready for the pleasure, waiting

for more. Eager…greedy. She arched her back and her head rolled to the side. His lips were hot on her skin… the heat radiated through her, warming her inside and out.

She thrust her hips toward him, rubbed her pelvis against him, reminding him that silk still separated them. He ignored her, switching his mouth from one breast to the other.

She groaned in a mix of frustration and pleasure, then hooked her thumbs in the tops of her pants and jerked them down. He smiled against her breast, but didn't turn his attention away from what he was doing. With her body bare and free to press up against him, she didn't mind—went about trailing her fingers down his stomach and toward his sex. She found his hardened flesh and ran her fingers lightly down its length. His lips paused and his fingers dug into her hips. She squirmed so the thatch of hair covering her sex brushed against him.

He lapped at the tip of her breast once, then sucked it into his mouth, pulling hard—so hard a cry escaped her lips and her body clenched with need.

She wrapped her fingers around his sex and ran her thumb over its tip, felt the bead of liquid that escaped— massaged it over the silky skin until she heard him cry and stiffen.

Power roared through her. She had never felt this in control, and…she stared at Raf, saw he was looking at her, too, his eyes still glowing, simmering almost…she loved him for it. Loved him for trusting her and allowing her to be herself. She slipped her free arm up his shoulder and around his neck, then pulled his mouth back to hers.

He leaned forward, lowering them both to the ground

and slipped his thigh between hers. The floor was cold, but Raf was so warm she didn't shiver, just clung to him.

His lips moved to her neck. He nibbled her skin and whispered to her—told her he loved her, that he would never leave her, that nothing could make him.

Her body tingled; for a second she thought he was shimmering them, but it was just her body's reaction to his words, *believing* them.

Her life of deception and being alone was over.

He traced the length of her body with his palms. His skin barely grazed hers, but energy pulsed everywhere he touched. She shoved her hands into his hair and turned his ear toward her—whispered that she loved him in elfin. She knew he didn't understand, but saying it was a relief, freeing.

He pushed his upper body up on his forearms and stared down at her. "I love you, princess, no matter the language." Then before she could respond, he thrust his length inside her.

Marina gasped. The pressure was so sudden and intense, her body flushed. She clung to him, arched herself toward him and wrapped her legs around his waist. Fully inside her, he paused and caught her lips in another kiss...long and lingering.

Heat built where they touched, inside and out. Power built—she could feel the magic swirling around them.

"Do you feel it?" he asked.

She nodded not sure if he meant the magic or the tension that threatened to explode inside her. She pushed her hips higher, pushed him even deeper.

They let out ragged breaths, both fighting the need to continue, and reveling in the building pleasure. Then, finally, when she thought she could stand it no longer, he pulled back just an inch. She gasped and he pulled back further. She clawed at his sides, doing everything she could to keep a scream from ripping from her throat.

With a smile, he pulled out fully, then thrust himself back in, and Marina clung to him, moved her hips with him, increasing their pace until her body began to quiver with unreleased tension. He drove deeper and harder and her body tightened more. The magic around them thickened to a cloud. She could see it, feel it, taste it—glowing, warm and sweet, like cotton candy that continued to spin and grow.

He grabbed her hips, tilted her even higher, moved even deeper. Her breath caught and her heart pounded. Colors and heat swirled around them until they exploded into pure white light. Marina cried out and grasped at Raf's back. He slid both arms under her, jerking her against him as he trembled with release. He held her like that until their orgasms had passed and their breath had slowed to rough pants, then he lowered them both to the ground, kept her cradled in his arms.

Her head snuggled under his, she lay there listening to his heart beat against hers, feeling his heat mingling with hers, and knowing everything would be all right.

There was pounding below—like someone ramming a log against a door. Raf trailed his fingers down Marina's arm. "Sounds like company is coming."

She smiled up at him. "Uninvited guests, don't you hate them?"

He brushed his lips over hers. "I do." Her scent of spring and flowers wrapped around him. Made him want to wrap his arms around her and stay right where they were.

But…something cracked below…things were about to get difficult here, and they had the rest of their lives to spend wrapped in each others' embrace.

It was time to get out of Alfheim.

He stood and pulled Marina to her feet beside him. "Are you ready to leave?" he asked.

She nodded and wove her fingers between his.

He handed her her clothes. While she pulled them on, he strode to the doorway and stared down the steps. The front door still held. He could hear yells coming from beyond it.

Marina stepped beside him and grabbed his arm in both hands. "I'm ready."

After a short discussion, Marina led him to the stairs and a window that overlooked the bailey. It was only one flight below the tower—three flights from ground level.

He shoved open the wooden shutters and placed his hand on the sill. "You trust me?" he asked.

She smiled. "We're past that question."

He lifted her onto the sill then wrapped his arm around her waist. She pressed her face against his. He pulled her closer, then dove from the window. They fell straight and fast in a nosedive toward the ground. Marina clung to him.

There was a scream from below, and elves rushed to their weapons. Ky stood in the middle, her mouth in an *O* and her eyes wide.

Marina's hair wrapped around them, cloaking them from her sister's view. The elves raised their bows, aimed their arrows. Ky lifted an arm, then dropped it.

Arrows pelted toward them.

His eyes glowing, Raf pressed a kiss to Marina's ear and shimmered them both to her uncle's mansion.

* * *

Marina stumbled as she and Raf materialized, held on to him to keep from falling, then kept her body pressed against his just because she could. After a few seconds, however, their surroundings interfered with her contentment.

They were in the mansion...or what was left of it. They were outside her room. She could see down the hall to the main entry. The front door was missing and there was daylight where there shouldn't be. The roof had collapsed over the south wing.

"What happened?" she asked.

Raf shook his head. "I'm not sure. When I was looking for your uncle, there was an explosion. I don't know if the mansion was the target or just a casualty of some unrelated conflict."

Marina turned in a circle. Returning to the castle had opened up old wounds she didn't realize existed, but seeing her uncle's home like this...the house she'd thought of as home, really...it was just as upsetting.

She opened the door to her room and walked in. All the pictures had fallen from the walls and the plaster was fractured from floor to ceiling. She stooped to retrieve a photo. The silver-framed image was of Ky and Marina when they were children. There was a crack in the glass separating the two. Marina stared at it for a second, thinking how easy it would be to replace the glass.

If only everything else could be healed as easily.

"What has happened to Alfheim?" she murmured. She asked the question, but she knew the answer. The Paladin had told her the answer. The throne was causing all this, would, according to him, continue to wreak this destruction until she sat on it, agreed to be part of Alfheim. Ruled alone, without Raf.

Raf stepped behind her, placed his hands on her upper arms and pulled her back against him. The warmth of his body should have been reassuring—but it wasn't.

It reminded her what else the Paladin had said…that Raf would betray her, or try. She didn't believe him, but still she stepped forward, out of Raf's embrace.

Over her shoulder, he frowned. She shook herself. What the Paladin said didn't matter. He was wrong. He had to be—about Raf and her destiny.

She was leaving Alfheim with Raf; the throne be damned. It would just have to choose another. With her out of Alfheim, surely it would choose another.

It would have to.

She placed her hand on Raf's face, then lifted herself on her toes to press a kiss to his lips. "Why are we here? I thought we were leaving."

He smiled, his eyes twinkling. "You think I should travel like this?"

She glanced down; she'd forgotten he was naked. She moved her hands to his chest and splayed her fingers over his bare skin. "I don't see why not."

His hand slipped behind her back and he tugged her against his body. She could feel his strength through the thin silk she wore.

His lips found hers. She opened her mouth and curled her fingers into the hair on his chest. His tongue pushed against hers, but gently, lovingly. She wrapped her tongue around his, willed the kiss to go on, but he pulled back and placed his forehead against hers. She could feel his heart beating beneath her palm; her own beat with it—loud, almost desperate for him to continue.

He breathed out and tugged her against him, into a hug. "Trust me, once we are out of Alfheim, I plan to spend more time unclothed than clothed, but for now I think pants at least might speed our escape."

While Raf went to his room to retrieve clothing, Marina wandered around hers gathering a few things. She left all but one change of clothing behind. She didn't intend to ever wear silk again if she could help it, but she took keepsakes, including the photo of Ky and herself. She held it for a second considering the image, but never once thought of leaving the memento behind.

Who was to say Ky was even to blame for her actions? Everything, all the madness, including her sister's, might be nothing but the throne's influence. Perhaps there was still hope, once Marina was gone and things had settled down, that the sister she'd known before would return. Marina put the photo into her bag and slipped the bag's strap over her shoulder.

Raf returned clothed and carrying a bag of his own. Marina looped her arm through his and was hit by a sense of overwhelming dread. She shuddered to a stop.

"What's wrong?" Raf dropped the bag and reached for her.

She held out a hand, stopping him. "What... Do you feel that? The sense of unknown? Lostness?" She shuddered again.

He glanced at the bag he'd dropped. "It's the stone. I wrapped it in the net and put it in the bag. I thought the net would mute its magic—at least make it more tolerable, but it must not be working. Maybe it's even worse if you can feel it from there."

"The stone?" She swallowed. Somehow she'd forgotten the stone, forgotten that Raf believed the stone was the key to finding out who murdered his family.

"I'm taking it with us—someone, somewhere besides your uncle, must know the key. If not, after you are settled, I can come back and locate him."

"You'd do that? Put off getting your answers?" She swallowed a knot of guilt that formed in her throat. The Paladin had said she could use the stone. That as the throne's pick it would answer for her. She should tell Raf...

But she didn't. She didn't want to believe the stone would work for her, that everyone was right, that she was destined for the throne.

She placed a hand on his arm. "Are you sure you need it? Isn't there some other way?"

He glanced at the bag, his expression darkening. "Perhaps. There's almost always another way. But in this case, I have no idea how to find it. After my family was killed, I spent every second of my life searching for answers. I wouldn't have resorted to dealing with the elf lords if I hadn't." He looked apologetic after stating the last, but she understood. No one outside of Alfheim chose to work with the light elves—not if they didn't have to. Elves were...elves—arrogant and difficult, like a world of headstrong thoroughbred horses. And many of them looked down on every being who wasn't an elf.

She pressed her hands together and nodded. "We'll bring it, then." She held out her hand. Raf hesitated and suddenly it was important he give it to her—important she see that the Paladin was wrong.

He frowned. "I'm used to it. Maybe if I hold it closer, lose the bag, it will focus on me." He pulled out a box wrapped in the net they'd used to hang her uncle from the chandelier.

She tamped down the moment of distrust and ran her fingers through a slit in the weave. "He cut it."

Raf's lips twisted into a wry smile. "I underestimated your uncle."

She shook her head. "We all did." Her uncle was like a cockroach who wouldn't die and couldn't be trapped. "I wonder if Ky's found him yet."

"Knowing Geir, he figured out some way to escape."

Marina nodded, but her attention was on the stone. Just looking at it made her knees shake with insecurity. Was she doing the right thing? How could she turn her back on Alfheim? Did Raf really love her or was the Paladin right?

She curled her fingernails into her palm until little half-moon impressions were left on her skin. She had to ignore the questions—they weren't hers. They were the stone's or the throne's or someone else's. "How does it affect you?" she asked. Did he hear the same nagging doubts she did?

He hesitated for a moment, then pressed his lips together. "Questions. Pounding questions."

Marina licked her lips, then forced her mouth into a smile and held out her hand. "Let me carry it."

He paused again. "It isn't your burden."

"It's elfin. I'm elfin. It won't bother me as much."

A line formed between his brows. She could see doubt in his eyes. Her own doubts flared in response.

Marina stepped closer. "Trust me. I can handle it." She held her breath and willed him to hand her the stone. If he didn't...

His gaze seemed to pierce into her, like a laser

cutting her apart and searching for truth. She pulled on her lifetime of training, kept her eyes wide, free of doubt.

He hesitated again, then handed her the stone.

The box was heavy; she pressed it against her stomach to keep from dropping it. He'd trusted her. She should be happy, but she wasn't—felt as if she'd betrayed him.

"Are you okay?" He reached as if to take the stone back.

Marina stepped away and slung the net-wrapped box over her shoulder. "I'm fine. I just needed a second to… adjust." Her smile was thin, another lie, but again he didn't seem to question it.

He trusted her, but could she trust him? She was about to find out.

Chapter 21

Marina convinced Raf to search the destroyed mansion—
to make sure no servants had been left behind.

While he was gone, she pulled out the box.

She ran her hands over the lid. The wood was worn,
unimpressive, but inside the stone pulsed. It wanted her
to open the lid, to show her its secrets.

She clenched the wooden top. Raf had told her what
Lord Sim had said, the danger of opening this lid...but
somehow she knew it would be okay, that the stone
wouldn't hurt her.

Which meant she also believed the legend—that she
was meant to rule.

She shoved the thought aside and lifted the lid.

The room she occupied was dark. The stone glowed
green. She waved her hand over it, waited for the pain.
There was none. A peace settled over her instead. The
questions stopped.

She set the box on her lap and placed both hands on the stone. For a second, she felt nothing but the cool, hard rock beneath her palms. Then her eyes closed and she was somewhere else—standing in the castle, the throne room...

Raf and the Paladin were there, as was the throne. On the wall behind them a scene played out, as the Paladin had shown her before. Alfheim was in chaos.

She stood by the throne, knew she had been sitting on it. There was uncertainty in her eyes; she glanced at Raf—fear. She held out her hand to him, but he ignored her, stalked toward the Paladin. He was going to kill the elf; she could see the intent in his eyes.

Power shot from her palms, curled up Raf's chest and around his neck. With Raf completely contained. She smiled at the Paladin. "See, no problem." She twitched one hand and sent Raf sailing into the wall.

Then she settled down onto the throne.

Marina jerked her hands away from the stone, sat blinking at it. Horror shuddered through her. The Paladin was right. If Marina took the throne, Raf would turn on her—or more accurately she would turn on him—attack him. Kill him?

Her hands shook; she held them over the stone. She should touch it again, ask the stone to tell more. But she was afraid—afraid of what she might see, afraid she was destined to slip, to destroy the one being she loved and trusted.

She folded her fingers into her palms, then hardened her resolve. She needed to see.

"The house is empty."

Raf's voice caused her to jump. She slammed the lid closed and turned.

He frowned. "Is everything okay?" His gaze moved to the box she held pressed against her stomach.

She nodded. "I just…the questions…but I'm getting used to them. I can handle it." She smiled and pulled the net around the box. "I thought the net might be amplifying them, but I was wrong."

Her hands shaking, she slung it back over her shoulder. "Let's go. Let's leave Alfheim."

If she left Alfheim, she wouldn't sit on the throne and she wouldn't betray Raf—again.

When Marina and Raf arrived at the portal, the crowds crushed around them immediately. Raf didn't believe the crazed citizens even realized a hellhound and Alfheim's princess had magically materialized in their midst. The elves were too caught up in chanting and holding images of elf lords and royals alike over their heads.

Smoke clogged the air. Raf pulled Marina against him, encouraged her to breathe through his shirt.

"What's happening?" she asked, her voice breaking and her eyes darting back and forth in her face.

Taking advantage of his height, Raf scanned the area. "There's a fire. I think they're burning those…" He pointed to a straw-stuffed image of what could easily have been Lord Sim that a group of boys had pinned in the gutter and were pummeling with their fists and feet.

"Oh." A tremor went through Marina. Raf ran his hand down her spine and pulled her closer against him. With the crowds as crazed as they were, he didn't want anyone to recognize her.

Two teens who had been watching the boys with the effigy and laughing, turned and gestured toward Marina.

Both wore simple denim pants and T-shirts not that different from what Raf wore. One had a black cap pulled low over his brow. He mumbled to his companion. Raf read his lips, something about Marina and the silk she wore.

The teens stalked forward.

They stopped a few feet away, just out of Raf's reach—if he had been dependent on his arm's length to grab them. Unfortunately for the boys, he could at any time shimmer and be inches away, rather than the three feet they seemed to think was a safe distance to taunt him.

The one in the hat made a loud sniffing noise. "I smell a royal. How about you El?"

El made a point of inhaling until his nostrils collapsed against his nose. "Yeah, royal. You think she's one of the ones that killed the Adals?"

At her parent's name, Marina jerked, but Raf held firm. The teens weren't interested in hearing reason. They were looking for someone to bully.

Too bad for them they'd come across a hellhound. There were no bullies in a hellhound world—there were alphas and everyone else, and these boys fell clearly in the everyone else group. It looked as if it was going to be Raf's job to make that clear to them.

He pushed Marina behind him and stepped forward. "Go away." He didn't move, stood tense and ready… for anything.

"You a royal-lover?" The capped one asked. He rocked forward onto the balls of his feet, then back on his heels.

His friend grinned.

Raf smiled back—then he grabbed them by the fronts of their shirts and held them overhead, one in each fist.

The smug expressions on their faces disappeared. They didn't even have the sense to struggle, just hung there, shocked that someone would call them on their idiocy.

Raf growled and jerked them both close. "Don't make threats you aren't willing to back up."

"We didn't...we just..." The capped boy stuttered.

Raf didn't have the patience or time for lies. He had to get Marina to the portal. He dropped both teens onto the pavement and turned.

But she was gone. As was most of the crowd, they were flowing through the street, past the building that housed the portal and toward billowing smoke.

With a curse, Raf jogged after them.

The smoke was thick and black. Tears ran down Marina's cheeks as she was pushed along by the crowds. She had to breathe through her sleeve to keep from coughing.

She should have stayed with Raf. She could have, but the smoke and the elves swarming toward it reminded her of another scene, from Gunngar.

That day she'd been the one calling the crowds. She'd been the one holding the torch. Her heart had pounded, like it did now, but she hadn't cried. She'd had to act her part, pray that the plan she'd worked out with Gal, the one elf she trusted, would play out correctly—that the smoke would cover the trapdoor opening. That no one but she would realize there was a portal there that lead to the uninhabited part of Gunngar. That the witch would be separated from her family, but alive.

The plan had worked and the witch had survived. Marina knew that now, but that day she didn't know for sure. The portal left no record of what it had done, and the fire had burned too hot to leave behind any sign as to whether a witch had really died there.

So, Marina had stood there feeling sick and hating herself, but she had still dropped the torch.

If she hadn't. If she'd refused to do what the elf lords had asked...

A female elf knocked into her, causing the net-wrapped box to bounce against her back. She winced as the corner gouged into muscle.

She lowered it from her shoulder, let it drag on the ground. If she hadn't done what the elf lords had wanted, they might have killed her. But was that an excuse for the risk she took? What she put the citizens of Gunngar through?

No. It wasn't.

Another elf bumped into her, this one shot her a look, let his gaze linger on her silk clothing.

She glanced around, realized she was alone—surrounded not by royals as she had been her entire life, but common elves dressed in cotton, wool and even cheaper synthetics.

Another stopped and stared at her, then another, until there was a small circle surrounding her. One by one they started to whisper, until their low words changed, became almost a chant. "Royal. She's a royal. Add her to the pyre."

She'd heard the words a dozen times before their meaning sunk in. *The pyre.* They weren't just burning straw images. They were burning elves.

She spun and raced toward the thickest part of the smoke. The elves who had surrounded her broke into a run, too. They were chasing her, she realized. Like dogs driven to hunt her down simply because she had run.

But she wasn't running *from* them or anything. She was running toward something—the fire she could now see blazing in the center of the street.

Flames lapped against dry wood that had been piled so haphazardly she wondered that it could burn. But burn it did. The flames had started on the outskirts of the pile where the citizens of Alfheim had tossed matches and torches; the center and what stood there— three elf lords tied back to back—were as yet untouched.

At the edge of the flames, Marina ground to a halt. The fire had formed a fence that circled the lords. The three males slumped forward; only the pole they were lashed to kept them from falling.

She screamed at them to look up, to acknowledge that they were still alive, but either they weren't or the roar of the fire and sound of the crowd drowned out her words. She glanced around, looking for something to throw at them, some way to get their attention.

Her gaze dropped to the net that seemed to cling to her fingers. She lifted it over her head and began to spin her arm, like a cowboy preparing to throw a lariat.

Then someone hit her from behind and she fell, the box hitting first. The wood cut into her abdomen, and the doubts she'd felt when she'd first seen the thing slammed into her.

These elf lords were going to die—because of her. The citizens of Alfheim were running wild because of her. Everything, every bad thing that had happened was because of her.

And she, selfishly, was choosing her own happiness over all of them, was choosing life with Raf away from Alfheim over all of them. If they died, if Alfheim died, it would be her fault.

She gritted her teeth and tried to block the thoughts from her brain. She shoved her palms against the pavement and pushed herself up, off of the box. The doubts subsided, but only slightly. The truth of her situation didn't go away.

The world whirled; someone, or many someones, grabbed her around the waist and dragged her toward the fire. "A royal! Add her to the pyre." She flipped and the faces of her attackers flashed in front of her. They blended into one mass. Young, old, male, female—they all had one thing in common, anger.

They wanted her dead. Like the citizens of Gunngar had probably wanted her dead. And this time she was the one who was going to be tossed on the fire.

It seemed right—just.

She went limp, let them carry her. Her fingers went limp, too, slipped free of the net's weave. The box fell from her grasp and dropped onto the ground. The fog that had surrounded her since taking hold of the thing lifted, but her outlook didn't change. Things still looked just as bleak, perhaps more so.

Heat flickered out toward her; she stared sightlessly at the sky. She had failed everyone, and by running away with Raf she was doing it again.

Her feet had reached the fire. Flames warmed the soles of her shoes until they burned against the bottoms of her feet.

Then somewhere behind her, muted by the crowd, there was a roar. Her eyes flew open and everything zoomed back into focus.

Raf or Alfheim? She owed them both and lying here, letting a crazed crowd toss her onto a fire wasn't the way to repay either. She sat up, startling the elves. Their eyes rounded and for a second alertness flickered behind their gazes—reminding Marina that they were victims, too, not cognizant of everything they were doing.

Then Raf solidified beside her and all hell broke loose.

The elves didn't move when Raf materialized behind them—just kept feeding Marina toward the fire like so much more fuel. He grabbed two and slapped their heads against each other. Those remaining stumbled— but, he sensed, not so much from fear as momentum. Still, two more moved in from the crowd to replace the ones he'd downed.

He stopped. What had at first seemed a crazed crowd, looked different up close—robotic rather than frenetic.

He frowned, not understanding what they were doing or why. They should be afraid, terrified. He had every intention of destroying each and every one who had placed a hand on Marina.

He reached for another elf, had his hand on the male's shoulder when Marina yelled.

"Save them." She pointed toward the center of the fire. Almost hidden in the smoke were Lord Sim and two other lords. It took a second for Raf to realize they were tied there, unable to escape.

He glanced at Marina; she'd sat up when he'd first arrived. Her upright position was deceptive, made it look as if the elves below her were carrying her, honoring her instead of toting her to her death. Or planned death. She was in no danger from the zombie-like elves whose hands shuffled over her legs as they tried to move her into the blaze.

He should have realized that from the beginning—

known that Marina could take care of herself, but he'd panicked, forgotten everything he knew about her abilities.

"Save them," she called again, begged. Her eyes were huge and filled with pain.

He glanced at the lords, the fire and Marina—realized she was reliving the day she'd burned the witch, or pretended to.

Was that why she'd allowed the elves to carry her so close, hadn't fought back?

With a sweep of his arm, he knocked four more elves to the ground, catching Marina as they fell. With her clasped against his chest, he murmured in her ear, "Why don't you?"

She stiffened and her eyes rounded.

"Show yourself, Marina. Not the princess or the elf lord's pawn—you. Show who you are to everyone including yourself."

He straightened the arm that held her legs and let her slide to a stand. For a second he thought she wouldn't do it, that she'd fall back on one guise or the other, but with one last glance over the crowd, she strode forward her hand held out in front of her and power, green and alive, pulsing against her palm.

"Stop!" she yelled. "In the name of the throne of Alfheim, stop!"

The elves parted. Their clouded gazes began to clear. Raf let out a breath, relieved for her. Marina was doing it—showing her powers to all of Alfheim. There would be no hiding them now, no denying what and who she was beneath the guises that had been forced on her in the past.

Now she could relax, accept herself.

While Marina held off the elves, Raf shimmered to

the center of the pyre. The flames had crept inward. He materialized on flames. Fire lapped at his clothing. His pants began to smoke. He ignored the flickering heat. He was in no danger from its touch.

The same, however, wasn't true of the elves, and the fire had reached the three lords. Raf strode forward, grabbed the three in a giant hug and shimmered.

He dropped them at Marina's feet. They lay pale and still. For a moment he thought the effort was wasted, that the smoke had already done its intended job.

Then they started to cough.

Sim was the first to recover. He rolled onto his back and stared up at the crowd surrounding them. Raf knelt beside him and wrapped his fist into the lord's shirt. "It appears someone took up the sword."

Sim blinked and started to speak, but a fit of coughs stole his words. Raf dropped him back onto the pavement and stood. He shimmered to where Marina had dropped the box and slung the net over his shoulder. Then turned to walk back to Marina.

She was standing with her hands at her sides, her face pale and unsure. Surrounding her were elves. Thousands of them, kneeling with their foreheads on their knees.

Raf froze. The stone's questions started pounding into him again, but he ignored them. It was easy this time. He was too focused on what was happening around Marina for the stone's questions to shake his concentration—too filled with his own questions.

He didn't know where the elfin masses had come from so quickly or what their appearance meant. Then he caught Marina's gaze, and saw the apology in her eyes.

He knew...somehow he'd lost her.

Chapter 22

Marina turned from Raf. She didn't know what else to do. She had no explanation for what had happened. But she knew she had made a decision—a commitment.

She stared out over the sea of elves. When she'd made her announcement, called for peace in the name of the throne, they'd flooded out of houses, stores, everywhere—and they were still coming. The streets leading to the pyre were packed. Elves had climbed onto the tops of cars and rooftops. They were everywhere and they were all kneeling.

She swallowed. She hadn't thought…hadn't meant….

The words had just come.

She folded her fingers into her palms. She could feel the power pulsing there—or was it her heart beating?

The two seemed the same. Her magic was just a part of her now, like any other part, and it felt natural.

She put her hands over her face and sucked in a breath. She didn't want to understand why the elves had dropped to the ground before her. They'd never done that to anyone, not even her parents.

She turned to glance at Raf. He hadn't moved; he was watching her, as was everyone else. Even with their heads down, the citizens of Alfheim were watching her, waiting for her to do something.

Her heart sped. What had she done? She didn't want to stand out. She didn't want to matter. She just wanted to be swept along the river of life, unimportant as a leaf caught in the current.

As the thoughts pinged through her head, the place grew quiet. No one moved; nothing moved.

Then the trill started—a high ringing noise like a hummingbird with metallic wings flitted around her. She spun, searching for the source. Silver flashed around her. She reached out to swat it away, but her fingers found only air.

Then the sound was gone and a heaviness settled over her, like a mantle had been thrown over her shoulders... weighing her down.

She looked up.

The Paladin stood twenty feet away. A circle of elves kneeled around him. An aisle of bowed heads had formed between them.

He stared at her, obviously waiting for her to do something. She didn't move. Despite what she'd said, she didn't want the throne. She wanted Raf. She opened her mouth to scream the words, but only a croak escaped.

She tried to see behind him. The throne...it had to

be here, too. Panic built in her chest. *She wasn't ready. She wouldn't do this.*

Her hands wrapped around her throat as she tried to force her voice to work. But nothing came out.

"Marina?"

Raf's voice. She swallowed, but didn't turn. Tears forming in the back of her eyes, she faced the Paladin. "You can't ask me to make this choice. It isn't fair. I shouldn't have to trade my happiness for the safety of Alfheim."

He shrugged, a strangely casual gesture for a moment that felt almost formal, processional. "Important choices are never easy. But the throne only does what is best for Alfheim."

In other words, it didn't care about her—just like Alfheim had never cared about her, or so she'd thought. She glanced over the crowd…saw old and frail, young and strong, all on bended knee for her. It was a lie, though, wasn't it? Alfheim had done nothing for her before this. They'd watched her, used her for entertainment, but none had ever tried to challenge her uncle's hold. None had ever asked who killed her parents. They had all just gone along the easiest path.

She clenched her fists. "What if I refuse?" she asked.

The Paladin cocked a brow. "You already made the choice. If you hadn't we wouldn't be here." He motioned to the elf lords lying on the ground behind her. "This would have ended very differently, but if you're asking what will happen if you back out…." He shook his head. "Look in your heart."

She dropped her gaze. She didn't want to look in her heart. She knew what was there—Raf, but Alfheim, too.

The Paladin stepped back. The throne was behind

him. It was as she remembered it, a simple silver chair.
But it no longer intimidated her. It seemed happy—if an
inanimate object showing emotion was possible—
glowing with warmth.

She held out her hand and looked for guidance from
inside herself. In her mind, power leapt from her
palm—formed into a vine like she'd used to overpower
her uncle and Anton, but this one was thicker with lush
leaves and flowers dangling from its length. She didn't
direct it, just let it grow. The vine zigzagged over the
elves' bowed heads, wove its way toward the Paladin
and the throne.

No one else could see the dancing vine, but Marina
could, and she knew what it meant. She held her breath,
afraid of what her own magic was telling her.

"Marina?" Raf touched her on the shoulder. She
jerked. The vine jerked, too, paused and raised up, like
a snake poised to strike.

Raf ran his fingers down her back, a soft stroke that
made her tilt her head and close her eyes.

"Princess?" The Paladin prompted.

Marina ignored him. Her heart ached, as if it were
tearing in two.

Raf didn't say anything. He seemed to sense she was
battling something.

"I can't leave," she muttered. The words hurt to say,
but she forced them out. She had to face the truth. She
had called the throne; it was her destiny. The vine
quivered in approval.

Raf's palm flattened against her back, warm and
tempting. "You want to stay here? In Alfheim?" She
could feel his frown; knew he was confused. She'd

never acted as if she wanted to stay in Alfheim. It wasn't right to spring it on him now, but she had no choice.

"What do you want, Raf? More than anything, what do you want?" she asked.

She knew what his answer would be; he'd never hidden his mission from her. Still, when he said the words it would hurt just a little.

"To find my family's killer. To right, just a bit, the mistake I made by leaving them unguarded. And you. I want you."

She let out a breath—not just revenge, he wanted her, too. This answer hurt even more than the one she'd expected, made what she had to do all the harder. "Me, too, but we can't have both." Raf had to leave. If he didn't, the stone's prophecy would come true—she would turn on him, betray him again.

Raf grabbed her by the shoulders and twisted her around. The vine snapped and danced over their heads. She closed her hand into a fist—cut off the power. There was a pop and the vine disappeared. The decision had been made; there was no turning back.

"What are you saying?" he asked. His gaze was intense, almost blazing. He lowered the stone to the ground.

She could feel the throne behind her, calling her. She licked her lips.

She forced herself to look at Raf to keep her gaze steady. "We can't have both. We have to choose. We can't undo our past mistakes and be together." Alfheim had shown her what would happen if she walked away. Gunngar amplified a thousand fold. She couldn't live with that.

Raf dropped his hands from her shoulders, stared at her as if she'd slapped her. Her stomach clenched. She felt his pain, but it was best this way, best he thought she was forcing him to choose. He could walk away without guilt.

"What game are you playing, Marina? I thought you wanted to leave Alfheim."

"I can't. I have to stay, and you have to leave."

He dropped his hands from her shoulders. The line between his eyes deepened. "You aren't telling me everything." The words were flat, almost dead, but there was a flicker in his eyes—hope.

She had to crush it.

"I'm choosing the throne. I wanted it all along." She waved at the crowd around them. "This was just build up. I had to put it off, to increase the excitement. But now, the throne's here and I don't need you anymore."

He said nothing for a second, then turned. His back to her, he ran a hand through his hair. The muscles of his back bulged.

He spun back. "You are lying. I don't know why, but you are." He held out one hand. "Let's leave, talk."

She stared at his hand, wanted to slip hers into it. But as she reached out, the Paladin called. "Your sister is coming. The throne won't wait."

A line of cars appeared in the distance, their drivers blaring horns and screaming at the elves who jammed the roads.

Raf stared at her, then lowered his hand. "Why are you doing this?" he murmured.

She gestured to the elves surrounding them and the line of cars approaching. "I'm the princess. I'm meant to rule, not spend my life in some other world with a hellhound."

His hands formed fists; his knuckles turned white.

The cars' horns grew louder. A woman screamed. Marina turned and saw a man disappear under the carriage of the first vehicle. A woman threw herself at the car's window, but the vehicle kept moving.

She was out of time.

Marina glanced back at Raf. "I'm sorry if I hurt you." She moved and the throne did, too—appeared before her. She touched the arm.

"Marina!" Raf called, but it was too late. She was already moving forward, could already feel the throne becoming part of her. A millennia of Alfheim history flowed through her mind. She staggered under the weight of it, grasped the throne's arms with both hands to keep from falling.

"Sit. You have to sit," the Paladin urged and he shoved her forward. Her body twisted and she collapsed against the throne's back. Everything went quiet for a moment, then faded. Her vision became a tunnel and she was zooming along it acquiring knowledge and experiencing things she didn't even know existed. A weight landed on her lap; she clawed at it. Knew she had to learn something, share something. Answers bubbled out of her; she couldn't speak fast enough. There was yelling, arguing. Someone trying to talk to her, but she pushed him away—couldn't concentrate on anything with all the knowledge and power whirling through her brain. There was tugging and more yelling.

None of it mattered. All that mattered was learning what the throne had to say. She collapsed into it, the metal collapsing with her until it was molded to her body, cradled her. The tunnel appeared again and she was hurtled through it, faster and faster, until all she could see was light—red, blue, purple, every color imaginable whizzing past her. She gave up watching them, gave up thinking at all, gave into the power of the throne and let her mind wander…let the world around her disappear.

Chapter 23

Raf lunged for Marina; his fingers wrapped around her arms and he tried to tug her from the throne, but the throne held on…seemed to have melded with her. He cursed and tried again. The Paladin appeared behind him with a sword and shoved it against his throat. "She made the choice. You can't undo it."

Raf ignored him. Marina's head fell back; her eyes were open but blank.

Rage coursed through Raf. He spun on the Paladin, grabbed the small male by the throat. "What is happening to her?"

"The throne has accepted her. It's sharing everything it knows with her."

Raf dragged the elf towards Marina—thrust him forward until he was almost lying across her lap. "Make it stop."

The Paladin gasped and shook his head. "No one can stop it, but she's fine. She'll be fine."

Raf didn't believe or trust him. His gaze swept over the crowd, searching for some weapon or tool he could use to separate Marina from the throne.

The Paladin held up one hand. "If you interfere, you will only increase the chaos, and I don't know how her body would handle an abrupt separation. It might kill her."

Raf's fingers tightened on the elf's shirt. He wanted to shake the male to force him to make whatever was happening to Marina stop.

"Do you want to help her?" the Paladin asked.

Raf lowered his brow. He didn't bother with an answer, just stared at the elf until the smaller male began to squirm under the pressure of Raf's gaze.

"If you want to help her, you'll leave. Alfheim is on the brink of civil war, disaster. If she sees you, her doubts may return. If there are rumors that she...that you and she..." He glanced to the side.

Raf growled. "What?"

The elf let out a breath. "Now is not the time to try and prove your place. Alfheim isn't ready for a ruler who..."

Raf pulled the elf close, mumbled into his face. "Loves a hellhound? Did you tell her something? Is that why she lied?"

The elf's eyes narrowed. "There's no reason to lie. You know how hard her job is going to be. Do you want to make it harder? If you care for her, leave, take care of what you came to Alfheim for in the first place."

Raf glanced at Marina. She'd quit struggling, seemed to have fallen asleep. Her breathing was smooth and easy and her color was good.

The Paladin gestured to Marina. "She's fine. Leave."

Raf crossed his arms over his chest, assessed what was happening around them. The other elves still sat with their heads bowed. The cars that had been approaching had stopped. Ky stood outside of one, her hands wrapped around her arms and a lost expression on her face.

Seeing the direction of Raf's gaze, the Paladin waved a hand. "It was the chaos. Now that the throne is claimed, Ky will return to the pliable child her uncle raised her to be."

Raf let his gaze linger for a minute on the female. Perhaps her actions hadn't been her own, but somehow he doubted she'd return to what she had been before all of this. How could she?

The elf gestured for Raf to release him. Thinking he'd seen reason, Raf loosened his hold. The Paladin took a few steps away and placed his hands on his hips. "The throne will protect her now."

Without warning, he jerked a sword from his belt and slashed it towards Marina's throat. Raf jumped, but the elf was too quick, too close. The blade sliced the air just above Raf's hand. The Paladin released his hold and leaped back, but the blade kept moving.

Raf's heart seizing in his chest, he roared and lunged. The elf danced backward, yelling and pointing toward Marina as he did. Afraid of what he would see, but unable to keep himself from looking, Raf glanced over his shoulder. The blade hung frozen in midair. It began to vibrate. A whining noise pierced the air.

Raf stepped back, confused. The Paladin smiled and gestured again. There was a snap, and another. Then the entire sword disintegrated, until a pile of metallic dust lay on the ground below Marina's feet.

The elf drew up onto his toes. "The throne will protect her far better than you. If you truly want to help her, there's something else you can do."

Raf cocked a brow.

The elf reached into his jacket and pulled out a piece of paper. "I've discovered her parents' killer. He's here, hiding in the human world while he gathers forces." He shoved a map into Raf's hands. "Marina won't truly be safe until her parents' killer is captured."

Raf glanced at the map. It was a large city in the United States that he had never visited. "Who is it? Have I met him?"

The Paladin's gaze darkened. "Of course. It's her uncle, Geir. He wants the throne for himself, always has. Once Marina's parents were gone, he thought the throne would accept him. But it didn't. It disappeared, waiting for Marina to be ready. Now that she is, now that the throne is back—Geir is determined to kill her and take it for himself."

Raf frowned. Some of what the Paladin said made sense, but some didn't. "Why didn't he kill her long ago?"

The Paladin made an impatient noise in the back of his throat. "He needed her to lure the throne out of hiding."

"And he's in the human world? Now?" It didn't fit. Geir hated humans.

"It's the last place you would look for him."

Raf stared at the paper again, then at Marina. Knowing who killed her parents...she deserved that. She could have the closure he had yet to find for himself.

Raf retrieved the stone and laid it on Marina's lap. Then shimmered all of them, Marina, the Paladin and the throne, back to the castle.

He turned his gaze on the Paladin. "If anything happens to her—"

The Paladin raised a hand, cutting him off. "Go. If you are quick you can be done before she awakes."

With one last unsure glance at Marina, Raf shimmered.

When Marina awakened, her hands were wrapped around the chair's arms and her breath was coming in puffs. The stone's box lay on her lap. She placed her hands on top, waited for the pounding doubts and questions to start. They didn't.

Slowly, she lifted the lid. Inside lay the stone, dull gray, cold and totally unimpressive in the room's bright light. She stared at it, hated it for showing her what it had.

She looked up, expecting Raf to still be beside her, to still be outside near the portal, but he wasn't and she wasn't.

She was in the palace, in the throne room and only the Paladin was with her.

She moved to stand, but the Paladin held out a hand. "Sit, adjust."

"Where's Raf?" she asked. Gone, she hoped. If he wasn't…she glanced at the stone. Dread filled her. She couldn't kill Raf…she wouldn't…

"He left."

She placed her hand on the stone's rough surface, waited for relief to wash over her, but it didn't. She felt sick and alone.

"Where did he go?" she asked.

The Paladin tensed. "He left. I don't know why. Forget him. You are ruler now. We have to start the broadcast, to let the people know. A switch is over there." He pointed to the wall by the door. "The broadcast runs automatically when the switch is up and you are sitting on the throne. One of your mother's later additions after she'd hired the elf lords to bring in technology." He glanced at her as if expecting a comment, but she had none. He nodded, pleased. "I just need to check something. Then we will start."

Marina watched him leave. So, that was it. Raf was gone and she was the ruler of Alfheim. Nothing left but to tell the citizens. Everything was as it should be. The throne should be happy.

She should be happy.

But she wasn't. She wasn't at all.

Raf stood outside the address the guard had given him. It wasn't what he'd expected—it wasn't a ritzy mansion or a sexy high rise. It wasn't the opposite, either...a sleazy bar or unoccupied warehouse (Raf's personal choice when hiding in the human world).

It was a nice, middle-class human home—brick with a two car garage, a swing set in the front and a minivan in the drive.

Raf stepped onto the concrete sidewalk that lead to the front door.

Had the guard made a mistake?

If so what other mistakes, might the elf have made?

Marina. Was she safe?

Just thinking her name, made Raf want to shimmer back to her. He took a step, let the first tingles of his shimmer begin.

A scream cut him off. His gaze darted to the house.

A woman was standing by the front window, her mouth open and her eyes huge. A dark arm shot into view and she fell out of sight.

With a growl, Raf let his shimmer take over—but his destination changed. He pointed himself to right behind that arm, to the back of whoever had just struck the woman.

Marina was glad to be alone. She needed time to adjust, to force her mind away from Raf, where he was and what he thought of her. He'd believed her lies or he wouldn't have left.

That hurt. Which wasn't fair. She'd meant for him to believe, but deep inside she'd hoped he wouldn't, that the two of them had been through enough he'd see through her deception.

But he hadn't and it was for the best.

She forced her spine to relax against the throne, forced her mind to relax, too. To her surprise, the second was easy. Her eyes drifted shut and her mind opened.

Images and thoughts flooded through her. She was standing in the tower, but she wasn't herself, she was her mother. The stone that had been resting on her lap was in her hands and her father stood beside her. The Paladin was there, too.

Something inside her tensed, but she didn't try to leave. She wanted to see what was in the stone.

The stone glowed green, the color almost blinding. Her father murmured something she couldn't understand. Then, "Are you sure? What do we do? Do we tell anyone? Is Alfheim ready?"

Her mother spoke, her voice seeming to come from Marina. "It's years and years away. The stone can't be wrong. By then Alfheim will be ready. We will make them ready."

"And Marina?" Her father again.

"She will be part of it—the biggest change Alfheim has ever seen."

"No!" The Paladin stepped forward and knocked the stone from her mother's hands. Marina watched it fall, desperate to see inside it as it tumbled. It landed hard, made a clattering noise as it rolled across the floor. "This is not the future of Alfheim. It can't be. We can't let it be."

Her parents looked at each other, their faces cautious. "It will work out. The stone, like the throne, knows best."

The Paladin shook his head. "Your daughter yes, but the other— That can never happen." He turned and strode from the room.

Marina's father bent and scooped up the stone, held it out so Marina, through her mother's eyes, could see inside.

Framed by the stone's green glow was an image of Marina sitting on the throne, but she wasn't alone, sitting beside her—holding the stone was Raf.

"A hellhound, a ruler of Alfheim. Who would have predicted it?" her father muttered.

Her mother sighed and took the stone. "Neither of us, but we'll do our part. We know our direction now. It is time for Alfheim to change, to grow—to accept other beings as we never have before."

Her father grasped her mother's hand. "We can do it."

"And if we can't, our daughter can." Marina's mother slipped her arm around her husband's waist and the two walked from the room.

The image faded. Marina looked up.

The Paladin stood staring at her.

Raf materialized inside the house. The curtains were closed now—must have fallen back into place when the woman tumbled—and the room was silent. It was a typical living room: couch, a couple of chairs and an oversized TV. There were toys scattered across the carpeting, but Raf couldn't say if that was unusual or not.

The woman lying unconscious beneath the window, however, definitely was. She was wearing a robe and house shoes. Raf guessed Geir had surprised her not long after her family left for school and work.

He flexed his hands, but didn't approach her. That would be the expected thing—a perfect time for Geir to attack him from behind.

He turned instead, spied an open door that seemed to lead to a kitchen. He shimmered.

The kitchen was dark, too—all the blinds were pulled. Some kind of stew bubbled inside an electric pot beside the stove, filling the air with the fragrant scent of meat. He ignored it, ignored the ticking of a clock that hung on the wall, too, concentrated on smelling elf, or hearing the whisper-light steps of Geir somewhere in the house.

Instead, he smelled something completely different, felt something he didn't expect to feel at all—the smoky scent of hellhound and the ripple of magic as one shimmered.

Chapter 24

Air whooshed. Raf dropped to the ground and rolled, then sprung back to his feet.

The hellhound/bounty hunter who had been hunting Marina grinned at him from a few feet away. "Nice of you to come to me."

Raf drew back his shoulders and lowered his head. "If I'd known you were waiting for me, I'd have been here sooner."

"Yes, I guess you would have." The hellhound shimmered. Raf shimmered, too. Both materialized—Raf just outside the kitchen door, the bounty hunter where Raf had been seconds earlier.

Raf nodded his gaze toward the woman who lay unconscious on the floor. "Was that necessary?"

The bounty hunter lifted one shoulder. "I didn't pick this place. My employer did, but I couldn't exactly leave her wandering the house could I?"

"You could have tied her up."

The bounty hunter shrugged again. "Takes time. I'm into efficiency."

Raf was, too. He lunged and shimmered. His target dropped to the ground; Raf overshot him and slammed into the stainless steel refrigerator. Both hellhounds were back on their feet immediately.

Raf sensed this could take some time. *He might as well learn something while he decided how to kill the other male.* And kill him he would. It's what he should have done in the first place.

"So, is Geir here, too, or are you waiting for him?"

"Geir? You mean the royal who hired me first time around? Can't say I know what he's been doing. Can't say I care." The bounty hunter grinned. "You don't know who hired me. Someone wants you dead, and you don't even know who—and that same person I hear sent visitors before. To a house, in the woods?"

Raf froze. There was only one house the bounty hunter could be speaking of—Raf's house where he'd lived with his wife and child, where he'd left them with his brother. Where he had returned to find them all dead. Rage roared through him. His adrenaline surged, felt like fire ripping through his veins.

He gritted his teeth and balled his fist, barely kept himself from throwing his body at the other hellhound. The male knew who was responsible for his family's murder. Raf had never been this close to learning the name; he couldn't blow this chance by giving in to the blood lust now. There would be time for that later— when he was staring into the eyes of whoever was responsible for his family's slaughter.

The bounty hunter watched him, seemed to measure

Raf's reaction. "So, it's true then? I heard stories when it happened—a female, a male and a child?"

"My wife, my brother and my son." Saying the words hurt. Raf struggled to push them out past the pain shooting through his core.

The hunter looked away. A stupid move that left an opening for Raf to attack, but he didn't, waited to hear what else the bounty hunter would say instead.

"I don't like working with elves, never had until the princess, but times are tough. I can't afford to be choosey." The other male blew air out of his mouth, in a loud disgusted breath. He laughed. "But when I checked the site for jobs I found your picture there. I couldn't pass that up. In fact, I can't say I've ever been more eager to take a job." He paused. "Everyone else had turned it down. When I asked around, I found out why."

Hellhounds were constantly fighting for position among themselves—but an outsider sneaking into a hellhound community? Killing a hellhound child? It had angered Raf's friends and enemies alike. Raf tightened his fist more, focused on the now to keep the pain at bay.

"Give me his name."

The bounty hunter, his gaze back on Raf, sighed. "We really need to quit talking and get fighting. I'm looking forward to my pay. Good thing about elves, they pay in gold." He lunged toward Raf.

This time Raf didn't move; he was ready to get done with this fight. He had a new plan, though. The hunter knew who had killed his family, or ordered them killed—one way or another, Raf would know soon, too.

The hellhound hit him in the midsection. Raf

hardened his abs and bent forward. He let the momentum of the hit carry him backward into a somersault, then used his leg to slam the bounty hunter into the ground.

The other male groaned. Raf leapt to his feet and pulled his leg back to kick the hellhound in the head. The bounty hunter grabbed Raf's foot and jerked him down to the ground.

The two rolled across the floor, knocking into the center island. Raf landed on top. He wrapped his hands around the other males' throat and squeezed. The bounty hunter's eyes began to glow; Raf could feel the blood lust coming over both his opponent and himself—but he needed more answers and then he had a bigger enemy to find, kill. He couldn't afford to get lost in this battle.

He lifted the male up by his throat and slammed him back down, smashing his head against the slate floor. The other hellhound growled, tried to shimmer, but couldn't—not with Raf touching him and blocking the move. Raf slammed his head down again. The hellhound brought his own hands up, fisted, and slammed one and then the other into Raf's sides.

Raf grimaced, but ignored the pain, concentrated on inflicting it on the male beneath him instead. "A name," Raf muttered through gritted teeth.

The bounty hunter glared back.

Raf lifted him, and dropped him down again. This time there was a crack—the floor or the bounty hunters' skull—Raf couldn't tell. He shook the other male. "Give me a name. My son was only five." Pain rolled over him, emotional, not physical. If someone had shot him through the heart he didn't think he'd feel it right then. He'd never been more focused on anything.

He lifted the hellhound again, but the last smash had been too much. The bounty hunter's eyelids flickered, his hands fell limp and finally, his eyes rolled back in his head.

Raf dropped him with a curse. The hunter was still alive, but out. Now Raf would have to bring him back around—get him to talk. He bent and levered the unconscious hellhound onto his shoulder.

Someone screamed.

He spun. The woman from the window hung onto the kitchen door's trim, her mouth open and a shriek racing from her lungs.

Without bothering to hide what he was doing, to give her an easy explanation for what she was about to see, Raf shimmered.

Marina could do nothing but stare at the Paladin. He'd lied to her, had said the stone showed Raf betraying her, when actually it had shown Raf beside her on the throne.

What else had he done?

She wrapped her fingers around the throne's arms and formed her words carefully. "The throne. Does it have any special powers?"

The Paladin hesitated. "Why do you ask?"

She fluttered her fingers, made a noise as close to a laugh as she could manage. "Just now, I saw something. Nothing important, my mother and father talking with you." She smiled, warmly she hoped. "They seemed fond of you."

He let out a breath, nodded. "Yes, like the stone, it does. It holds memories."

She tapped her fingers on the arm, tried to look trusting. "Whose?"

"Every ruler's. The throne is part of the trinity—the past. The stone is the future and the current ruler the present. All three together and Alfheim is whole." He smiled, seemed pleased, but nervous.

"All memories?" she asked.

He shook his head, looked more confident. "No, just ones important to present-day choices. The throne is too wise to not filter out the unnecessary, it isn't flawed like the—" He pressed his lips together.

"The stone?" she prompted. "The ruler? Is the throne wiser than both?"

The Paladin opened his lips to answer, but before he could reply, there was a noise in the bailey. He turned and scurried toward the doorway. Marina rose, intending to follow, but before she could move more than a step Raf appeared in the doorway, the bounty hunter who had pursued her in the human world hanging across his shoulder.

The Paladin stopped, blocking his entrance into the room. "What does it take to kill you?" he hissed. "I've tried Svartalfars, serpents, even your own kind. Why won't you die?"

Raf's eyes flared. He dropped the bounty hunter onto the ground and stepped over him. "You?" he asked. He glanced up and saw Marina.

She took another step, to join him, but his eyes told her to stay where she was.

The Paladin grabbed a stick from the floor and slapped it against the palm of his hand. In his fury, he seemed to have forgotten Marina, forgotten everything except venting his rage. "Because of you, Alfheim suffered. Over one hundred years with the throne empty. Do you see what you caused?" He waved his hand and the scenes he'd shown Marina, the destruction that had encompassed Alfheim in the last few weeks appeared on the wall.

Marina fisted her hands; pieces fell into place. The Paladin was behind it all—the snake, the murder of Raf's family, the murder of her parents. He'd done all of it to keep a hellhound from sitting on the throne.

Raf's eyes glimmered red; Marina could feel the magic building in him. He was on the brink of changing, of throwing himself on the elf and ripping out his throat.

The Paladin deserved it; she knew that. But if Raf killed him without a trial, without the citizens of Alfheim being given a chance to hear what the Paladin had done, they might never accept Raf. The Paladin might die, but he'd get what he wanted—no hellhound on the throne. Instead, Raf would be tried and executed.

She moved back to the throne and sat down. She had to activate the broadcast.

"He wanted to stop you from being with me, from ruling Alfheim," she said, her voice calm, but her mind racing through ways to keep the Paladin talking while starting the broadcast.

Raf frowned. "Ruling Alfheim? I'd never been to Alfheim when he ordered my family killed. I don't think I'd even met an elf."

She closed her eyes and shook her head at the irony of what the Paladin had done. He'd brought Raf and her together—killing his family had sent Raf to Gunngar, just as killing hers had ultimately lead her to Gunngar, too.

Power zipped through her. She put her hands behind her back, hiding the glow. The Paladin had yet to see her magic; she might be able to use that last little surprise to their advantage.

The scenes the Paladin had playing on the wall changed. They weren't the same as she'd seen before, they were new, had to be what was happening in the streets of Alfheim right now.

Elves pressed into the area surrounding the castle. Her uncle, her sister and the elf lords were there, too. For now all was peaceful, but she could see elves glancing from one to the other, see their lips moving as they murmured among themselves. They were ready, waiting for the broadcast; time to bring it to them.

She stood and waved for Raf to approach.

The Paladin frowned. "He shouldn't get near you."

She smiled, tried to look as if she didn't hate the elf, didn't want to kill him herself. "He's no threat to me. Let me show you." Power shot from her palms and wrapped around Raf like a vise. He stiffened. His eyes glowed and she could feel him shifting.

Praying her plan would work, she sent a tendril of power curling up his chest, around his neck, let it flicker against his ear, then in her mind she mumbled her message to him, over and over. Willed it to flow through the line of magic like a voice through a taut string.

He glanced at her, nodded.

She smiled at the Paladin. "See, no problem." Then she flipped her palm and sent Raf sailing into the wall.

The Paladin's gaze locked on to her. Behind him, Raf reached up and flipped a switch. Marina settled back against the throne. *Let the show begin.*

"You're a witch," he muttered. "If I'd known—"

"What? You'd have killed me, too, along with my parents?"

"Elves aren't witches." His hands tightened around the stick he held. She could see a war being waged behind his eyes.

She held out both hands, showed the power snapping there. "This elf is, and the throne accepted me. Would you kill me, too?" She moved as if to rise from the throne.

The Paladin screamed and pointed the stick at her head. "I would. I will. I didn't go through this to see an abomination on the throne. I am the Paladin. My job is to protect the throne." A yellow bolt of energy shot from the stick, and barreled toward her.

Raf lurched toward Marina. Sitting on the throne she was safe, or should be, but his body didn't wait for his mind to process the thought. He leapt and shimmered, materialized in midair. The bolt hit him in the chest, knocked him into the wall beside the throne. He landed on the floor with no breath in his body. The smell of torched skin filled the space. He ignored it and pushed to stand up. His shirt was burned through in the front and his skin blistered.

Without pausing to think, he changed.

Hair sprouted and his bones bent. In full hellhound form, he sprang across the room, his jaws opened and directed at the Paladin.

Marina yelled, but he couldn't hear her words. Blood was rushing through him, hate filling him. The time for revenge was here. He couldn't wait any longer—wouldn't wait and give the Paladin another chance to hurt Marina.

The Paladin pointed the stick again, this time at Raf.

Raf didn't hesitate; he leapt. But the Paladin moved. Marina stood by the throne, vines of magic curling from her palms. She had brushed the Paladin aside like an ant.

"He's mine," Raf said in her mind.

She shook her head. "He belongs to Alfheim. Don't take him from them. Let them decide his fate." She gestured to the scene still playing out across the wall.

Elves sat on car roofs, stood hip to hip, their eyes all focused one direction, all watching one thing.

"They're watching us." Her eyes flickered. "The Paladin did all of this—killed your family, my parents, tried to kill you to keep us from sitting on that throne. If he dies, if you kill him now, he wins."

Raf growled. He didn't care if the Paladin won; he just wanted him dead.

Marine closed the fingers of one hand, cut off the power flowing from her palm. "It's your choice. Revenge?" She glanced at the Paladin who was gripping the stick with both hands, seemed to be waiting for the scene between them to play out before acting again. "Or me?"

Raf closed his eyes. Her words hurt, the reality of what she was saying hurt. He'd waited so long, dedicated his life to finding his family's killer and now revenge was so close. He could taste the villain's blood, hear his screams.

He lowered his head. As he did, the Paladin raised his stick, and Raf made his choice. He leapt, knocking Marina backward, onto the throne.

A yellow bolt of magic flew from the Paladin's stick. Raf spun, ready to lunge and fight, but Marina grabbed him by his fur, held him in place. He snapped, tried to pull free and fell to the side, onto the throne's seat.

He froze. The throne had expanded, was now big enough for Marina and Raf to sit side by side. He stared down at it, not believing what had happened, what this meant. He changed into his human form; the throne shifted again.

The Paladin cursed and flew toward them, bolt after bolt of yellow energy shooting from his stick. The throne blocked them all, sent them ricocheting back into the room. The Paladin screamed, cursed the throne for betraying him, for not seeing that what he was doing was right, for the good of Alfheim.

Elves began to pour into the throne room—Geir, Ky, Tahl and others. A group dropped a net on the Paladin from behind and dragged him still swearing from the room. The space was suddenly busy—too busy.

Raf ignored him, ignored all of them. His only desire was to be with Marina—alone with Marina. He placed his hand on her thigh and shimmered them to the tower.

They materialized on the cold floor where they'd made love before.

"If I'm going to help you rule Alfheim, this no shimmer from the keep thing is going to have to be fixed," he murmured, pulling her toward him.

"So, you'll stay? You'll stay in Alfheim, and make history with me?" she asked, her words soft…unsure.

He cupped his hand around her cheek. "Will it make you happy?"

She nodded.

"Will it piss off your uncle?"

She smiled, confident again, and nodded again.

He leaned forward and whispered against her lips, "Then I wouldn't have it any other way."

Epilogue

Raf took the stone out of its box and held it up to the light. Marina, lounging on the grass next to him, cocked an eyebrow.

"Are you planning on using that?"

He rolled the sphere around in his hands then sat it down on the grass, stared at it. "Wouldn't you like to know what the future holds?"

Marina, her gaze on her uncle and Lord Sim who were engaged in yet another battle of wills and words, sighed. "Knowing the future didn't help the Paladin any, did it?"

Raf placed one finger on the stone and rolled it a bit. "He wasn't interested in doing what was right for Alfheim, not really." He lifted his finger and nodded toward Ky who sat surrounded by a diverse group of admirers—a group made of both royals and lords. "It would be good to know if we could trust her."

Marina switched her gaze to Raf. "Would the stone tell us that?" She shook her head. "I don't think so." She brushed bits of grass off her hands onto her jeans, then scooted over the ground to lay her head on his chest. "Life can't be planned, or avoided. It just has to be lived."

Raf placed his finger under her chin and tilted her face toward his. "Well, then, I'm glad I get to live it with you."

"Me, too," she murmured.

As their lips met, Raf placed his hand on the stone and rolled it away. He didn't need magic to tell him the future; he'd found his, here with Marina.

As Alfheim's first hellhound king.

* * * * *

Rancher Ramsey Westmoreland's temporary cook is way too attractive for his liking. Little does he know Chloe Burton came to his ranch with another agenda entirely....

That man across the street had to be, without a doubt, the most handsome man she'd ever seen.

Chloe Burton's pulse beat rhythmically as he stopped to talk to another man in front of a feed store. He was tall, dark and every inch of sexy—from his Stetson to the well-worn leather boots on his feet. And from the way his jeans and Western shirt fit his broad muscular shoulders, it was quite obvious he had everything it took to separate the men from the boys. The combination was enough to corrupt any woman's mind and had her weakening even from a distance. Her body felt flushed. It was hot. Unsettled.

Over the past year the only male who had gotten her time and attention had been the e-mail. That was simply pathetic, especially since now she was practically drooling simply at the sight of a man. Even his stance— both hands in his jeans pockets, legs braced apart, was a pose she would carry to her dreams.

And he was smiling, evidently enjoying the conversation being exchanged. He had dimples, incredibly sexy dimples in not one but both cheeks.

"What are you staring at, Clo?"

Chloe nearly jumped. She'd forgotten she had a

lunch date. She glanced over the table at her best friend from college, Lucia Conyers.

"Take a look at that man across the street in the blue shirt, Lucia. Will he not be perfect for Denver's first issue of *Simply Irresistible* or what?" Chloe asked with so much excitement she almost couldn't stand it.

She was the owner of *Simply Irresistible*, a magazine for today's up-and-coming woman. Their once-a-year Irresistible Man cover, which highlighted a man the magazine felt deserved the honor, had increased sales enough for Chloe to open a Denver office.

When Lucia didn't say anything but kept staring, Chloe's smile widened. "Well?"

Lucia glanced across the booth at her. "Since you asked, I'll tell you what I see. One of the Westmorelands—Ramsey Westmoreland. And yes, he'd be perfect for the cover, but he won't do it."

Chloe raised a brow. "He'd get paid for his services, of course."

Lucia laughed and shook her head. "Getting paid won't be the issue, Clo—Ramsey is one of the wealthiest sheep ranchers in this part of Colorado. But everyone knows what a private person he is. Trust me— he won't do it."

Chloe couldn't help but smile. The man was the epitome of what she was looking for in a magazine cover and she was determined that whatever it took, he would be it.

"Umm, I don't like that look on your face, Chloe. I've seen it before and know exactly what it means."

She watched as Ramsey Westmoreland entered the store with a swagger that made her almost breathless. She *would* be seeing him again.

Look for Silhouette Desire's
HOT WESTMORELAND NIGHTS
by Brenda Jackson,
available March 9 wherever books are sold.

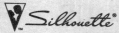

ROMANTIC SUSPENSE

Sparked by Danger, Fueled by Passion.

Introducing a brand-new miniseries
Lawmen of Black Rock

Peyton Wilkerson's life shatters when her
four-month-old daughter, Lilly, vanishes.
But handsome sheriff Tom Grayson is
determined to put the pieces together and
reunite her with her baby. Will Tom be able
to protect Peyton and Lilly while fighting
his own growing feelings?

Find out in
His Case, Her Baby
by
CARLA CASSIDY

Available in March wherever books are sold

REQUEST YOUR FREE BOOKS!

2 FREE NOVELS PLUS 2 FREE GIFTS!

Silhouette

nocturne™

Dramatic and Sensual Tales of Paranormal Romance.

YES! Please send me 2 FREE Silhouette® Nocturne™ novels and my 2 FREE gifts (gifts are worth about $10). After receiving them, if I don't wish to receive any more books, I can return the shipping statement marked "cancel." If I don't cancel, I will receive 4 brand-new novels every other month and be billed just $4.47 per book in the U.S. or $4.99 per book in Canada. That's a saving of about 15% off the cover price! It's quite a bargain! Shipping and handling is just 50¢ per book in the U.S. and 75¢ per book in Canada.* I understand that accepting the 2 free books and gifts places me under no obligation to buy anything. I can always return a shipment and cancel at any time. Even if I never buy another book from Silhouette, the two free books and gifts are mine to keep forever.

238 SDN E37M 338 SDN E37X

Name	(PLEASE PRINT)

Address		Apt. #

City	State/Prov.	Zip/Postal Code

Signature (if under 18, a parent or guardian must sign)

Mail to the **Silhouette Reader Service:**
IN U.S.A.: P.O. Box 1867, Buffalo, NY 14240-1867
IN CANADA: P.O. Box 609, Fort Erie, Ontario L2A 5X3

Not valid for current subscribers to Silhouette Nocturne books.

Want to try two free books from another line?
Call 1-800-873-8635 or visit www.morefreebooks.com.

* Terms and prices subject to change without notice. Prices do not include applicable taxes. N.Y. residents add applicable sales tax. Canadian residents will be charged applicable provincial taxes and GST. Offer not valid in Quebec. This offer is limited to one order per household. All orders subject to approval. Credit or debit balances in a customer's account(s) may be offset by any other outstanding balance owed by or to the customer. Please allow 4 to 6 weeks for delivery. Offer available while quantities last.

Your Privacy: Silhouette is committed to protecting your privacy. Our Privacy Policy is available online at www.eHarlequin.com or upon request from the Reader Service. From time to time we make our lists of customers available to reputable third parties who may have a product or service of interest to you. If you would prefer we not share your name and address, please check here. ☐

Help us get it right—We strive for accurate, respectful and relevant communications. To clarify or modify your communication preferences, visit us at www.ReaderService.com/consumerschoice.

SN10

SILHOUETTE

SPECIAL EDITION

FROM *USA TODAY* BESTSELLING AUTHOR

CHRISTINE RIMMER

A BRIDE FOR JERICHO BRAVO

Marnie Jones had long ago buried her wild-child
impulses and opted to be "safe," romantically
speaking. But one look at born rebel Jericho Bravo
and she began to wonder if her thrill-seeking side
was about to be revived. Because if ever there was
a man worth taking a chance on, there he was,
right within her grasp....

*Available in March
wherever books are sold.*

Silhouette Desire

THE WESTMORELANDS

NEW YORK TIMES
bestselling author

BRENDA JACKSON

HOT WESTMORELAND NIGHTS

Ramsey Westmoreland knew better than to lust after the hired help. But Chloe, the new cook, was just so delectable. Though their affair was growing steamier, Chloe's motives became suspicious. And when he learned Chloe was carrying his child this Westmoreland Rancher had to choose between pride or duty.

Available March 2010 wherever books are sold.

Always Powerful, Passionate and Provocative.

SD73013